Deliver Me

Deliver Me

ASHLEY HAWTHORNE

*To Maria for encouraging me
Robert for supporting me,
And Mom for making me everything I am*

Content Warning

Contains physical and sexual violence, racism, and homophobia. A complete list is available at ashleyhawthorne.net

Part One

Chapter One

Summer

The letter that changed Gabriel's life arrived on a Tuesday. The first one he'd received in over a decade. It landed in his bunk just after the evening mail delivery, aided in its flight by his smirking cellmate. Alex knew he didn't get mail.

Everyone knew it.

Yet there it was, out of place on his threadbare blanket. There was nothing suspicious about the envelope. Black ink, a stamp, and a return address he didn't recognize written in looping feminine script ... but scrawled across the front were two words written in black marker, clearly added after the original writing. The last letter of it even covered the corner of the stamp.

His name.

Gabriel Myers.

"What the hell is this?"

"I don't know, man. You've got to open it."

"Yeah? Well, *no shit*, genius," Gabriel snapped, but he stood for a moment tapping the letter against his thigh.

Alex merely shrugged, unimpressed by the outburst, and turned his attention back to his own mail. Gabriel had known more than a few people who were seriously fucked up, even before he landed himself in this hellhole, but Alex Hayes was colder than most. Lean and wiry, with pasty white skin and vividly orange hair, Gabriel figured it came from too many years of getting his ass kicked as a kid, but he didn't ask, and Alex didn't tell.

He sat down on his bunk, holding the letter up to analyze it before taking out the contents. It had been opened already, obviously, and everything inside already read and examined for potential threats or clues of misconduct. The guards were all nosy, disgusting pigs but for once it didn't bother him. There were too many questions tumbling around in his mind.

When was the last time anyone bothered to write to him? Surely it hadn't been long after the trial. The letters of support had stopped rolling in once the verdict came down. Maybe they couldn't sympathize anymore, or maybe it was because the news stopped blasting his face nonstop across every channel, but either way he had lost all contact with the outside world a long time ago.

He ignored Alex's curious stare—there was never a single moment of privacy in this place—and tore the top off the envelope.

The letter inside was written on a single sheet of clean lined paper, folded in even thirds, and composed in the same dark black ink and feminine handwriting that had been used to write the addresses on the envelope.

Dear inmate,

I realize you don't know me, but I'm hoping that this letter might change that. I hope that it finds you well and you are at least willing to read it and consider the offer of friendship that it contains.

My name is Mia and I volunteer with my local church in their women's Bible study group. We meet on Wednesday evenings to pray and organize our efforts for various charities.

One of our members has a cousin that has spent the last few years in the same facility that you're in now and he mentioned that some of you don't have anyone on the outside to write to. That sounded terribly lonely, so she suggested we start a letter writing campaign through the warden. Each member of my prayer group wrote a letter, and the prison distributed them to those who seemed most in need of a friendly pen pal.

My letter found its way to you, and I hope that you'll write back and let me offer you some semblance of comfort and friendship during your stay in prison, however long that may be.

I'll keep you in my prayers,

Mia Anderson

The words were plain enough but did little to ease his confusion. No reasonable person would be writing to him. There wasn't a redeemable bone in his six-foot, three-inch frame. Gabriel ran a hand through his hair, ruffling the thick black waves as he looked around the cell, taking in the dirt, grime and the peeling paint. The whole place had an aura of filth and he had cigarettes stashed in his toilet, for Christ's sake.

Whoever this lady was, she had no clue about how the real world worked.

She'd keep him in her prayers? Fuck that. He'd seen how little prayer could do. At best, God didn't exist. At worst, he was a sadist who got off on the suffering he let run rampant in innocent people's lives.

"Well?"

"Just a pity letter from some uppity religious bitch who

thinks she can save my soul," he said as he crumpled the letter in his hand.

~

The heat was brutal in the late afternoon. There was no place to hide from the Texas sun and the temperature had been in the triple digits for weeks. Walking to the mailbox was a short trip to the end of the dirt driveway and back, but even that was enough to have sweat dripping down Mia's sides and her brown hair hanging limply down her back. The loose blue sundress she wore was the nearest to naked that a decent woman could be while lounging on a Saturday afternoon, and it still clung damply to her skin as she hurried back to the house, making a messy bun with the elastic hair tie she always kept on her wrist in the summer months as she went.

She'd have to make a pitcher of sweet tea this evening before her dad came home. The air conditioning at the church wasn't always reliable and he liked to sit outside on the shaded front porch in the evenings, sipping a cold drink and watching the lightning bugs dance through the yard. Things cooled off a touch once the sun went down and, if they were lucky, they might even get a faint breeze.

This time of year, everything smelled like honeysuckle, and she plucked a white blossom from the vine near the door. A quick twist at the end to separate the petals and a downward tug pulled the stamen out, bringing with it a single drop of clear nectar that danced sweetly across her tongue.

She let the screen door slam behind her, welcoming the ceiling fan's cool air over her skin as she sat down at the kitchen table to flip through the mail.

Advertisements.

Bills.

A thank you card from a parishioner that was addressed to her father.

Her hand stilled on the last item, buried at the bottom of the pile. The envelope had her name on it, inscribed neatly in blue ink, the kind that reminded her of cheap Bic pens like the ones they use at the bank downtown because they knew everyone stole them.

Her stomach did a slow roll as she chewed nervously at the corner of her thumbnail. There was no return address but there was really only one thing this could be, and the person who wrote it might not be entirely friendly. None of the other women in the prayer group had gotten a response yet, so they were all unsure if their attempts to communicate had been welcomed by the recipients.

She ripped open the envelope and pulled out half a sheet of white legal paper that was ragged and uneven at the edges where it had been torn.

Mia,

Next time you write you should ask the warden to give your letter to someone else. I didn't land in prison for tax fraud or stealing some old grandma's pension. Save your prayers for someone who deserves them.

I'm one of the dangerous ones.

Gabriel Myers

Chapter Two

The small church was one of Mia's favorite places. The linoleum floor was cracked and peeling, and the faded yellow paint on the nursery walls needed to be redone soon, but it didn't diminish the comfort she felt every time she walked through the doors. She had spent so much of her childhood in this building that it was like a second home.

Her mother had been a pastor's wife and that came with responsibilities. She'd devoted her days to record keeping in the office, baking sweets in the kitchen to be delivered to elderly neighbors, and teaching Sunday school in the nursery as children sat on the floor and listened to fantastical tales of rainbow-colored coats and boats big enough to hold two of every animal in the whole world.

Mia had loved it all, but none of it had captured her heart like those stories. For a lost and frightened child, the promise of miracles and God's love had been a profound revelation. She wanted nothing more than to make the same positive impact on the lives of others as her mother had made, and she intended to start right here with this same congregation. She always arrived early to set out desserts and help to set the room up for their Wednesday night meeting.

"Are we ready?"

Mia smiled and set a stack of paper cups on the table. Mrs. Mitchell was the head of the women's Bible study group, a sweet white-haired lady in her late seventies that wore the thickest glasses Mia had ever seen. Firmly independent and spirited, she always smelled like nipped afternoon rum cake and old woman.

Mia adored her.

"That's the last of it," she said. "Everyone should be showing up any minute now."

As she predicted, the room filled quickly as women talked and snacked on cookies and lemonade that Mia had made herself. There were young girls newly graduated from high school, some in college like herself, recent brides still flush with new love, tired moms with hastily wiped spit up stains, and women that were old enough to be grandmothers who liked to hand off advice to the rest of them.

There was a feeling of community, a connection that Mia was grateful for as talk moved quickly over the latest town news. There was a pregnancy, a death, an amicable divorce. Someone mentioned the often hoped for dream that they might someday get a Taco Bell in town, and Mia couldn't help but smile.

They'd been hearing that rumor for five years and still had to drive all the way to Abilene for a late-night burrito.

Mrs. Mitchell let them ramble aimlessly for a few minutes before clearing her throat and standing up from her orange plastic chair to call the group to attention.

"We've got a lot to cover tonight," she began. "We have the upcoming bake sale to raise money for the food pantry, the Fourth of July celebration that still needs volunteers to work the tables, and Ms. Durand has suggested that we might want to consider starting now to gather donations of school supplies for the kids when classes start back up in the fall."

Almost everyone nodded and Mia knew her best friend's newest project would also be a success. Lilly had joined the church when the girls had been in middle school. Back when Lilly's family had recently moved from Louisiana, and she'd been dealing with a new school on top of middle school mean girl attitudes. It hadn't been easy, especially for her in a small town like this one, but nothing had been able to wipe the smile off Lilly's face and Mia had loved her immediately. Lilly had lost the braces in the years since, but she had maintained her round cheeked grin and determined attitude.

Mia shot her a quick, encouraging smile as Mrs. Mitchell continued.

"The first thing on the agenda, though, is to see if anyone has gotten a letter back from the prison? I got mine in the mail yesterday," Mrs. Mitchell confirmed.

Across the circle from Mia, Mrs. Newberry sniffed indelicately. Middle-aged and still beautiful, she'd been a regular church volunteer since her youngest child had left for college the previous year. She'd been openly opposed to Lilly's suggestion from the start, refusing to participate and quoting fire and brimstone to everyone who would listen at every meeting since.

"Felons will meet their justice at the hands of God," she had insisted. "We must be vigilant and not allow these criminals to corrupt our hearts and minds. Their dark thoughts have the ability to let the devil into our lives."

Everyone had ignored her then, and Mia ignored her now, though she noticed Lilly's eyes narrow as she reached for her own letter and knew she hadn't been the only one to notice Mrs. Newberry's behavior.

One by one each of the other ladies held up a similar envelope to the one in Mrs. Mitchell's hand.

"Wonderful. Did anyone have any problems? Issues?" Mrs. Mitchell scanned the group, but everyone shook their heads, denying any upsetting interaction with the prisoners. They had been polite in their responses, and most had seemed genuinely grateful for the letters. "Then the Lord must have ensured that our letters found their way into the right hands."

The rest of the meeting went smoothly, and soon the only people left were Mia, Lilly, and Kennedy Daniels. Kennedy was the third member of their friend group and had been since she'd started coming to their church in high school. Her parents didn't let her come every week—making her go to the one they attended on the other side of town at least once a month—but when they did, she was reluctant to leave and always stayed after to help with the cleaning.

"I love that Mrs. Newberry objects to all of my suggestions by pretending she doesn't actually want to help people in trouble and thinks that's better than admitting she's a racist who hates me because my grandmother is Vietnamese," Lilly muttered, tossing her long black braid over her shoulder as she stacked the orange chairs a little too forcefully in the corner.

"She gives everyone a bad attitude and I guess that makes it easier for her to hide it," Mia mused. "She's never been easy to get along with, but I've noticed we're having more problems with her since she started volunteering."

"She does always seem to have something negative to say when she's not the center of attention," Kennedy said. "Mrs. Mitchell's talked to her about it but..."

Mia glanced at Lilly as Kennedy let the words hang meaningfully. "If she makes you uncomfortable, we can talk to Mrs. Mitchell or my dad about her."

Lilly pondered that for a moment, the plastic chair in her arms cradled against her chest. "Not yet," she said. "If she does anything more obnoxious than whine about my project ideas then we can, but I want her to see the success of the programs for herself."

"Are you sure?" Mia asked. "You don't have to prove anything to her."

"I'm sure," Lilly said, setting down the chair and tossing the last of the used paper cups in the trash. "I don't want her to cause bitterness in my heart, but I do kind of want to watch her sit there every week, knowing she can't stop us from doing good things and being kind to people."

Mia laughed. "If that bothers her then it's a misery that she brought on herself."

Kennedy nodded in agreement, and they went back to working in silence until she looked over her shoulder and said, "I noticed you didn't say anything about the guy who got your letter." She huffed a strand of blonde hair out of her face with a grimace. It hung loose nearly to her waist, softly curled at the ends. With her strikingly blue eyes and even ivory complexion, the pink dress she wore made her look like a porcelain doll and everyone knew how much she hated it. Kennedy would have cut her hair years ago if her parents would have allowed it.

Mia reached her hand into her pocket and rubbed her fingers over the stiff paper. "I was going to, but I haven't decided yet if I should write him back or ask the warden to send my next letter to someone else."

"What?" Lilly said in surprise. "I thought you agreed that it seemed like our letters went to the right people?"

"I didn't want to worry the other ladies and put a damper on your project," Mia admitted.

"Did he say something mean to you?" Lilly looked ready to fight, her usually cheerful face set in angry lines.

"He barely said anything to me at all," Mia said quietly. "He says he's dangerous and I should write to someone else, but he didn't give me any more information than that."

Kennedy's expression was doubtful. "I guess you should

stop writing to him if that's what he really wants but maybe he's not used to having someone care about what happens to him?"

Mia nodded. She had gone into this because she wanted to reach someone that might otherwise have been unreachable. After all, someone had once reached out to her, taken on a difficult challenge with no promise that things would work out in the end, and it had made all of the difference.

"I'll pray and ask God for guidance," Mia promised them, and she listened with a smile as the conversation turned to Lilly's boyfriend and Kennedy's excitement about going back to college at the end of summer. These women were a blessing to her, and she was convinced God had helped them find each other, knowing they would help guide one another through life's challenges.

Perhaps that was what He had planned for Gabriel Myers. Maybe he needed someone in his life to encourage him and guide him toward God. She had gone over every inch of his letter several times since it arrived yesterday, looking for clues to what kind of person had written it. The evidence didn't paint much of a picture. Neat handwriting and evidence that he lived as she imagined a prisoner would—cheap pens and scraps of paper that smelled vaguely of cigarette smoke.

There was nothing to tell her what kind of man he was, or how he spent his days, or what he'd done to deserve being sent to prison. All she knew for sure was that he must be lonely if no one wrote to him.

~

3:30 am

He didn't need the wake-up call anymore. After so many years on the same schedule, he woke on his own at exactly the same time every morning, allowing himself a few seconds to become oriented to his surroundings before the rest of the prison began to stir.

There was no need to think about what to wear since all inmates were stripped of their individuality and made as indistinguishable from one another as possible in white jumpsuits and black shoes, and they dressed in silence before filing into the dining hall. Breakfast was questionable oatmeal, browning apple slices, and shitty black coffee all served precisely at 4:30 and eaten elbow-to-elbow on long metal tables. They ate in silence as well, though this was as much from habit as lack of desire.

Talking during mealtime was prohibited.

By 6:00 a.m. they had been shuffled along with most of the other inmates to their shift in the prison's garment factory. The shifts were long, twelve hours a day, and the work was hot, sweaty, and miserable.

It was also mandatory. Every able-bodied prisoner was required to work. Some worked the kitchens, or the laundry unit, and a lucky few even got to work outdoors in the garden. The rest came here, to a large room that was loud and busy and filled with complicated machinery and rows of sewing machines, where they would spend their sentences making clothing and textiles that would be used in their prison and others around the state.

None of them were paid, Texas didn't bother giving their inmates financial compensation for their labors, but while the other inmates hoped that they might at least earn time credits for an earlier release date or a good behavior stamp that would increase their chances of parole, Gabriel's only benefit was a way to kill the endless stream of time that threatened to drive him mad.

At least his work went toward the prison itself and he wasn't sewing bras for Victoria's Secret, unlike prisoners in some other institutions he'd heard about. It was a good system for the prison and the company, maximizing profit under the guise of giving the prisoners job skills and a way to pay for their own room and board, but it was an obvious labor scam. He'd been around enough shady deals to know one when it hit him in the face.

He settled in behind an industrial-sized sewing machine, and the hours passed in a blur of stitching on white fabric. There was only a short break for lunch—if two hot dogs with sauerkraut tossed on top, a slice of white bread, and a scoop of cold canned carrots could really be qualified as a meal—to break up the monotony until late in the afternoon.

He glanced up from his machine as the sounds of fighting erupted behind him, barely audible over the roar of the machines, despite the proximity of the beating that was happening a few feet away. A young man was curled up on the floor, arms wrapped protectively around his head as an older inmate with a shaved head and a swastika tattooed on his neck rained down a series of vicious kicks.

"You think you can get away with bumping into me and not paying attention to where you're going, you dumb piece of shit? You worthless—" The rest was cut off as the guards finally reached him and wrenched him away from his victim.

He left the room in restraints, destined for disciplinary action that likely meant nothing to a man already serving a life sentence while the young man he assaulted was sent to the medical ward for stitches and ibuprofen, blood running over his dark skin and onto his white uniform.

Gabriel went back to his sewing.

There was nothing he could have done to help that wouldn't have made things worse for the kid and gotten himself written up, too. The kid was new, and he was going to have to get hard or do his time with a target on his back. He was lucky that this had been a beating, instead of a stabbing or worse. Prison was a living hell for anyone identified as an easy target.

There were cameras everywhere and the guards patrolled constantly, monitoring for signs of contraband or the violence that was never far from the surface, but it wasn't enough. It didn't stop the beatings or the drugs. Prisoners were nothing if not inventive, and they had plenty of time for scheming, especially if they considered the reward sufficient. The guards didn't run this prison, the gangs did.

Gabriel had resisted the pressure to join up with any specific gang, having had his fill of that bullshit before getting arrested, but plenty of others hadn't and the slightest misstep was enough for a man to end up dead. Hell, sometimes the way you looked was enough, as the kid currently getting stitched up had found out the hard way.

By the time they made it back to the day room, Gabriel was in a bad mood. As usual he opted to skip the limited opportunity they had for TV or social interaction and withdrew to his cell. Everyone in here had something that helped keep them sane. Some had drugs, Alex had a surprising love for reality TV, and he had art. Paper, like everything else in here, was exorbitantly expensive but at least his stone-cold cunt of a mother kept his commissary card full every month, even if she hadn't spoken a word to him since he was fifteen years old.

He lost himself in the smooth glide of his pencil and ignored his cellmate when Alex finally threw himself down on his bunk not long before lights' out.

"Looks like I got a letter from my brother," Alex mused, rustling the day's mail in his hands before realizing Gabriel wasn't going to answer and tossing a letter onto his bunk with a smirk.

Gabriel sighed, holding it up to find that she had written his name on the envelope herself this time. The woman was obnoxiously persistent, and he knew the type. Probably middle-aged and mousy, sure that her own husband and children were flawless and therefore convinced that she knew how to fix everyone else's problems, too.

One of his childhood friends, the rich kind that he'd known before he was sent to live with his Uncle Richard, had had a mom exactly like that. Sanctimonious. Pious. Obnoxious. He used to get high in the garage with that kid while his dad fucked the babysitter and he wondered now if she'd ever figured out how little she'd actually had to hold over the rest of them.

He pulled out the letter, curiosity getting the better of him but still prepared for an unwelcome lecture.

Gabriel,

I don't know what you did to be in prison, but no one deserves to be lonely for the rest of their lives.

I think you wrote that last letter to try and scare me and it worked for a little while, but I know that God commands me not to fear and to love my neighbor as myself.

I'm ashamed that I considered complying with your request to write to someone else, and I'm sorry you feel undeserving of someone to talk to.

I'm not afraid and I'd like to continue to write to you if you don't mind?

Mia

He didn't know what to think about this lady and her odd determination to put herself at risk trying to be friends with a dangerous stranger, but her response bothered him. He'd signed his letter with his real name, hoping to frighten her when she realized the extent of the crimes he had been convicted for, but she hadn't responded to that information at all. His trial had been plastered all over the TV for months and he didn't think there was a single person in the country that didn't know his name and his face by the time it was all over.

There were several possibilities in his mind but only one of them made sense.

He wrote a single sentence before stuffing the slightly crumpled piece of paper in an envelope.

How old are you?

Chapter Three

Mia's brows drew together as she sat, curled comfortably in the center of her bed, and read Gabriel's most recent letter.

You're a child and whoever allowed you to write to dangerous prisoners is a fucking idiot. You'd know that if you were even old enough to remember who the hell I am. It's not like what I've done was a secret. Go back to your church group, little girl, and save yourself the trouble. You shouldn't be talking to monsters like me.

There was no greeting, no signature, but even with the obvious hostility she seemed to be making some progress. At least it was a full paragraph this time.

She'd been flabbergasted by that last letter.

How old are you?

Receiving a reply at all had surprised her, but if he was going to write she had expected more than one blunt question with no context.

She'd answered in the same way, unwilling to give him the satisfaction of asking for an explanation.

I'm twenty.

She sighed and chewed gently on the end of her pen as she rescanned this most recent correspondence with a frown. Most of his anger seemed centered around her age, if the liberal sprinkling of offensive language was any indication, though she didn't understand why.

Little girl.

Hmph.

He seemed unreasonably determined to scare her off and this letter definitely seemed to hint that what he had done was bad enough that it might even have made the news.

Maybe …

She dropped the letter on the bed beside her, letting the paper flutter down and land on a white blanket patterned with small daisies in her favorite colors of blue and yellow, and reached for her laptop. Her jaw dropped as a simple search for the words "Gabriel Myers" brought up more than half a million results.

She scanned the top few, all of which were news stories with horrifying headlines—

"Gruesome Crime Rocks Nation"

"Shocking Violence Among America's Elite"

"Teen Killer Gabriel Myers Faces Justice"

She placed a hand on her stomach, fighting the urge to be sick as the last headline jumped off the screen and swam dizzyingly in front of her eyes.

"A Family Demolished—How Patricide Destroyed a Legacy"

Patricide …

Her mind flashed to the only parents she could remember —the father who loved her, the mother she had lost. Gabriel Myers really was a monster. He hadn't even bothered to try and deny it.

She slammed the laptop closed, only to reopen it seconds later and peer intently at the small thumbnail image beside the first article. The boy in the photo stared back at her without remorse.

He might have been a handsome kid if she hadn't known what he'd done. Wavy black hair framed a long face with defined cheekbones and a prominent nose. The sharp lines and sculpted jawline would have made his appearance harsh if his lips hadn't been so full and the ears poking out from his hair so large. She couldn't make out the color of his eyes, but they were hard and emotionless as he stared at the camera.

Why would God have guided her letter to someone like this?

Unable to ignore her curiosity, she scrolled the results, skimming past the YouTube videos of old news reports for now, and filling her screen with articles and images. She scanned the page, taking in a series of pictures taken after his arrest. In each of them he looked young, almost childlike, but his eyes were always cold.

She bit her lip as she considered his mugshot—a boy with dark circles under his eyes and hair that was cropped too close on the sides, revealing those ears that were a touch too big. He showed no fear, none of the terror that she knew she would be experiencing if she were in his place.

His face was equally impassive in a newspaper photo of him wearing a blue juvenile detention jumpsuit as he stepped out of the back of a police car, flanked by officers with stern expressions. The handcuffs on his wrists and ankles were connected by a long chain that made his attempt to stand look awkward and emphasized the youthful lankiness of his arms and legs.

She almost laughed sadly at a court drawing of him in a black suit, an obvious but failed attempt at making him look presentable for the courtroom. He didn't look old enough to attend prom, much less be on trial for murder.

Her amusement faded when she found the only picture that showed a smile on his face. A candid home photo of him as a child in front of a Christmas tree, arms wrapped around the waist of an older man with an identical grin—his father she realized with a jolt.

The man he'd killed.

She didn't understand how anyone could do such a thing to another person, especially at such a young age. He looked so happy in that Christmas photo—his smile so enthusiastic, his hug so pure.

The shadows on her walls grew long and the sun sank below the horizon as she sat on her bed with its pretty floral blanket, searching the internet's memory as though it might have answers to a mystery that humanity itself still hadn't solved.

What made someone a killer?

The media had done their best to find out while he was on trial, scouring through every inch of his personal life searching for one incident that might have explained it all. They interviewed his friends, his acquaintances, his teachers ... None of them had answers. He was a decent kid—maybe a bit lonely, certainly wild and prone to mischief, but never violent. That hadn't stopped the reporters from digging, turning over every facet of his life, his family's lives.

She would have been seven when he was arrested, too young to remember the story, but the whole thing had been quite the scandal. There didn't seem to be anything about his life that wasn't splashed across the front page of some magazine or newspaper. He was the only child of a career politician and her handsome playboy husband. His mother, Lilah Miller, was from an extremely wealthy family and Gabriel had been raised surrounded by the finest things money could buy. If the media's assessment of his early years was to be believed, he was a spoiled rich kid that had been provided with the best education, the fanciest homes, the most expensive vacations.

His family was small—a father, a mother, an uncle—but they were reported to have been close and happy, despite his father's rumored affairs. There had been no sign of problems and as Mia clicked on another link, she discovered his mother's brother was apparently a famous Evangelical pastor named Richard Miller, now deceased. His death had gotten quite a bit of national attention the year after Gabriel was convicted.

Lilah had apparently been elected to the US Senate when Gabriel was twelve and there were plenty of photos of her, too. There didn't seem to be much of her in her son—he obviously got his looks from his father—but she was beautiful. A petite brunette with a charming smile, she appeared determined and sophisticated as she stood beside her family at press conferences and political events. There was never a hair out of place or a jacket wrinkle to be seen.

His family's shimmering public image hadn't helped Gabriel during the trial. His only supporters seemed to have been young women impressed by his looks or his fortune, and they had been widely mocked for their willingness to overlook his crimes for a pair of pretty eyes.

Every reporter, news anchor, and celebrity that had decided to weigh in on the subject—which had been almost all of them—had deemed him a spoiled brat with an anger problem that deserved to rot in prison and never see the light of day again.

Mia thought he was a spoiled rich kid that obviously needed better lawyers.

His mother, understandably upset about the circumstances of his arrest, had apparently refused to pay for his legal team, and his public defenders had done embarrassingly little defending. There was never even an attempt made to claim that he hadn't committed the crime of which he had been accused. It was freely acknowledged that Gabriel Myers had stabbed his father seven times in a dimly lit alley in Houston.

His reason, told through his lawyers because they didn't allow him to take the stand, was rooted in family problems. There had apparently been prior behavioral issues, and his parents had sent him to live with his uncle, a decision that Gabriel had not handled well. When his father finally tracked him down after he had spent six months living on the streets with a group of runaways, he hadn't wanted to return. There had been an altercation and it had gotten out of hand. They portrayed him as an impulsive child, panicking over a punishment and lashing out without thinking.

The jury hadn't seen it that way—it had taken them less than three hours to return with a verdict.

Guilty.

He'd been too young for the death penalty, even in Texas, but that meant there was only one possible punishment remaining and he was sentenced to life, without the possibility of parole, at the age of sixteen.

There were plenty of videos from inside the courtroom since the trial itself was well televised, and his reaction—or lack thereof—to the verdict had been the cause of speculation for weeks. He had stood beside his lawyers, clean cut and stoic in his suit, as the rest of his life was taken from him. There had been no tears, no sudden slumping of his too stiff shoulders, no looking around for support or escape or even a friendly face.

Not that there would have been a friendly face anyway. His mother and uncle hadn't attended the trial. The court had been forced to appoint a guardian for him, with one parent dead and the other still attending to her political career several states away and refusing to even acknowledge his existence.

Mia let the video play to its end, and another to take its place. It was even more obvious in the videos how cold and empty his eyes were now that she could see him move and breathe. He was emotionless as the legal teams called their witnesses and presented their evidence and wrangled fancy words at a jury that should have been somber but looked instead like they might secretly be enjoying the attention as they held a young man's life in their hands.

But then, as yet another video played and the clock on her bedside table ticked relentlessly toward two a.m. and she felt her eyes begin to droop against her will, she saw it.

The prosecution had put up a large photo of his father in the courtroom to play on the sympathy of the jury—to let them see the humanity of the man who was murdered in a dirty alley by the child he had loved and raised—and Gabriel, who had spent most of the trial staring straight ahead and ignoring the proceedings entirely, turned his head to look at the face of his father.

She leaned forward and paused the video, staring at Gabriel in that one brief moment when the mask of indifference slipped. Her heart pounded and her breath caught painfully in her throat because there was a lost child in his eyes.

It was a look she recognized immediately—pain, anger, fear ... and beneath that the kind of desperate shock that only comes from a loss that is so deep and so profound that you cannot speak of it.

The wood floor creaked beneath her feet as she padded down the stairs, skipping the loudest one by habit and guiding herself only by the light of the moon that streamed in the windows so that she didn't wake her father.

It took her a few minutes of careful rummaging in the

downstairs office to find what she was looking for, but when she did, she said a quick prayer of thanksgiving and ran nimbly back up the stairs to her room, a small photo album now tucked under her arm.

She crawled back into her bed and began to skim through it in the low light of her laptop screen. It was full of old photos of herself, most of them unremarkable with her wide smile and normal family, but those weren't the ones that she was looking for. She finally pulled out two, taken several years apart, and held them up beside the computer. She looked at each of them in turn and then back again to Gabriel Myers' face, still frozen on the screen.

The first, taken when she first arrived with the Anderson's, showed a small and sickly little girl with mouse-brown hair and too many freckles in a pink dress that hung limply off her body. She was so thin that even in pictures her bones poked painfully at her skin. Alone and frightened, she'd been traumatized from being bounced from foster home to foster home as each deemed her unruly and difficult to discipline.

The second was taken the day of her mother's funeral. It was a bit blurry, a quick snapshot someone had taken of her and her father, both dressed in relentless black and standing helplessly in the sea of flowers that had been given in futile hopes to help ease their grief. She had changed, gotten long-limbed and healthy by the time of the second photo, though she'd kept the soft brown hair and the freckles.

In both of the photos, she had the same broken look in her eyes that Gabriel did sitting in that courtroom looking at a picture of his father. If God worked in mysterious ways, perhaps he had led her to Gabriel because she was the only person in the world who would have seen that look and recognized it for what it was because she'd felt it herself.

She clicked on her bedside lamp, creating a little pool of

light to push back the darkness, and pulled a sheet of paper and a pen from her desk drawer.

Gabriel,

I was too young to remember it when it happened, but you were right, a little time on the internet today showed me your trial was quite a spectacle. You got your fifteen minutes of fame out of it, anyway. I think they must have splashed the horrifying details all over every newspaper and TV show in the country.

You stabbed your own father, left him lying dead in a pool of his own blood because you didn't feel like going home to your nice house and your pampered life. You were obviously spoiled, out of control, and dangerous.

Is that what you wanted me to say?

God doesn't ask me to judge you for what happened, He only asks that I treat you with kindness and compassion, but I made a judgment anyway. I watched the trial and I know that look in your eyes.

You're not a monster.

Maybe it's easier for you if you tell yourself that you are, maybe it makes it easier for you to deal with your secrets and whatever really happened that night, but I know what it looks like when someone's whole world has crumbled beneath their feet.

You can fool yourself, but you can't fool me.

Mia

Chapter Four

Gabriel had been in a piss poor mood for three days. Fury pulsed in the air around his large frame to such an extent that even Alex had wisely kept his mouth shut and stayed as far on his own side of the cell as possible. The other inmates, already intimidated by the sheer size of him and his unpredictable temper, gave him even more space than usual.

Three days.

That's how long it had been since he'd last received a letter from *her*. The obnoxious woman—not woman, *child*—that had shown up in his life from out of nowhere, hellbent on disruption and acting like she knew one single fucking thing about him.

You're not a monster.

The words repeated endlessly in his mind since he had first read them and the sheer audacity of it was still difficult for him to wrap his mind around. She'd watched the damn shows, read the fucking articles ... she knew exactly what he'd done.

He'd never denied it.

You're not a monster.

But he was. Why didn't she understand it? That it didn't matter at all what the hell she thought she'd seen or how he'd felt or why it had happened. It only mattered what he'd done. They'd made that clear to him in abundance, hadn't they? His family, his friends, the courts ... all of them. He'd been left to rot in a juvenile detention center for a year because his mother and uncle, the thought of whom still sent fresh coils of rage rioting through his veins, refused to post his bail. He'd turned sixteen in that hellhole, all alone and with no one to acknowledge him.

It was only the hope he'd clung to that had gotten him through that. He had been open with his lawyer about what had occurred, and the psych evaluations had resulted in a diagnosis of severe PTSD related to events that had occurred before the stabbing, about living conditions that clearly fell within the definitions of mental, emotional, and sexual abuse.

It painted a clear picture and it seemed like it should have been enough ... but it wasn't. Not once the lawyers had decided that his version of events wasn't credible. He'd spent years wondering if they had simply been too overworked to bother investigating his story or if they had simply been fans of his uncle's, unable to wrap their minds around his role in what happened.

Gabriel could still feel it, the weightless absence of sensation when he'd realized none of that evidence would be used, the way shock and disbelief almost made it feel like he was floating, how the words themselves were muffled as they reached his ears, the dark metallic taste of fear on his tongue when he realized what it would mean. He'd never gotten a chance to speak, to explain, to lay out his reasons and be judged fairly for his crimes.

The verdict had been unsurprising, such a foregone conclusion in his mind that it hadn't even been able to penetrate the hopeless numbness. The press had gone crazy over his lack of reaction. It was one last thing to demonize him for before they locked him up and threw away the key.

Not that he was sure it would have mattered anyway. The public had already gotten the story they needed, the media spreading the details for everyone else's entertainment, and he'd been made to understand exactly what he was. They had wanted a monster, and he had become one, the last of the hope inside him dying as the trial progressed.

How dare she show up now, years after it had all stopped mattering to him, to try and tell him he wasn't a monster?

On the third day, simmering with rage and unable to hold his emotions inside any longer, he scribbled another hasty note on a torn scrap of paper, breathing heavily through clenched teeth as he slammed a stamp on the corner of the envelope.

What the hell do you know about anything, kid? You think I'm a nice person even after everything I've done? After all the shows you watched you should know exactly what kind of monster I am. Did your parents keep you so tightly bundled up in your nice little house and your nice little church that no one ever bothered to teach you stories about the boogeyman?

That's a serious flaw in your education, princess, so let me do you a favor and fill in the gaps. The devil you should be worried about isn't the kind that lives in your Bible and thinks that saying 'fuck' is a sin. The devil you should be worried about lives next door to your house and thinks about peeling the skin from your bones. He's the friendly guy at the grocery store that pays to watch strangers do unspeakable things to kids on the internet, or the nice lady at church who goes home and beats her own children, but only in the places where their clothes cover their bruises.

Hell is empty, sweetheart, all the devils are here.

~

Alex smirked when he handed over a new crisp white envelope.

"Fuck off," Gabriel snapped, but there was little heat to it.

It had been longer this time, long enough that he really thought that maybe his last letter had finally gotten through to her, that she'd moved on, but she was stubborn.

It was almost as impressive as it was irritating.

He tore the top off the envelope and quickly scanned the letter inside, noting with surprise that there appeared to be a few spots near the bottom where the rich black ink had blurred and the paper looked thinner, more fragile.

Tear spots.

Fuck.

He hadn't meant to make her cry.

Gabriel,

Mark Twain quotes, huh? I'm impressed.

You're not a monster or a devil, even if you do try to act like one. I've been so nice to you, and I think you owe me an apology for being so mean all the time, but I forgive you.

I forgive you because it's what I'm supposed to do. As a Christian it's what God commands me to do, but more than that, I forgive you because I think you're a man who has a lot of hurt in his heart. Have you seen those devils, Gabriel? The kind that you told me about in your letter? I think you have, and I think they hurt you.

You asked me what I knew about anything, and I guess that's fair. No one expects someone like me to know about hurt or how it can dig around inside you and scoop out everything else until there's nothing left but the numbness and the anger. They keep you safe because it means no one can get close enough to hurt you.

No one expects me to know it, but I do.

I learned about it the day my birth parents left me alone in a run-down motel room and never came back. I was three, and they left me behind like garbage they didn't want anymore. The state thinks they were probably junkies, but no one knows for sure.

I learned it again in every foster home they put me in for the next three years. They bounced me around from place to place because no one wanted to deal with my issues. I guess my parents hadn't fed me very well because I was always stealing food, no matter how much the new families gave me. I got into a lot of fights with the other kids, and I bit people a lot. My adoptive dad still has a scar on his arm that I gave him the first week they took me in.

I thought that was it when my last foster family adopted me. That pain would never be able to find me again because I had a family of my own, but I learned it again a few years ago when my mom died. That one probably hurt the worst. She was good, and kind, and she wanted me when I was so wild and angry that I was practically feral, and she loved me anyway. She didn't deserve to die, but she did. I couldn't stop it and it hurt.

I don't know why I am telling you this, I probably shouldn't, but I said we could be friends and I guess I think friends might talk about these things, the kind of secrets that weigh on their hearts and leave scars.

I have other friends, but I don't talk to them about stuff like this. They don't understand what it's like to hurt this deep and if I talk about it, they look at me with pity. I don't think you would pity me. I think you'd understand that even when things look okay on the surface, they might not be okay on the inside.

Maybe you don't have many friends, and I hate the thought of anyone feeling like they're alone. I know what it feels like to be alone and Gabriel ... you're not alone.

Mia

Her heart beat a little faster when she pulled the letter from the mailbox. She bit her bottom lip as nervous butterflies flitted around her stomach. She had no clue what she'd been thinking, sending him that last letter. She'd poured her heart out to him, an angry and resentful stranger, on impulse and with nothing but a stray hope that maybe there could be some connection there.

Now the results of that decision were in her hands.

If he was still angry at her, still not interested, then she would have no choice but to ask the warden for a different name, no matter how strongly she felt that God had brought her to Gabriel for a reason.

"Hey," her dad called from the kitchen, "don't let the screen door ... slam." He sighed, good natured even in perpetual disappointment, when the door reverberated against its hinges behind her, as he had done at least once a day since she'd moved into this house. She'd always been a little bit careless, but he never really seemed to mind.

"Anything good in the mail today?" He stood at the stove, sleeves of his white dress shirt rolled up as he made dinner. There was a little salt in his pepper dark hair, and a few wrinkles around his eyes when he smiled, but he was still a handsome man. Mia attributed most of it to the kind twinkle in his blue eyes—everyone loved her dad.

"Hmm? No ... I mean, yes, there was but it was just a letter from that pen pal program with the Bible group."

He brought a spoon of spaghetti sauce to her lips for her to sample and she nodded. The flavor was good, better than anything she could have made. Desserts were about the most anyone could expect from her in the kitchen.

"Is it going well? The program? I've heard so many good things about what's happening in the Bible group lately."

She slipped the letter into the pocket of her jeans, hoping he wouldn't ask her about her own experiences. "I think so.

Everyone's pretty satisfied with it so far and most of the inmates were very enthusiastic about the idea."

"That's good, honey," he said, clearly distracted as he looked around the kitchen for a clean spoon. "Why don't you grab us a couple of plates? I think this is almost ready."

She sighed in relief, pressed a kiss to his cheek, and set the table for dinner.

As they ate, they chatted happily about her upcoming plans for the Bible group now that the Fourth of July picnic had come and gone, and his upcoming sermon for the week. The relationship between them was comfortable and easy, and she knew how lucky she was to be so loved and unconditionally supported, even though there was still a permanent ache around her heart when she looked at her mother's empty chair.

Maybe she'd handled things badly in her letter and she should have focused on her blessings. Gabriel was going to tell her how spoiled and ungrateful she sounded. How spoiled and ungrateful she *was* ... complaining about her life to a man that would spend the rest of his behind bars. The guilt she felt was sudden, sticky and unwelcome as it clung to her ribcage and soured her appetite.

Unable to face him, she left the letter sitting unopened on her desk until morning, when her curiosity finally overrode her anxiety and she had to see his response even if it *was* a blistering lecture on her own privilege. She could apologize if he was angry and try again, she decided, forgetting her plan to leave him alone if he was still reluctant to write to her. It didn't make sense for his opinion to matter so much to her, but it did.

Mia,

If I'm not alone, then neither are you ...

Chapter Five

If I'm not alone, then neither are you...

He didn't regret telling her that, not exactly. He didn't even regret what he said after that—

Maybe you were right, maybe I do know what it's like to feel that kind of pain, that kind of anger. There were secrets the trial didn't talk about, things that happened to me before I killed my father. I'm sorry for what I said to you. There's no point in talking about what happened to me. Not anymore. But if you're determined to keep writing to me, we could talk about something else.

You could tell me about something that makes you smile because I didn't mean to make you cry.

—though he probably should regret it because he just *knew* she was going to write back and say something calm and understanding. His worst tactics hadn't been enough to shake her off, she was apparently immovable when she'd set her mind to something, and now he'd gone and been nice to her. He was definitely stuck with her now.

No, the part that he regretted was that talking to her meant thinking about things.

Lots of things.

Especially now that most of his irritation with her had begun to fade into curiosity, maybe even a grudging sense of connection. It was impossible not to wonder what she looked like or how she spent her time. Did she enjoy school? Did she have friends?

He reached into the envelope where he had stored her letters, rereading the first one for the hundredth time, careful not to bend or wrinkle the pages too much. She was part of a Bible study group, which sounded like a fucking nightmare to him, but meant she probably knew people and had friends.

That was nice for Mia, that she had people who cared about her, even if there were some things that she chose not to share with them ... things that she had only shared with him. He hadn't had a connection to anyone in such a long time that he'd almost forgotten what it felt like to be curious about someone else and to have them be curious about him in return. It was nice for him to know something intimate about someone, and she'd already shared so much, while he had shared so little. At least, nothing that the whole world didn't already think they knew, anyway.

His eyes drifted to Alex, lounging in his bunk and reading some book that was probably dumb as all fuck, and tried to imagine what would've happened if he had even bothered to ask what it was about. Alex would've told him to piss off and that would have been the end of that. There was nothing for him here, he was absolutely alone and had been for a long time. Now, suddenly, it bothered him.

Maybe it wouldn't hurt, to tell her something about himself, to try and connect with another person. She was safe on the outside, away from him and anything that could happen, any way that he could hurt her or let her down.

He went to sleep wondering what he might tell her when she wrote him back this time because he was sure that she would. It was odd to admit that he was almost looking forward to it.

That night he had one of the dreams again for the first time in a long time and it hurt even more than he remembered.

He was never sure exactly what happened in the dreams, his waking mind only able to recall broken fragments that didn't fit together . His uncle's face, smug and terrible, and his own impotent rage. The cry of a baby he'd never hold. Pleas from people he'd never see again as they begged him to save them. Pain and betrayal as he looked into the eyes of a monster and realized he couldn't even save himself. Places he'd been flashed across his consciousness, his memories vibrant snapshots speeding toward an inevitable end he couldn't avoid, and then the world turned dark and red, and someone was screaming, and he didn't know if it was him or his father.

The scream was the last thing he heard in the dream, it always was, right before he bolted upright in his bunk with sweat pouring off him and a real scream stuck painfully in his throat. He always had a desperate urge to run, but he knew in real life he hadn't run. He had stayed there, holding his father's body and staring into his lifeless eyes until the cops found him a few hours later. He'd often wondered if he was still screaming when they got there.

Twelve years later, curled up in a bunk in the prison cell that he would never leave, he could still feel the rawness of his throat and the tears on his cheeks when they'd slapped him in cold, biting, metal handcuffs and dragged him away. Maybe he'd been a little insane then.

Maybe he was a little insane now, thinking that someone like Mia would still want to talk to him if he told her about all that shit. The shit he'd killed to keep hidden away because of the guilt and the shame and the fear that it had laid on his heart and soul.

The shit she'd lived through ... it was shit that had happened to her, through no fault of her own, because life and fate were bastards to everyone. The shit he'd been through, though. That was his fault. His and Richard's and Seth's. No, he couldn't tell her about all of that. She didn't deserve to be dragged into that world, not even through his memories.

The next letter he received reassured him that he'd made the right choice. She was bright and happy and optimistic, and he'd be damned if that was ruined because of him, not after everything she'd already been through to come out shining on the other side.

Gabriel,

I understand that you aren't ready to let me in and share what happened. I'll be here if you do ever want to talk about it. Okay?

You didn't really make me cry, I just miss my mom sometimes, but if you really want to know what makes me smile? Let's see ...

Food, always and any kind. I can't cook but I love to eat, especially sweets. Peach cobblers and cherry pies will get a smile from me on even my worst days!

Music! I love music, but my favorite is contemporary Christian, and I don't think you'd enjoy that. I like classical and opera, too.

I'm going back to college this fall. That makes me smile a lot these days. I attend the same school as both of my best friends which helps make it exciting even though I'm still not completely sure I made the right choice about my major. My dad thinks I'd be a good teacher, and I like kids, so early childhood education seemed like a good choice ... We'll see, I guess.

What else makes me smile? Oh! Getting letters from you! Is that weird? I know you weren't exactly thrilled about it at first, but I know God sent you my way for a reason and I'm always happy to find a letter from you in the mailbox.

His stomach fluttered. It felt damn good to be the reason someone smiled. It settled over him, something he hadn't realized he'd been missing, a new sense of purpose. Make Mia smile.

He kept reading.

I don't want to upset you, and I know that it may be part of what you don't want to talk about, but why doesn't anyone else write to you?

Mia

He sighed and tipped his head back against the pillow, debating how honest he should be when he answered her last question.

~

Mia,

First of all, any food? What about liver? Haggis? My mother made me eat escargot as a kid. I was not a fan.

A laugh bubbled up inside her. She couldn't wait to tell him how disgusting that was. Someone needed to feed him some real food. Except they couldn't, she remembered with a jolt, because he was never getting out of prison.

Second, contemporary Christian is not my favorite. I like most music, but not that. Or opera. Did your parents let you listen to normal music?

Congrats on going back to college! I think you'd be a great teacher. You seem like the kind to dig until you find the best of someone and not let them give you anything less. Kids need that, someone to have faith in them.

Had he needed that? Why had no one helped him?

She nibbled on the jagged edge of a broken thumbnail, frowning as she read the rest.

Maybe I wasn't the nicest person when you started writing me, and I'm sorry. You aren't what I thought you'd be, and you don't make me feel like I'm not human because of the mistakes I've made. Thanks for that.

And about your last question ... my mother didn't even come to the trial and my uncle died a few years ago. So even if he wanted to (which he didn't) now he can't, and she won't.

It's okay, though, they aren't the kind of people you really want around anyway. I'd rather have you.

Gabriel

"What are you smiling about?"

She looked up in surprise, clutching the letter to her chest and meeting the kind and familiar face of James Prescott, the youth pastor at her father's church.

At twenty-five, he was a few years older than she was and handsome. Short brown curls surrounded a perfectly sculpted face—high cheekbones, firm jaw, sensual lips over even white teeth. He had a passion for sports and the outdoors, and the sun had given him a perpetual burnished glow that deepened in the summer months. He was friendly, never wasting an opportunity to talk to her or tease her when they bumped into each other at church, but she wasn't used to seeing him at her house.

"Hey, James," she said. "Are you here to talk to Dad?"

"Yeah, he said I could swing by tonight and have dinner." His eyes were still on the letter, but she didn't appease his curiosity, turning instead to back slowly toward the stairs, only finally turning her back on him when she set her foot on the first stair.

He watched her go with an amused smirk and she knew

that she had just set herself up for an endless stream of him picking on her about her secret. "Please excuse me, I need to run upstairs and clean up before we eat."

"Sure," he shrugged. "See you in a bit."

She called back over her shoulder when she was halfway up the staircase, "Dad's in his office. Go on back since he's expecting you."

It wasn't a complete lie. She was going to clean up for dinner ... as soon as she finished writing another quick letter.

Gabriel,

Liver is disgusting. You should be ashamed for suggesting that it qualifies as a food...

Chapter Six

"I can't believe summer is almost over already."

Mia hummed noncommittally at Kennedy's comment, eyes pressed shut against the harsh glint of the afternoon sun. Sweat was already beading on her skin and she had just stretched out on her towel after climbing out of the water. The skin of her fingers was still wrinkled, and she was already thinking about jumping back in to escape the heat.

"It doesn't feel over," Lilly's boyfriend complained, leaning back against her legs as she sat behind him. Bryce had been in love with Lilly since she'd first moved to town, but it had taken him until their senior year of high school to find the courage to ask her out, when he'd been the quarterback of the football team and a hometown hero. His parents were so proud of his athletic and academic success that almost everyone half expected Mr. Wheeler's head to pop clean off his shoulders one day, but Mia secretly suspected having Lilly at his side was the thing Bryce was proudest of. They'd been inseparable ever since they'd started dating and Mia watched wistfully as Lilly caressed his cheek and rubbed a fresh layer of chalk white sunscreen into his warm brown skin.

He pressed a kiss to her fingers when she was done and tugged playfully on the ends of her hair. Bryce towered over Lilly's tiny five-foot frame, long and lean from years of sports training, but his manners around Lilly were always gentle and quiet. The ferocity he showed on the football field disappeared whenever she was around.

They were an adorable couple, and it always sent a little frisson of jealousy through Mia to see them curled around each other so affectionately. She didn't begrudge them their easy intimacy, but she did wish that just once someone might look at her with interest.

Nobody in this small town really wanted to date the pastor's daughter and she was too focused on her classes to really notice anyone while she was at school. James was the only person she'd ever wondered about, and he certainly wasn't interested in her.

"You two are so cute," Kennedy said wistfully. She lounged on a towel beside Mia, eyes hidden behind the lenses of her sunglasses. "I don't think you've stopped touching for more than five minutes since you started dating."

"It's because Lilly's so *sweet*," Bryce said with a grin. He nipped playfully at Lilly's thigh while she slapped at him and turned her face away in embarrassment.

Mia turned her gaze back to the water. It was obvious that they were talking about something intimate, but her knowledge about sex was restricted to the little she'd been taught in the school's sexual education classes, which came down to nothing more than instilling fear of disease and pregnancy while insisting on abstinence. She rarely had a clue what her friends were talking about when they brought it up, but she was too embarrassed to admit it. She'd made an early commitment to wait till marriage before she had sex, and she knew it would make dating a challenge even if she could find someone who might like to try.

"Someday, when I'm done with college and I can move out of my parents' house, I'm going to find someone who looks at me that way," Kennedy mused. "Like I'm all she wants in the world."

"You shouldn't have to wait until you move out to do that." Mia reached out, wrapping her fingers around Kennedy's, and giving them a small squeeze. "I'm sorry."

"Don't be," Kennedy said. "It's not your fault. Your Dad's never made me feel bad with any of his sermons, not like the church my parents go to."

"It's awful that they think God's love is a way to hurt and condemn anyone different," Lilly said. "Are your parents still mad that you like going to church with us now, instead of with them?"

"Kinda, I guess?" She shrugged, unbothered. "It's not exactly a secret that your church is the most open-minded one in town. They don't agree with a lot of the stuff your dad says but church is church to them."

Mia knew quite well that plenty of the older people in town were not pleased that her father chose to focus more on God's love and forgiveness than his wrath, and that Kennedy's parents were definitely among them. She'd never understood how two people with such a cold lack of empathy had managed to produce such a kind and loving daughter.

"We still have plenty of people like Mrs. Newberry, though, don't we?" Lilly asked. "That woman uses her faith as a weapon on everyone around her. She's been a total bitch to me—sorry, Mia—and I know she'd make your life hell and probably out you to your parents if she got the chance."

Kennedy winced at the thought. "They'd kick me out, you know? That's why I don't date."

"You could live with me," Mia told her, not for the first time. "My dad wouldn't let you live on the streets. He's not like that, you know he isn't."

Kennedy smiled but shook her head. "I wouldn't do that. I don't want everyone in town gossiping about me or being mean to your family because of it."

"It's not fair that you have to hide who you are," Mia assured her, wrapping her arm around Kennedy's slender shoulders before turning her gaze to Lilly. "Mrs. Newberry is seriously still giving you a hard time?"

Lilly nodded; face wrinkled in dislike. "I think she gets worse every time the group agrees with one of my suggestions."

Mia sighed. "It's way past time for her to find some joy in her heart. Imagine spending so much time at church and leaving with nothing but bitterness and hate."

"There's far too much hate in the world," Lilly agreed.

"More than I realized," Mia admitted. "I feel so stupid because I thought that people like Mrs. Newberry were really horrible, and she *is*, but ... but some of the stuff Gabriel's told me about being in prison ..." She shuddered.

"My cousin said things were bad," Lilly agreed.

"It's supposed to be a punishment, right?" Bryce asked. "It's not like people go there to have a good time."

Lilly smacked him in the arm. "My cousin got arrested for stealing a car. He doesn't deserve the stuff that goes on in there. Besides, you know the system is incredibly broken and has always been racist."

"You don't have to remind a young Black man that the system is unfair," Bryce said. "But he just straight up murdered his own father. You don't think he should be punished?"

"He was a kid," Mia said, cutting in before Lilly could answer. "A literal kid. I've seen the trial footage."

"He killed his dad," Bryce repeated, shaking his head a little in bewilderment. "Does it really matter when or why he killed him?"

Mia lifted one slightly burnt shoulder in a short, dismissive shrug. She regretted ever telling them anything about Gabriel or what he had done. Every conversation about him somehow circled back around to that, and it was frustrating.

"You two have been writing a lot, haven't you?" Lilly asked quietly.

"Yeah? He's lonely. That was the point, remember?"

"Sure, we wanted to help some people out, make their sentences a little less miserable. It's just ... we all got car thieves or people locked up on petty drug charges and you got a murderer who is never getting out of prison."

"Yeah," Kennedy agreed. "Dan got picked up for possession charges, so he'll be out soon. They might even parole him and move him to a halfway house before his sentence is over."

Mia stared at her. "So?"

"I don't want you to get too close with this guy," Lilly explained. "He seems dangerous."

"You said so yourself, he's never getting out," Mia reminded her. "He can't hurt me. All he does is draw me pictures and talk to me about music and stuff."

Lilly fell silent and a stern look from Mia kept the rest of them from speaking up again. The conversation turned to other topics as Mia leaned back in her chair and pretended to nap.

It irritated her, how quickly they'd dismissed him once they'd found out why he was in prison. She'd tried to explain to Lilly about her connection to him and her theory that God had brought them together, but Lilly hadn't understood. Every conversation about him ended up much as this one had, and her worries had quickly gotten under Mia's skin. She knew they loved her, but Lilly was being far too overprotective.

Mia let her mind drift as she listened halfheartedly to her friends as they talked about the last few fleeting days of summer and their return to college classes. It left her feeling strangely hollow and sad inside that Gabriel had missed out on all of that over the years, the good and the bad.

~

"Jesus Christ," Alex snapped irritably. "You'd think keeping us in decent air conditioning would be considered a basic fucking human right in this heat."

The dark wet spots down his spine and beneath his armpits gave silent witness to the truth of his discomfort.

Gabriel hummed, too hot and miserable to do more than that. The heat was intolerable in early August, leaving them all feeling like they were crammed into this hell like sardines in a tin can that someone had stuffed into an oven.

The whole place smelled like stale sweat and aggression.

His fingers left damp imprints in the paper as he read Mia's most recent letter.

Gabriel,

Thank you so much for the drawing you sent with your last letter. I can't believe you remembered my favorite colors and that daisies are my favorite flower! That was so sweet of you!

I have a wall full of your art now (I have to admit I've framed every single one of them because they're so beautiful) but I think that one is my favorite so far. We've already written quite a few letters, haven't we? It's almost time for my classes to start and I can't seem to figure out where summer has gone this year.

It's a bit disappointing if I'm being honest.

Summer is supposed to be something magical, right? I didn't feel any of that this year, it was just more days hiding inside for the air conditioning and hanging out at the pool with the same friends I've always had. It was identical to every other summer. I thought getting older was supposed to change things, but I feel stuck in the same place I've always been. Like I'm not really growing up and becoming an adult like I thought I would.

It seems like there's something missing in my life, and I can't figure out what it is.

Maybe it's because I'm not really set on my major so I'm not excited about finishing school and starting my career?

I feel so restless, and I know I always end up rambling to you about something unhappy and I'm really sorry about that. I hate writing to you about this stuff, especially knowing that you didn't get to have any of this for yourself.

You'd probably give anything to have the things I take for granted and it makes me feel awful. It's so easy to talk to you and I forget that it makes me seem like an ungrateful brat when I whine to you about my life.

I wish you could have been with me at the pool today. I think that would have made it a great day for both of us.

Mia

If things had been different, if his parents hadn't sent him to Richard's or he hadn't ended up running the streets for Seth ... Maybe they would've met some other way in that hypothetical life, and he could have been with her.

Maybe he would have made something of himself, and she wouldn't have been ashamed to be his friend if he had. He could have been someone she could introduce to her friends, instead of someone she had to hide. She'd never told him exactly what had been said, but he knew her friend Lilly had discouraged her from writing to him too often or sharing too much.

Just looking out for her, he knew, concerned about her safety, but it hurt, and it made him nervous. He didn't like the idea of someone trying to take her away from him, this first friend that he'd had in so long, not when life had already taken everything else from him.

His mind slipped away, flashing back to his first days in juvie after he'd been arrested and how terrified he'd been when he realized that the inside of a prison might be all he ever knew.

He looked around, taking in the small cell and Alex still ceaselessly bitching about the heat, the putrid smell, and the inescapable feeling of hopelessness. He'd been right, this was all his life would never amount to, but he didn't want her to know that, or how much it hurt him.

Mia,

You should know by now that I like it when you tell me about your life. Even the boring stuff is a welcome distraction from what happens in here. Nobody is happy all the time and I bet once you figure out for sure what your major should be, you'll feel much better.

Do most people have magical summers?

I think that might be some made up TV bullshit. I bet your friends think their summer was pretty typical, too, even if most of us in here would love to hang out by the pool all summer. Our air conditioning is pretty unreliable, so it would be a welcome relief from the heat.

If life has its magical moments, I doubt they come on a schedule, it just happens when it's the right time. There's no fucking TV show or movie on Earth that would have predicted that this summer would be anything special for me, but it's the summer you found me.

Your letters have become a bright spot in my shitty life. I'm happy that you get to enjoy your life so don't waste any of your time being sad about me being stuck in here, okay? Promise?

You shouldn't waste your life wishing for things you can't have.

Gabriel

He stared at his last sentence and wondered if he would be able to take his own advice. There was always a sinking feeling in the pit of his stomach when he thought for too long about whether she would keep writing to him once she went back to class.

What if she got too busy?

He'd gotten used to having someone to care about over the past several weeks and the thought of losing her now made his heart ache.

Chapter Seven

Fall

The stack of her letters had grown thicker and new ones arrived on a predictable schedule that gave rhythm and reason to his days. The prison itself had not changed—the reality of incarceration was as unpleasant and endless as it had always been—but the monotony had been broken. She wrote to him at least twice a week, usually not even waiting to receive a response to one letter before composing the next.

She'd gushed happily about her first weeks back at college, boundless in her enthusiasm for every experience. He knew she must be smart because she found the work stimulating and enjoyable. He loved to learn but always hated sitting in a classroom, and he was glad that she was different. That her life wasn't a cage for her and that she was all of the bright and happy things, bringing the world joy where he had only ever brought pain.

Prison offered him few interesting things to discuss, so he answered her questions if she asked directly, but never volunteered more than necessary about his barren existence. He preferred to talk to her about her life, which was rich and vibrant and full.

To compensate, he continued to draw for her. Always cheerful things like flowers and sunsets and interesting faces that he remembered from before he came to this place. He wondered often what her face looked like, but he could never summon the courage to ask.

Alex had given up on mocking him for his 'little girl pen pal' when he realized how much Gabriel's attitude had improved with the regular arrival of her letters. The lack of heat in Gabriel's temper had turned Alex into her biggest fan.

"Mail from your girl," he said now, handing it over and snorting out a laugh when Gabriel extended his middle finger in reply.

"I'm stuck in here for the rest of my life, remember? Not everyone is lucky enough to have an actual release date. Lucky bastard."

"Some women are into that. Intimacy issues or some shit, right? Or maybe she can't get a man on the outside."

"Watch your mouth," Gabriel warned. "You don't know a damn thing about her."

"Neither do you, really. Do you even know what she looks like?" Alex's look was condescending, and he already knew the answer.

"No, I don't," Gabriel admitted, not really looking at Alex anymore, his gaze fixed on a spot of peeling paint beside his cellmate's head, "but I know she's smart and funny. She wouldn't have any problem getting a boyfriend if she wanted one."

Mia deserved to be loved. She was always positive and happy—who wouldn't be drawn to that vibrant energy?

"Do you think he'll try and stop her from talking to you if she does?"

"What?" Gabriel's gaze snapped back into focus on Alex's face.

"Would you want your girlfriend writing to some stranger? Especially one in here?" Alex gestured vaguely to their surroundings with a pointed look.

"Shut up, Alex," he muttered, and Alex shrugged, his point made. Gabriel hadn't thought about the implications of her being in a relationship, figuring that since she kept writing him after she went back to school that he was in the clear, at least for a while.

But Alex was right ... If he had a girlfriend, he certainly wouldn't want her to spend her time writing to a murderer.

He tucked his unease away as he opened her letter. There was nothing he could do about it now, so there was no use worrying about it.

Gabriel,

My classes are still going well. My humanities class has been the most interesting so far. The class focuses on learning about social issues and injustices. It's been unpleasantly educational, but fortunately I wasn't the only one in the class that was surprised by what we learned. There are so many horrible things most of us had never realized before.

We've spent two weeks focusing on the justice system, which made me think of you. There are significant problems, of course, with the structure of our laws and the way that they're implemented, but one thing in particular caught my attention.

Did you know that you can still appeal your sentence if you were not properly represented? I don't know all the details, but I know that something happened to you, something bad, and it was never brought up during the trial.

Your lawyers did almost nothing to defend you, they let you take the fall as an out-of-control rich kid and if you were abused or your lawyers had information about something that happened to you and they didn't do anything about it, you could petition the court to reverse your conviction and let you go. It's too late for you to just appeal the conviction (why is the deadline for that only thirty days after the trial ends anyway??) but it's not too late to file a petition for a writ of habeas corpus. The constitution guarantees you a legal defense and if your lawyers didn't do their jobs, then you have a legitimate reason to challenge the results of your trial.

I'm doing my semester paper on ways the public defense system fails the public because it's infuriating and there are so many examples. My professor says that it'll make a good paper because I feel so strongly about it, but I wish there were ways I could help people like you that have been unfairly treated in some way. Not just that you shouldn't be in prison for life, which I really don't think you should, but also the complete media frenzy around your trial. The judge shouldn't have allowed all of that, Gabriel. You were a minor and you deserved protection and privacy.

It's not much but I hope you're doing well today, and every day, and you know that I'm always thinking of you. I try to cheer you up and let you experience as much of college and normal life as I can through these letters.

There are a million little things that I notice every day that I probably wouldn't notice otherwise, because I keep track of them in my mind to share them with you.

She went on, and each word kept the smile on his face for another minute longer.

~

You're right.

He'd written back to her about college and friendships but all he had said about something that could have altered the course of his entire life was—

You're right. I tried to tell the lawyers and the guardian the court appointed for me about what happened, but they didn't believe me and there was nothing I could do about it. I was sixteen and in prison, how was I supposed to track down witnesses?

I wanted to challenge the conviction after it happened, but I couldn't. Did your classes tell you that Texas doesn't offer public services after conviction? There was no way I could find a lawyer to represent me for free within that thirty-day deadline. I couldn't file an appeal all those years ago and I can't do anything about requesting a new trial now for the same reason. Petitioning the court would mean hiring lawyers I can't afford.

She was still fuming the morning after reading it, tapping her finger in irritation on her thigh as she listened halfheartedly to the day's lecture. Sure, maybe she should be glad that he'd resigned himself to the inevitable—since apparently there was not one single thing at all that he could do to change it—but that went against every instinct she possessed. It wasn't right, it wasn't fair, and he should not be made to suffer this way, no matter what he had done.

"Mia?"

"Hmm? Oh!" Mia looked around with dawning realization to find that most of the class had already filed out the door, leaving only her instructor. "I'm sorry," she said, shoving her laptop and her water bottle in her bag and jumping to her feet. "I must not have been paying attention."

"I was going to ask if you mind staying behind for a moment?" She smiled when Mia hesitated nervously. "I'd like to talk to you about your paper."

Dr. Fischer had always been easygoing, and they all liked her well enough, but their final paper was worth a full 30% of their final course grade. "Is something wrong with the outline I turned in?" Mia asked when the door had closed behind the last student.

"Quite the opposite actually," the professor responded,

turning in her seat to face Mia with a wide smile. "I knew from our class discussions that this topic was something you were passionate about, but the paper that you are proposing is very in depth and already well researched. Truthfully, I've had many students come through my class with law school aspirations and not one of them was demonstrating work at this level."

"Oh, thanks." Mia shifted uncomfortably, tugging the strap of her backpack higher on her shoulder, and tightening her grip on the phone in her hand. "I appreciate that, but I've never even considered being a lawyer."

Dr. Fischer nodded politely, but her eyes were keen. "Yes, I remember you said your primary interest right now was early childhood education. Is that right?" She waited for Mia's mumbled agreement before continuing, "That's an admirable field and I'm sure you'll excel if that's truly where your passions lie. I wouldn't be doing my duty as your teacher, however, if I didn't tell you that it would be a waste of your potential to go that route if your heart isn't in it."

"My heart is in helping people," Mia told her honestly. "It's in making a change in the world."

She may have been uncertain of what exactly her future career might consist of, but that much she had always known. After all the challenges she had gone through in her life, it wouldn't be right to hoard the gifts she had been given. She had been helped, and loved, and she wanted to pass that along to others.

Dr. Fischer looked at her for a moment before setting her glasses on top of her head and leaning back in her chair. "Not all lawyers are the bloodsucking leeches that you hear everyone making jokes about," she said carefully. "There are two sides to every case, two sides to every policy. My husband is an environmental lawyer and works for a firm that handles litigation against companies that are engaging in pollution or destruction of habitat. There are also nonprofit organizations, pro bono cases, and many other ways that someone with an interest in the law could have a positive influence on the world."

Mia tucked her bottom lip between her teeth, her mind flicked to Gabriel as she stood there, considering a possibility that had never occurred to her before. "I'll think about it," she promised.

"That's all I can ask," Dr. Fischer said with an encouraging smile. "And don't forget about the quiz on Monday." Mia recognized the dismissal when the professor turned back to her papers.

She said a hasty goodbye and slipped out the door, wondering if she still had time to catch Bryce and Lilly in the library and get some research done, and turning that way when she stepped outside onto the sidewalk. Her choice of college had been an easy one once Bryce had received a full-ride football scholarship. Lilly had wanted to go with Bryce, and Mia and Kennedy had both followed Lilly. There were other colleges close by that were just as good, but none of those had her friends and that had made the decision easy for all of them.

September had not done much to cool the air, and the leaves on the trees outside were still green, but something about being back at school always made things feel like fall. They'd be carving pumpkins and picking costumes by this time next month, and Lilly was already planning a Christmas toy drive for the prayer group.

After all, she'd insisted, you can't start too soon on those types of things.

Mia knew everyone was hoping that she'd step in and do more for the group as Mrs. Mitchell got older. Her father was the pastor and her mother had run the group until she died, so it was a logical assumption but as happy as she was to provide snacks and chip in for events, Lilly was really the one that came up with the good ideas and enjoyed being involved in the planning.

It was something that had been tumbling around in her head for a while now. She was worried her father would be disappointed if he found out that she wasn't living up to her mother's precedent when it came to church involvement, but Lilly deserved more credit than she was being given. Maybe she could talk to Mrs. Mitchell about making Lilly an official co-leader for the group. If that wasn't a thing, then Mia was sure they could make it one ...

She set the thought aside when she swung open the heavy doors that led to the blessedly air-conditioned sanctuary of the library. She was sweating through her T-shirt from the short walk and paused gratefully just inside the large well-lit room, letting the cool air blow over her as she looked for her friends. She should have sent a text to ask if they'd be here, but she doubted Lilly would check her phone inside the library.

The large room was lined all around with shelves of books, with sections on the interior that divided the space into further book storage, rows of computers, and neat little tables that provided comfortable study space to a few dozen students. Mia passed several that seemed to have fallen asleep in their books, and she chuckled as she walked by.

Next to church, Mia had always thought that libraries were the most likely place to find God. There was always a feeling of quiet contemplation, an atmosphere of knowledge and wisdom and peaceful rest. Even though every library was different, the smell of books was always comfortingly the same. It was like an infinite number of homes waiting to welcome you in with the turn of a page.

Lilly and Bryce were already seated at a table, talking quietly as they leaned over an open textbook. They both looked up expectantly when she dropped into a chair across from them.

Mia leaned forward to whisper, "I had to stay and talk to my professor. She wanted to talk to me about my final paper."

"She asked you to stay behind for that?" Lilly asked, peeking around to make sure no one was looking before stuffing a piece of chocolate in her mouth. "Isn't it a little early to be worried about finals?"

She pressed a chocolate into Mia's outstretched palm and Mia popped it into her mouth before answering. "I guess she also wanted to suggest that I look into changing my major and doing something law related, instead of teaching."

Lilly laughed and shook her head. "You've never wanted to be anything but a teacher."

"My dad wants me to be a teacher."

"But isn't that what you want, too? To be a teacher like your mom?"

"I'm not sure." She pulled out her laptop and looked at them with a frown. "I figured my dad kinda knew what was best since I didn't know what I wanted to do."

"Law is pretty cool, I guess," Lilly said. "Lots of years in school, though, and I've heard it's very competitive."

"Do you think I can't get into law school?" Mia paused at that—she hadn't considered the possibility that she might not be successful if she did decide to pursue it and she bristled a little at the thought.

"That's not what I meant," Lilly said, oblivious to the tumult going on in Mia's mind. "I wonder if the motivation for law school will still be there, once you aren't writing to Gabriel anymore."

"What does Gabriel have to do with law school?" Mia asked, and Bryce turned to look at Lilly, also clearly wanting her to explain the connection she saw between the two.

"I assumed that's where this sudden interest came from," Lilly said, looking to Bryce for confirmation that her assumption made sense. He nodded and she sat back in her chair, appeased that he agreed with her.

"Maybe some of it," Mia admitted, "but why would I stop writing to him?" She knew her tone was surly, but she had gotten tired of these conversations.

"I didn't think you were gonna write to him forever because it was a charitable gesture, not a real friendship."

"It *is* a real friendship," Mia said defensively.

"Okay, maybe it is *for now*, but what are you going to do when you get a boyfriend that doesn't want you writing to a convicted murderer that's serving life in prison?"

"I wouldn't want Lilly doing that," Bryce said as he placed his hand protectively over Lilly's. "It sounds dangerous."

"I guess it's a good thing I don't have a boyfriend," Mia snapped, loudly enough to have heads turning in the quiet room.

Lilly leaned forward to whisper, "Not yet, but you want one, right?"

"I'm not interested in dating," Mia insisted stubbornly, ignoring that she had seen plenty of attractive men on campus that she *might* have considered dating if they had asked prior to this very irritating conversation.

"Yeah? What about James Prescott?"

Mia leaned back in her chair and crossed her arms over her chest. "What about him?"

"Oh, come on!" Lilly prodded. "You've always been interested in James and surely you've noticed how much he's been at your house lately?'

"Talking to my dad—" Mia began.

"And looking at you." Bryce said, wiggling his brows suggestively. "I think *someone* has caught his attention."

"He doesn't look at me like that," Mia sputtered.

"He has no reason not to," Lilly reminded her with a pointed look. "And I wouldn't be surprised if your dad was really supportive. He loves James, and he knows James would be a good husband. He's always been nice and he's a stable guy, isn't he? You'd have a good life."

She absolutely would, Mia knew that. James wasn't the kind of man to raise his voice or his hand. He was great with kids and loved animals. He worshiped God and respected his mother and would provide his wife with a nice house and a large family. Mia had always wanted that—a home and kids of her own.

Lilly's expression was grave as Mia nibbled uncertainly on her bottom lip. "You know how he'd feel about Gabriel and this law school stuff. If he's going to be the pastor at a church of his own, he's going to need a wife that can help with that. It's something for you to think about."

Chapter Eight

She thought about her uncertain future for weeks, in the quiet spaces between her classes when she was alone and late at night as she lay awake and watched the moonlight and shadows dance across her ceiling.

There was no denying the joy she experienced as she worked her way through the research for her paper. She was fascinated and horrified by the things she discovered as she dug deeper into the processes of the criminal justice system. It was large and lumbering and unequal in ways that she found incredibly frustrating. It was clear that there was a desperate need for change and for people willing to fight for those who were treated unfairly or did not have the means to escape their circumstances. It would be a difficult career and require years of investment in her education, but it would be deeply rewarding.

The work she put into her class paper was equally emotionally draining and mentally stimulating. She passed hours alone in the library soaking up all the knowledge she could and huffing in frustration as she encountered case after case of kids who deserved so much better than the fate they had been dealt. Some days she wept quietly, but she always wondered if she might be part of the change that was so clearly needed.

She came home energized and excited from her schoolwork but even her new distraction couldn't keep her from noticing how often she now found James at her house. Nothing significant had changed in his behavior toward her, but she watched him closer now and she soon realized that Lilly and Bryce may have been picking up signs she hadn't been experienced enough to see. He smiled at her whenever she entered a room, made excuses to stay close to her while she was there, and watched her intently whenever she left. The Wednesday before Halloween he volunteered to help set up for their annual trick-or-treat event, something that she was nearly certain he had done only because he knew she would be there.

Some of the other local churches frowned on their participation in a holiday with such pagan origins, but Mia always loved seeing the kids in their costumes. They were adorable dressed up as superheroes and bumblebees. She'd always been grateful that her father believed in accepting the idea that you couldn't stop people from celebrating, so you might as well join in on the fun. All he asked was that they refrained from dressing as monsters and devils, and most were happy enough to show up in more wholesome costumes.

Mia had already spent over an hour attaching slips of paper with encouraging bible verses to the sticks of black and orange suckers that put temporary spider tattoos on your tongue, when Lilly showed up with several more huge bags of candy.

"We can't forget to pick up the apples on Saturday," she said, her smile big as she dropped the bags on the table with a thump and looked around. "The kids really enjoyed bobbing for apples last year."

"It's on my list of chores for that morning already," Mia

reassured, dropping the last sucker in a big orange bowl and opening the first bag of Lilly's candy. It was chocolate, and she grabbed a piece for herself once she had emptied the contents into the next bowl. She was going to end up eating her weight in candy this week, but she had no regrets.

"Any problems so far?" Lilly asked, grabbing a candy and biting into it with a satisfied hum.

"Not really. The usual complaints from Mrs. Newberry, same as every Halloween."

"We told her she could stay home."

"I wish she would have," Mia sighed. She was already tired of listening to her complain about how they were all celebrating the devil's birthday and corrupting children in the process.

Lilly was the new co-leader of the bible group, and Mia wanted tonight to go especially well since she was eager and excited about the first task in her new role. Her father had been surprisingly supportive of the change once she explained how much work Lilly had put into the group, and he hadn't questioned Mia's own commitment as she feared he might, but she still wondered if she had let him down.

"I see you've brought company," Lilly said, interrupting Mia's worries and tipping her head across the room to where James stood on a small step stool with his arms stretched high to hang orange and black streamers from the ceiling.

"He offered to help carry all the decorations from the attic," Mia said, a blush riding hot on her cheeks. "He was at our house anyway, so he said it wasn't a problem."

"Yeah, I'm sure he had nothing better to do tonight," Lilly giggled. "I *told* you."

"I know you did. Now, *hush*, before someone else hears you," Mia looked around to make sure no one else was close enough to eavesdrop, but she knew she was smiling. "What do I do?" she whispered frantically.

"Go offer to help him hang those streamers."

"I mean, he's been doing it himself for ten minutes ..." Mia said, glancing at him again and then away just as quickly when she found him already looking at her.

Lilly rolled her eyes. "He doesn't actually need help, just go hold the tape and streamers and don't forget to smile!"

Mia was afraid it would be awkward, but it was easy to hold the supplies and smile when he looked at her. His hand brushed hers every time she handed him a new piece of tape, soft and warm where it skimmed hers.

By the time the decorations were hung, and James went home, she was riding high on excitement and success. Almost everyone had already left, the rest were standing around in small groups chatting as the evening wrapped up. It didn't take her long to spot Lilly on the other side of the room, fixing a cheap plastic tablecloth with smiling jack-o-lanterns on it over where it had fallen off their folding dessert table.

Mia hurried toward her, but her steps faltered when she overheard Mrs. Newberry whispering loudly to a group of the other women, all of them clearly unaware that she wandered so close. "She hardly participates," the older woman sniffed disdainfully. "Her mother never had such problems. Kate Anderson was devoted to the church, and she would have been ashamed of that child if she had lived to see this. Did you see the way she was throwing herself at Mr. Prescott tonight?"

Unable to listen to another word, Mia turned and fled, tears blurring her vision as the words she had not been meant to hear amplified her own self-doubts. Mrs. Newberry was mean and a terrible gossip, but maybe she was right, maybe she would have disappointed her mother.

She sank down in her father's chair, hiding in his office in the dark as she let the tears flow. She was crying so hard she didn't hear the door open.

"You don't have to be exactly like your mother for her to be proud of you."

Mia jumped and looked up to find old Mrs. Mitchell standing on the other side of her father's desk, watching her from behind the thick lenses of her glasses. She sniffled and rubbed her tears away with the back of her hand.

"She was perfect, and everyone loved her ..."

"We all loved her, but she wasn't perfect. You loved her so much that you couldn't see the flaws. Nothing wrong with that, all things considered, and she loved you just as much. More importantly she *knew* you. She took you, chose you, when you were wild and mean, and she loved you anyway. She wouldn't want you to be an unhappy woman that's trying to be something you're not. She'd want you to be the best version of yourself, because that's what God created you to be."

"But Mrs. Newberry—"

"I already gave that woman a piece of my mind, and it's not the first time. She's upset my girls too much already. Don't you worry about what she said. Not about your mama and not about Mr. Prescott. She was the biggest flirt in this town when she was your age and she might have forgotten that little fact, but I assure you I haven't. I'm old enough to remember plenty of things that she'd rather were forgotten."

Mia giggled a little, almost as surprised by Mrs. Mitchell's fierce protectiveness as she was with the idea that Mrs. Newberry had once been a flirt.

"There's never been anyone interested in me before," she admitted. "Maybe I *was* too flirtatious."

"If you were being flirtatious, so was he. I don't think there's a thing wrong with talking to a nice man that wants to get to know you better." She was quiet for a moment, pensive as she looked at Mia. Sometimes it felt like Mrs. Mitchell could see right through to the heart of a person. "I'm going to give you one more word of unsolicited advice from an old woman," she said eventually. "James Prescott is a good man, but you need more than a good man to have a happy life. You need the *right* man and that'll be the one who fits into what God calls you to do and sees after your happiness as much as he expects you to see to his own."

Impossible dreams of law school flitted shamefully through her mind. "What if *this* isn't what I'm supposed to do?" she asked, waving her arm around to indicate the small office. "Would God call me away from the church?"

"From your seat on Sunday? I don't think so. But not everyone is meant to marry a pastor and spend their lives worrying over a congregation. Kate was happy with that life, and I know you saw how fulfilled it made her, but you are not your mama. Open your heart to God, really listen to Him, and you'll know what He has planned for you."

Halloween at the church went well. The adults had nearly as much fun as the children, and because it was a Saturday night, many of the parishioners stayed later than they might have done otherwise.

Mia was having so much fun that she offered to stay behind with her friends and clean up so her dad could leave early. He had to be up to get ready for the morning service and she wasn't ready to leave.

"How are you going to get home?" he asked. "Can Lilly drive you?"

"I can bring her," James said from behind her, and Mia turned to find him standing there with a shy smile. "It's not a problem."

Her father didn't hesitate, and Mia really wondered for the first time if he might support the idea of her dating James. She mulled it over as they swept up discarded candy wrappers and wiped the tables clean of spilled juice. Bryce caught her eye with a meaningful look, and she fought to stifle a nervous giggle.

After they were done, James walked out to the parking lot and opened the door to his sensible white sedan. It smelled clean and pleasant, like air freshener and his cologne, but having him so close to her in such a small space made her heart pound and she kept her hands folded tightly in her lap during the short drive. The lights inside the house were already out when they arrived, and her father had clearly already gone to bed. He obviously trusted that James would bring her home quickly and safely.

"Thank you," she said, breaking the tense silence in the car as she reached for the door handle.

"Mia, wait," he said softly, wrapping one warm hand around her wrist. She stilled, her skin tingling under the soft caress of his fingers on her arm as he laid his lips gently against her own. His kiss was warm and inoffensive, but he didn't linger for long, nor did he attempt to part her lips for a more thorough exploration.

"I'd like to spend more time with you," He cupped her cheek with his hand. "You're exactly the kind of woman I'd like to build a life and a family with."

It wasn't unexpected with all the time he'd spent hanging around lately. She'd always known he was the kind of man that believed dating was for the purpose of testing compatibility for marriage, but something inside her shifted as her budding interest dimmed. She wanted a husband and a family, but his words left her cold. "What kind of woman is that exactly?"

"The kind that puts their faith in God, where it should be. You're kind and generous and I've never known you to be rebellious or disrespectful. You're a good, modest Christian woman, exactly the kind that any man would be proud to have for a wife."

It was a very practical assessment and it left her feeling cold, even though his hand was still warm on her cheek. She couldn't fault him for it, not really, not when they had all been encouraged to seek those qualities in a spouse, but ...

"Can I see you again?" he asked. "Alone?"

"Alone?" She thought it over quickly, knowing how seriously he would take it if she agreed to start seeing him privately.

"I can talk to your dad tomorrow, ask him for his blessing."

"That would be great." She wasn't sure where her doubts were coming from, but she wasn't going to throw away the attention of a man who seemed to be strongly considering the possibility of fulfilling her dreams of a husband and family when she couldn't even put a name to her hesitation. "I'm sure Dad won't mind at all. He trusts you."

"Good, I'm really glad," he said. He kissed her again, a quick press of lips, and watched until she was safely inside the house before he started to leave.

She closed the door and slumped against it, thoughts racing.

He seemed sincere in his intentions, but was he interested in her as a person? Or was he looking for someone that checked off the boxes of what he believed would make a good wife? His kiss had been soft and sweet, but had he felt anything at all? Had she?

She sighed as she sat down at the dining room table and began to flick through the day's stack of mail until she found a letter from Gabriel. Here she was, feeling sorry for herself, when she had certainly still had a better day than he'd experienced. She'd wanted to send him some candy for the holiday, but they weren't allowed to send food to the prisoners. She knew because she had looked up the rules.

Mia,

I'm not surprised that you're considering changing your major. You were never excited about teaching, and you've been excited about law since you started that paper you're working on. Your teacher obviously has faith in you, and I am sorry that your friends can't see how smart and capable you are. You're going to kick ass at anything you do.

She giggled, shaking her head. Her father would probably be upset about his language and her ready acceptance of it, and she really ought to be trying to discourage him and set a good example, but it was so uniquely Gabriel. She didn't want him to change it.

I'm the last person who can give you advice, but I think you should follow your heart. You shouldn't be tied down by what someone else wants for you, not when you have a whole life of freedom ahead of you. Chase all of your dreams, and to hell with anyone who doesn't like it.

She quickly scanned the rest of the letter, shaking her head when he promised to try and have a good Halloween because she knew he had *not,* and then let the paper fall back onto the table. He had such faith in her, and it felt so good to have someone on her side even if he didn't know everything. She'd already explained her concerns about her father's disappointment and her mother's legacy, but she hadn't told him anything at all about one of the biggest reasons behind her hesitation.

She'd told him about everything else in her life, but not James. She wasn't sure why she'd kept that a secret since she'd finally noticed James' attention, but every time she'd tried to bring it up the words had refused to come, like she couldn't find the right way to tell him. She was sure that something so simple wouldn't change their friendship, and she wasn't ashamed of her interest in James, but she felt uneasy at the idea of those parts of her life connecting.

She never actually mentioned Gabriel around James

either, she realized with a frown, and her friends had thankfully stopped asking about him when they realized that she couldn't be swayed from her decision to keep in touch with him. Gabriel would probably have been happy for her if she'd found a way to mention James, but she doubted very much that James would feel the same way about Gabriel.

Over the past few months Gabriel had become something of a sanctuary for the rebellious parts of her desires, the parts that didn't fit into the neat boxes of everyone else's expectations. He encouraged her in everything she wanted to do because he didn't care about anyone else or what the world wanted. He only cared about her and what made her happy. He knew all of her flaws and ugly parts, the parts she kept hidden away from everyone else, and he still wanted to be friends with her.

Somehow, she thought that if she asked Gabriel what he liked about her, his answer would be very different from what James had told her in the car.

She picked up the letter and looked at it again.

Follow your own heart.

Everyone else had told her to heed God's guidance, and God had directed her to Gabriel. If he thought that she should follow her heart, then maybe that was exactly what God wanted her to hear.

Chapter Nine

T he letter came not long after Halloween, her words bubbling with a palpable excitement that nearly jumped off the page.

Gabriel,

I did it! I submitted my change of major form! I'm now a political science major! It's not going to be easy getting into law school, but I feel so good about taking that first step.

I haven't told my dad yet, he might be supportive, I just think it would be a good idea to wait until I can show him a few semesters of good grades to prove to him I'm serious about this.

Lilly and Bryce were decent about it, if not exactly excited. They think I should tell my dad now, but they've agreed not to mention it until I've finished a few more classes.

Thanks for encouraging me and believing in me. I don't think I would've had the courage to do it without you.

It felt good, the idea that he had truly changed someone's life for the better. There was someone out there that was glad that he had been there for them. It wasn't pity or charity that kept her writing to him now, it was a shared connection. A hard, dark place inside opened more than he had been willing to let it open in a long time.

But now I need you to do something for me. I need you to think about trying to find a way to petition the court and challenge your conviction. I'll help you myself if I have to but you deserve to be heard. You deserve a fair chance.

He thought about her words all night, staring at the ceiling as unfamiliar hope pushed against his carefully guarded heart. His experiences had warned him against believing in anything too much, the cost of faith was too high. It knocked the breath out of you when it crumbled from under your feet. He understood why she felt differently, why she still believed in God and good things, and he didn't want his failures to be what robbed her of it.

Mia,

I'm so proud of you.

I don't know if I've told you, but it's my birthday coming up. I'm going to be twenty-eight and it's been more than twelve years since they put me in here. I asked around after you told me about it, some of the guys in here spend a lot of time trying to help everyone with their cases, and they made it pretty clear that Texas doesn't like to let go of you once they have you in a jail cell. Even if the state overturned my conviction, there's almost a 100% chance that they would charge me with the murder all over again and make me go through a new trial. Don't waste your time on me.

He was afraid that she'd be angry at his refusal but when the next letter came, it brought only understanding and an unexpected gift. He didn't recognize it for what it was at first. A paper that was thicker and stiffer than what she usually wrote on fell out of the envelope to land by his feet. It was a plain white rectangle with a single line of script written neatly on the back in Mia's handwriting.

Just to let you know I was thinking about you!

Puzzled, he turned it over in his hands to find a glossy photograph. The background was a neat and tidy kitchen with bright sunlight streaming in the windows but dominating the image was a cupcake with red frosting and a single lit candle in the hands of the most beautiful woman he had ever seen.

His breath caught in his throat, his fingers trembled, his heart began to pound as he drank in the details of her.

A slender build, brown hair that tumbled just past the shoulders of a dark blue dress, and a simple gold cross that hung from a chain around her neck. But it was her face that captivated him. A pert nose dusted with freckles. A soft mouth, pink and turned up in a wide smile. Hazel eyes with long lashes that sparkled with laughter.

The sounds of the prison faded away, a dull buzzing of insignificant noise as he stared at her. His eyes roamed the photo again and again, trying to memorize every line of her as though someone might try to snatch the picture away from him.

This was Mia.

His Mia.

He rubbed his thumb over the image, careful not to smudge it as he imagined what it would be like to have her actually smile at him with such warmth and then hung it on the wall beside his bed. He could see her now when he woke up and when he drifted off to sleep.

"What's that?"

Gabriel sighed and flopped back down in his bunk. Alex had become increasingly annoying since Mia's letters had started arriving and there wasn't much he wouldn't do for an ounce of privacy at this point. "Nothing, it's none of your business."

Alex ignored him, standing up to crowd Gabriel's bunk and peer over him at the photo tacked to the wall. "Is that her?"

Gabriel shrugged. "Yeah, that's her."

Alex laughed, the rumble shaking his whole body so hard he had to sit back down on his own bed again.

"Something funny? There's not a damn thing to laugh at, she's perfect."

"That's what's so funny. You were already half gone over this girl and now you find out she looks like *that*. You're *so* fucked."

Gabriel pressed his lips together and swallowed hard. "She's just a friend."

Alex nodded. "Yep, and it kills you. It would kill me too if I had a girl that looked like that on the outside and I knew I was never getting out of here." For a moment, there was something on Alex's face that looked like pity, but it was gone so quickly that Gabriel was sure he'd imagined it.

Gabriel didn't answer, but he didn't take her picture down off the wall as he settled in his bunk to read her letter.

Gabriel,

I know this is a poor excuse for a birthday gift but I couldn't send the actual cupcake so it will have to do. I take personal exception to the prison's rule against sending you food. First no Halloween candy, and now no birthday cupcakes? It's cruel, evil, and inhumane. Unfortunately, due to this, I was forced to eat your cupcake for you. I'm sure you understand that I couldn't allow it to go to waste!

He shook his head, a laugh bubbling up from deep down inside that helped push his worries out of his mind. She loved food and he would've given her a hundred cupcakes, a thousand, one every day of her life if it kept that smile on her face.

Is there anything I can get for you for a real present? Surely, there's something you want?

He glanced at the picture and pushed the thought away. He couldn't let Alex be right about this, he couldn't think of her that way when she was...well she wasn't thinking of him that way, that was for damn sure. She was his friend. His closest and only friend. He had nothing at all beyond that to offer her, had no right to think the kind of thoughts that were creeping at the edge of his mind.

I'm sorry I only have time for a short letter today, but I wanted to tell you that I understand how you feel. I don't want to get your hopes up and then have the system let you down again. Even if all it got you was another chance to tell your story in front of a jury, I think you deserve a fair trial. I'm still willing to do whatever I can to help, but I won't push you if you aren't ready.

I'll write more soon, and I may have some exciting stories to tell when I do because I'm going to a party with Lilly and Bryce! A real party, for the first time ever! I've never done anything like this before and maybe it's ridiculous to be this excited, but I don't care!

I promise I'll tell you all about it in my next letter!

Mia

But the next letter didn't come.

He didn't get worried when the first few days passed, but by the end of the first week he'd grown concerned. By the end of the second week, he was terrified.

Alex avoided him as much as possible, giving him space to sit broodingly on his bunk and glare at the picture of her on his wall.

The letters he sent her weren't being returned to him, so she must have kept them, but he couldn't figure out why she wasn't answering them. His biggest fear, though he knew he had no right to it, was that she had abandoned him, moved on at the request of her friends or her father or some boyfriend she hadn't told him about.

He'd sagged in relief when a letter finally came, and he tore it open, eyes scanning hungrily ... his joy turning to despair when he recognized the tears stains that marked the words.

What could he have done to cause her such pain?

His stomach twisted, and he swallowed down the bile that crawled up his throat as he forced himself to read, to try and make sense of what she was saying.

Gabriel,

I'm sorry, so sorry, that I haven't written. I read your letters, and I know you've been worried about me, but I didn't know how to explain.

Something happened, something bad, at the party that night.

People were drinking when we got there and Lilly wanted to go home but I wanted to stay, just for a little while, because I'd never been to a party before. I should have listened but we weren't drinking, I never drink, and I thought everything would be fine, you know?

He squinted trying to make out the next few lines, tears had fallen heavily there, and it was hard to read what she had written.

I lost Lilly and Bryce in the crowd and there were some guys I had never met before. I was trying to get through, to find my friends, but they wouldn't let me. They said, well it doesn't matter exactly what they said ...

He knew exactly the kind of bullshit they'd said and if he wasn't already in prison, he would have landed himself in one for using his fists to teach every single one of them how to watch their fucking mouths around her.

... but it was awful. They were pulling on my clothes and laughing. I told them to stop, but they didn't listen, and I just wanted to leave. I wanted to find Lilly and Bryce and go home, but they wouldn't let me. They were blocking my way out of the room, and I was so scared of what they might do to me.

They needed more than their mouths fixed and his blood bubbled with rage. He looked around, momentarily blind to his surroundings, chest heaving with fury and the need to *do* something. It took a moment for him to realize how trapped he was, how helpless. He was no good to her in here, couldn't even protect her when shit like this happened.

He pushed a hand into his hair, chest rumbling with impotent anger as he read the rest, his fury rising with each word.

I hit one of them, it probably didn't even hurt him, but they weren't expecting it and I ran out of the room while they were distracted.

I couldn't talk to my friends about it because I was embarrassed and they'd know it was my fault for not wanting to leave, and I didn't want to tell my dad because he'd probably never let me leave the house again. I tried but I couldn't keep it bottled up inside and I ended up telling James.

I know I haven't told you about James and I'm sorry about that, but I've been on a few dates with him. He's our youth pastor and I'm the pastor's daughter and it all seemed so perfect on the surface. Everyone thought we'd be the perfect couple and I wanted to think that, too.

He asked me what I wore to the party and then said that maybe it had been a bad idea for me to go wearing that dress and maybe I should have worn a sweater over it or picked a longer skirt. He said that maybe I needed to try harder not to cause someone else to stumble. He agreed not to tell my dad because he didn't want anyone to know and be ashamed of what I'd caused.

He wants to be a pastor someday like my dad and I don't know how I can help him run a church if I'm leading others into sin and it causes them to do such horrible things. I mean, he might not have wanted to marry me anyway because of law school, but I hadn't even had a chance to talk to him about that.

I'm so mad at everyone right now, but especially myself and at first, I thought that I should never talk to anyone else about it because I couldn't handle anyone else looking at me the way that James did. It was so lonely, and I was having such frightening nightmares, but then I realized that of all the people in my life, you were the one person that I could say anything to, and you'd never judge me.

I don't know what I need you to do, but please don't let me be alone in this. Please tell me it's going to be okay.

Mia

Gabriel buried his face in his hands, rage coiled uselessly in every muscle of his body. He wanted to hurt someone, to rip and tear at them and make them bleed for what they'd done to her. She'd been so innocent, so full of light, and now the world had put its disgusting fingerprints on her, and she blamed herself.

Alex walked into the cell, his brows lifting as he saw the paper in Gabriel's hands. "You finally get a letter? I thought for sure she'd finally gotten smart ..." He trailed off at the snarl of rage on Gabriel's face. "What the hell? What happened? Did she get married and break up with you?"

Gabriel's teeth were clenched, his fist tightening over and over again reflexively.

"That son of a bitch made her feel like it was her fault."

Chapter Ten

She carried his letter in her purse, so it was always with her and when the guilt and shame started to creep in, she pulled it out to read again. The paper was soft now, and the words faded, but it didn't matter. She'd already memorized the exact phrases that had been most comforting and where she could find them on the page.

Are you alright?

He'd asked about her first, how she was doing, how she was feeling. It made her feel warm and safe, knowing she mattered to him more than any rule she might have broken. He didn't care if her judgment had lapsed or mistakes had been made, he only cared about her.

This was not your fault.

He'd told her that so clearly, so emphatically, that the sick feeling in her chest had begun to abate for the first time since the party. He knew what had happened, the real ugly truth of it and not the glossed over version that she'd told James, and he didn't blame her.

I can't believe that asshole actually tried to blame you. I'd like to knock his teeth down his throat and blame him for not wearing a helmet. I need you to know that what he said was bullshit.

She had laughed out loud at that, a trembling hand pressed to her mouth. She didn't feel bad about Gabriel's anger toward James. It wasn't like Gabriel could actually hurt him. He just wanted her to know that he'd protect her, keep her safe, and he wanted to make her laugh, like he always did.

Don't ever let someone make you feel like another person's sins are your fault, especially not some self-righteous, Bible-thumping bastard. He doesn't deserve you if he treats you that way.

People that hide their cruelty behind a mask of piety are even more terrible than the ones that are openly evil. You don't see them coming until it's too late, and even when they hurt you, they blame you for it.

She'd considered that, worried over what he meant, until she'd given in to the urge to ask him.

Did someone hurt you that way? Did they blame you, too?

She wasn't sure he'd answer, it was such an intimate and personal thing to ask, but he surprised her.

They hurt me and other people I cared about, and no one believed any of us.

She felt less alone knowing he'd experienced the same kind of hurt, and she wondered again what had led to him killing his father. She was so certain about his pain, that he hadn't really been the spoiled brat the media had depicted, but she didn't want to press too hard.

She had written only

I'm so sorry.

And

I believe you.

and then, thinking of Mrs. Newberry and Kennedy's parents

I know so many people of faith that have good hearts and love God, but I also know people who pretend to have faith as an excuse to hurt others. You expect kindness and love, but they spew hatred and judgment. You deserved better than whatever happened to you.

She wasn't sure what impulse had overtaken her, but she'd scrawled her phone number hastily on the bottom of the letter and put it in the outgoing mail before she could change her mind. She wasn't sure if he'd call and there was nothing she could do but wait.

"You look jumpy," Lilly sat down beside her as the other members of the Bible group roamed around the room nibbling on snacks and talking about the plans for the Christmas toy drive.

"I am," Mia admitted with a smile. "I haven't felt like myself the past few weeks."

"Have you told your dad about changing your major yet?"

Mia could hear the hesitant worry in her voice, and she shook her head as she picked at a piece of lint on her skirt. "I'm sorry, I know it bothers you, keeping my secrets."

"I'm worried and I don't think I'm the only one that's noticed you seem off lately. You aren't really talking to anyone, and you haven't been out with James at all. I think he's starting to wonder if you're still interested."

"I think *I'm* trying to figure out if I'm still interested."

"Really?" Lilly's face crinkled in concern. "Did the dates not go well?"

Mia shrugged and shot her a small, reassuring smile. "I think he's only interested in me because he thinks I would make a good pastor's wife. He doesn't seem to care much about who I am or what I want out of life."

"Oh."

She sounded so disappointed that Mia bumped her shoulder affectionately. "I want what you have with Bryce.

Someone that knows me and loves what I am, not what he wants me to be."

That soothed the worry from Lilly's brow. "I really did get lucky with Bryce, didn't I?"

"You truly did," Mia muttered, but her attention was on Mrs. Newberry as she made the rounds with her usual gossip. Heads were turning too often in their direction, and Mia had the unpleasant feeling that they were the subject of the night's discussions. "Why is she always causing problems?" Mia asked, jerking her chin toward Mrs. Newberry.

Lilly turned to look and rolled her eyes. "She's not happy about my new role in the group. I guess she thinks she should've been next in line to take over after Mrs. Mitchell, even though all she's done is complain about every single project."

"Bitch," Mia mumbled beneath her breath, and her cheeks turned hot when Lilly sucked in a breath and looked at her in horror.

"Mia," she hissed. "You can't say that in here! What's ... How did ... Where did you even pick up a cursing habit?"

Mia shrugged. "Probably Gabriel," she admitted. "He swears a lot in his letters."

"Seriously? You're supposed to be encouraging him with your good habits, not picking up his sinful ones. I can't believe you're still talking to him and letting him be a bad influence on you. Is there something going on with the two of you?"

"No," Mia shook her head sharply. She suspected that Lilly's objection had less to do with worrying about her vocabulary and more to do with not liking Gabriel. "He's never getting out of prison, remember? We're just friends."

The look Lilly gave her was skeptical, but she let the subject drop.

~

It took a few back-and-forth letters before he called her for the first time because it was harder to set up phone calls with an inmate than she'd anticipated. It wasn't as simple as picking up the phone and dialing her number.

She'd had to register her number on a website for the Department of Corrections before he was allowed to call her and then he'd had to put money in a special account with an outside provider to cover the costs since cell phones don't receive collect calls and her house didn't have a landline. In fact, she didn't know anyone whose house still had a landline, and they were both angry at the inefficient system long before they'd worked out all the problems.

In the end, despite his insecurities and all the obstacles, he told her he would call between 8 a.m. and 11 p.m. He couldn't give her an exact time because inmates couldn't use the phones during lockdowns or emergencies, so she pretended to have a stomachache and skipped class, instead sitting beside her phone nibbling at her fingernails. There was no way she was going to miss his call after all of the effort they had put into setting it up.

He didn't keep her waiting too long, and her phone screen lit up, displaying an unfamiliar number, at 10:17 that morning.

She swallowed hard, and her hands shook as she answered it. "Hello?"

There was a brief silence so intense she could hear the blood rushing in her ears. Her body felt weightless and numb and her fingertips cold as she waited for him to answer.

"Hi, is this ... is this Mia?"

Everything inside of her slid sideways at the sound of his voice. The images she'd had of him in her mind, the ones she'd carried since she'd looked up his trial, shattered. He'd been a kid, long and lanky and awkward, younger than her and fragile for all the brutality of his crime. That was how she'd pictured him in her mind when she wrote to him, when she read his letters, when she thought of him and how he spent his days.

This ... this was not the voice of a child, and the deep, rumbling timbre of her name on his lips shook her to her core. She hadn't paid much attention when he'd mentioned his birthday and said he'd turned twenty-eight, but now it was painfully obvious that he was a grown man nearing thirty.

She pressed her thighs together against an unfamiliar sensation and cleared her throat. "Yes, it is. It's nice to finally hear your voice. I feel like I already know you so well."

He chuckled and she bit down hard on her lip, terrified that he could hear the way her breath trembled on the exhale. "I feel the same way. I'm not interrupting your classes, am I?"

"I stayed home today. Tummy ache."

"Mia ..." His voice dropped, got impossibly lower and her body was suddenly hot all over, a flush rising under her skin. She bit harder on her lip and tried to focus. He was her friend and nothing more.

It was obvious he didn't approve of her skipping classes for his sake. They both knew the importance of her education, but she wasn't going to apologize. "I'm not going to skip class every time, but this was important, and I didn't have a specific time to expect your call. I'll send you my class schedule, so you'll know when I'm free for next time."

"Next time? You mean you want me to call you again?"

She scowled at the walls full of his artwork. "Of course, I do. Do you not want to call me again?"

"I do! It's just ..." He paused and when he continued his words carried the weight of years of rejection. "No one else wants to talk to me."

"I want to talk to you." She was careful to keep her tears from carrying in her voice, knew he wouldn't want her to feel sorry for him. "In fact, I'm hurt that you could think so little of me and just for that I'm going to eat your birthday cupcake next year, too."

He exhaled softly, and she could sense the tension as it flowed out of him. "That *is* cruel and unusual punishment."

"It really is, but you know you deserve it. Is it expensive?" she asked, changing the subject abruptly.

"The cupcake?"

She sighed. "No, calling me? Is it expensive?"

"Yes, but it doesn't really matter. The one thing my mother does for me is put a monthly deposit into my general account. I use it to buy stuff from the commissary, but I have enough to spend on phone calls if I want to."

"How often are you allowed to call?"

"I get twenty minutes per call, but a max of 300 minutes a month so that's ... uh, about three a week."

"That's good," she said. Her foot tapped nervously on the floor. "I think I'd like to hear your voice three times a week."

"I'd like to hear yours, too, but what about James? Or your dad?"

"What about them?"

"Will they be mad? I know you said there was something between you and James—"

"There isn't anymore," she said quickly, having decided right that moment that she wouldn't be going out with him again.

"There isn't?" he sounded ... surprised maybe, or relieved. She wished she could see his face, the look in his eyes, so she could know for sure. "Why not?"

She huffed out an impatient breath. "He just ... he doesn't make me *feel*. I don't think I make him feel anything, either. That's important, right? For a relationship?"

"Yeah, I guess you should love them."

"Yes, definitely." She agreed, foot tapping away as she hedged. "But you should feel ... other stuff. Intimate stuff?"

He paused and she was afraid she'd said the wrong thing, but then, "You mean, should you want to fuck the person you're in a relationship with? Is that what you're asking?"

She laughed, embarrassed and almost hysterical. "Yeah, I guess that's what I'm asking."

"I've been in here for a long time but, yeah, I know that's definitely something you should want. Do you ..." He coughed, hesitated, "Do you not want to fuck James?"

She shook her head before she remembered that he couldn't see her. "No," she said quickly. "At least, I don't think I do. He's nice to look at but ..."

"But he doesn't turn you on."

"I've never really been turned on, so I'm not sure, but I don't think so." He made a strangled noise on the other end of the line and coughed quickly to cover it up. "Gabriel, are you okay? I'm sorry I'm even telling you this, I just don't know what I'm doing at all and I needed someone who wouldn't think I was making a big mistake by breaking it off with him."

"I don't think that," he promised.

"Thank you." She glanced at the clock on her phone. Not much time left for today. "I'll send you my schedule," she reminded him. "But maybe you could call Saturday next time? I'm free that day."

"Yeah, I'll call Saturday."

"Gabriel?"

"Hmm?"

"I know you probably can't but ... is there any way you can take pictures? Of you, I mean? I'd like to know what you look like these days."

"It's not unusual for friends and family to want pictures and I can have some taken, but on one condition."

She frowned and sat up straighter on the bed, prepared to fight him for that photo. "What's the condition?"

"You send me another one of you."

She relaxed back against the pillows with a smile. "Oh, I can do *that*."

~

He kept his promise to call her Saturday and the picture came the following week. She studied it carefully before tucking it out of sight in her bedside drawer, away from the prying eyes of any visitors. The man in the photo was nothing like she'd expected, he was older and far more attractive than anything in her imagination. The skinny teen she'd seen in the videos had filled out into a large man that had grown into his big ears and prominent nose. His skin was still pale, and his hair was still black, now curling softly down to the collar of a white prison jumpsuit. His posture was awkward, unsure, and she knew this was the first time in a painfully long time that anyone had cared enough to ask him what he looked like.

His own mother didn't know what her son looked like as a man and now Mia couldn't stop thinking about it.

She nibbled her lip, trying to concentrate on her homework at the dining room table, but she had reread the same page three times, unable to keep her traitorous thoughts from drifting back to the image and how big Gabriel's hands were, or the thickness of his neck and thighs, the plump pink pout of his lips.

"Hey."

She jumped, startled and embarrassed, and pasted a bright smile on her face as she turned to face James. He was still handsome, but her pulse remained steady as she looked at him.

"Hey, haven't seen you at the house for a while."

He sat down in the chair beside her and picked up her book to examine the cover. "Yeah, well, things seemed a little awkward between us. I thought maybe you might like some space."

"That was very kind of you."

"You seemed upset," he said, pushing gently for an explanation that she wasn't certain she wanted to give, "like maybe you were angry."

"I was," she admitted, knowing it wouldn't do her any good to pretend otherwise.

"Why?" He looked genuinely shocked.

"You blamed me for something that wasn't my fault. The sin those boys committed was their own ... and your answer was bullshit."

He leaned back, frowning at her uncharacteristically combative tone and vulgar language. "Look, what I said ..."

"Was wrong." She leaned over and took her book from his hands, returning it to the pile as he bristled defensively.

"You know, Lilly told me about that guy you've been writing to. The murderer. She's worried about you and maybe she was right to be. I didn't want to have to go to your father, but your behavior lately ..."

"Please, do tell my father. I'm sure he'll think it's a fascinating story since he's been well aware of my participation in that particular church program."

She made no attempt to conceal her animosity as she gathered her things. "You don't actually know me, and I don't need your protection. Now, if you'll excuse me, I'm expecting a phone call."

She swept from the room without a backward glance, but her teeth were still clenched with rage when she answered Gabriel on the first ring, blurting out the whole confrontation as he listened quietly.

"How dare Lilly tell him about you? This is none of his business!"

"Maybe she thinks I'm competition," he teased.

"Who said you aren't?" she asked, words tumbling out faster than her inhibitions could stop them.

"What?"

"I just ..." She cleared her throat nervously. "Forget it."

His voice on the other end of the line sounded strangled. "Mia—"

"We're almost out of time," she interrupted. She shouldn't have said it, shouldn't have brought it up. "I'll talk to you next week?"

"*Mia*," he repeated. "You can't just say something like that and pretend it never happened."

"I don't know what to say," she admitted. She chewed absently on her thumbnail and watched another minute slip by on her bedside clock.

"Can you write it down? Send it to me?"

She closed her eyes, tipped her head back. Her words had been impulsive, but they hadn't been untrue and maybe it was time they both stopped pretending otherwise. "Yeah, I can do that."

Chapter Eleven

"You look tired."

"Hmm? Oh, yeah, sorry." Mia shot her father a quick smile, but she couldn't deny that it was probably tired around the edges. It had been two days since she had talked to Gabriel, and she had barely slept at all. "Is it alright if I go ahead and head up to bed? I'm not feeling well."

It would have been impossible to miss the concern, or the way his eyes traveled over her, looking for an explanation for her odd behavior lately. It caused a pang in her heart, the secrets she was keeping from him, but she knew he would only worry more if she told him now, before she had the words to explain it all.

"I don't mind. Get some rest, I'll make you pancakes in the morning."

"You make the best pancakes." She lingered over the hug she gave him, misty eyed with exhaustion and uncertainty about her future. He had always loved her, but she knew he wouldn't understand what was keeping her up at night.

There were crumpled papers crunched under feet as she walked across her bedroom, failed drafts of a letter she couldn't seem to get quite right. She'd spent every free minute writing and rewriting it, but she couldn't find the words to express her complicated feelings.

The image of Gabriel in her mind had shifted from a lost and lonely boy to an attractive man. She was afraid that their relationship had shifted, too. It had begun as a friendship, but now there was a connection between them, a hot and bright line that held more than friendly affection.

She had stared at her picture of him until she'd memorized every detail of his face. She knew the exact location of every freckle and the precise shade of his eyes, could have drawn the slope of his lips in her sleep. If he'd been able to, she would've wanted him to press those lips to hers, so she could discover the warmth and the taste of him.

They had never even seen each other in person, and it surprised her that her thoughts had become so impure, but Gabriel knew her deeply, all of her faults and her flaws, and she trusted him despite his circumstances. The way he treated her was a stark contrast to James' superficial interest, a distinction that she was finally able to recognize and appreciate for what it was. James cared about her impact on his image and Gabriel cared about her as a person.

It was easy to fantasize that his interest would carry him to wanting to know her more intimately, that his kisses would not be polite requirements but demonstrations of passion. Kissing James had been tedious, but kissing Gabriel ...

Would he really want that? Could he feel that way about her? And was it fair to either of them, considering his circumstances, for her to ask? She wanted to hope that she could convince him to ask for a new trial, but even if they gave him one, there were no guarantees that the jury would give him a different sentence. She might not have happily-ever-after hopes, the kind that would take some kind of miracle to achieve, but maybe it was better to grab onto what little they could get right now. It might be better than nothing at all.

She reached into her bedside drawer for a pen and paper, but let it drop when her phone rang. Her brief hope that it might be him died away when she saw another familiar name on the screen. She silenced the call with a swipe of her thumb and turned her back on the caller. There was no way that she could stay mad at Lilly forever for telling James about Gabriel, but she couldn't devote the mental and emotional energy to deal with her friend right now.

The bed creaked under her as she flopped down on her stomach, pen and paper in hand. She had been trying to write this letter using her head, and that would never work because what she felt for him wasn't rational. He had told her once to follow her heart, and there was nothing left for her to do.

"Are you going to open it?"

"Yeah."

"Sometime today?"

Gabriel looked at Alex, sitting on the side of his own bunk, watching. He'd been sitting here staring at the envelope for at least five minutes, so the question wasn't entirely unreasonable. "Probably ... Maybe." He winced, rolling his shoulder in an uncertain shrug. "I don't know."

Alex shook his head and leaned back against his own pillow. "It's going to say the same thing no matter when you open it. You might as well stop being a coward and get it over with."

"Yeah. Maybe I just won't open it." Gabriel tapped the envelope against his thigh. He knew he'd crossed a line during their last call. She'd brought it up, and he didn't know why, but he'd fucked it up worse by saying something that might have made her uncomfortable and ruined their friendship.

"That's really fucking stupid, you know that right? What if she actually has feelings for you? Isn't that kind of what you two were hinting at the last time you talked to her?"

"I don't know, but that would be the worst fucking thing for her. Because then what? We can't be together. I can't marry her or give her a family. She'd be wasting her fucking life. If I was a decent man, I would throw that letter in the trash, and never write to her again."

"Good thing you aren't a decent man. You're a murderer and a prisoner, *for once* use it to your advantage and open the damn letter."

Gabriel's fingers shook as he tore the envelope and swallowed hard against the urge to run away from facing what she had to say, convinced that it would kill him, no matter what it was.

Gabriel,

I've started this letter over more times in the last two days than I can count and it's the hardest thing I've ever written.

Dread settled in the pit of his stomach like a stone, and he was suddenly numb and cold. She regretted what she'd said and was going to do the right thing and free herself from him before he could ruin her life. He understood but the loss of one more thing that he cared about might be more than he could bear.

I know what I said to you on the phone wasn't fair.

You've never acted like you wanted to be anything more than my friend, and I put you in an uncomfortable position. I realize now that you might have worried it would jeopardize our friendship if you told me that you don't think of me as anything more than that. That was not my intention, and it was especially unkind of me, because you have come to depend on me to be your only connection to the outside world, and I don't want you to be concerned that I would take that from you.

He couldn't believe her, how caring she was and how sensitive to his feelings. She thought he might feel taken advantage of and she was worried about him. Was she afraid that he didn't want her, but he'd feel obligated to pretend otherwise? He wanted to pick her up and hold her, to kiss her until she knew that nothing, she wanted could ever feel like an obligation to him. Not with the way he felt about her.

Our friendship has become one of the most important things in my life. That will be true no matter what you have to say to me after reading this letter. I mean that, and I hope that we can be honest with each other about our feelings, even if you don't feel the same way that I do, because I need to be honest with you about something.

I lied to you.

When I told you that I wasn't sure about my relationship with James, I said it was because I had never been turned on by anyone before but that isn't true.

I've been turned on by you.

Alex chuckled at the choked sound he made, and Gabriel glared at him before turning his attention back to the page.

I feel something when I hear your voice, when I see your face in the picture that you sent me, when I read the words that you've written to me over all these weeks. Friendship, yes, but it's more than that. It's a heat beneath my skin, a fluttering in my stomach, an ache in my body that I've never felt for anyone else, and I needed you to know.

He reread her words again, sure that he must have misunderstood, but their meaning didn't change, and he glanced at Alex, suddenly uncomfortable that he was so close and watching with such interest. Sharing such a small space was hard enough when it had been his own vulnerable emotions on display, but it was worse somehow when Mia was talking to him about this. She was inexperienced and must have felt so exposed to speak to him so openly. Alex's presence felt like a violation of her privacy, even if he couldn't see her words.

He would have waited to open the letter until his cellmate wasn't around, but he hadn't expected her to tell him this. He'd been denying and fighting his own attraction for so long, sure that she would never feel the same. His only hope had been that Mia felt some kind of emotional connection to him, a friendship and someone to care what happened to him, the idea that she might feel something sexual for him simply had not occurred to him.

They'd never met, but her pictures on the wall mocked him, a potent reminder that lust was perfectly able to flourish from something as simple as a photo and a phone call. He would never forget the way he had felt when she'd answered the phone for the first time. Hearing her sweet lilting voice had been one of the best experiences of his life.

He'd been ashamed of it, had felt like a creep for the way he'd felt about her, but if she felt the same way ...

I needed you to know that no matter how you feel about me, I have strong feelings for you. I know I said I wouldn't push for you to ask for a new trial, but I'm going to do it anyway. Please, if you feel the same way I do, if you want the chance to see what there might be between us, fight for your future. I'll help you.

I'll always be your friend, but I wish I could be more.

MIA

"If I were a decent man ..." But the letter was clutched protectively in his hand, and he didn't know how to let her go.

"You're not." Alex reminded him. "And I don't think she wants you to be. Seems like she had one of those and decided she liked you better. So, whatever she said to you, say it back. Then ask her to send nudes.”

Gabriel glared at him. “You know the guards would confiscate that shit, besides she’s not like that.”

Alex snorted. “Women in love do crazy things.”

Gabriel’s heart, already pounding impossibly fast, somehow beat faster. “She’s not in love with me.”

“Isn’t she?”

Gabriel looked at Mia’s letter again. He was a selfish man and he wanted that from her, even if he only ever had her through the letters she sent.

“She didn’t say that she was,” he clarified carefully.

“Did you? Because we both know that you’re in love with her.” Alex didn’t wait for an answer before he shook his head and gestured at the letter. “It doesn’t matter if she said it, you know it’s true.”

~

She was too happy to be angry anymore. Her most recent phone call with Gabriel had pasted a smile on her face that didn’t waver when Lilly pulled out a chair and sat down beside her in the library.

“You’ve been avoiding me.”

Mia nodded. “I have and I’d say that I was sorry, but it would be a lie. You told James about Gabriel, and you did it without talking to me about it.”

Lilly winced, but she didn’t deny it. “I thought I was helping you. This thing with Gabriel ...” she drifted off, and her brows drew together in disapproval. “I’m worried.”

“I know you meant well which is why I’m not avoiding you anymore.”

Lilly relaxed, a soft sigh escaping her as she reached into her bag. “Does this mean that you’ve worked things out with

James?" She pulled out a bar of chocolate and split it between them

"No," Mia said with a laugh. Several of the other students turned to glare at her, but she ignored them. "It means I've forgiven you because I don't care at all what James thinks anymore."

"He's a good man—"

"He didn't love me," Mia cut in. "I'm not even sure he liked me, really, and I deserve someone who does."

"Of course you do," Lilly agreed. "I just wanted you to be happy."

"I *am* happy." The memory of Gabriel's phone call flashed through her mind, how he hadn't even bothered to say hello when she answered.

"I want you," he'd said breathlessly. "I want you *so much* and I didn't know how to tell you and I didn't think you'd feel the same. I don't know what the hell we're doing, and you have a whole life ahead of you that I don't want to ruin but if you want me, I'll try everything I can to get out of here. The guys that spend all their free time helping the other inmates with legal shit agreed to help me file the petition. If they approve it and I have to go through a whole new trial, then that's what I'll do."

"What are you smiling at?" Lilly asked. "Did something happen? Wait, do you have a new guy?"

"No, not a new one," Mia considered not telling her, but it was bubbling inside her, a secret that begged to be shared. "It's just ... it's Gabriel."

The look of horror on Lilly's face was almost comical. "No ... Mia, I don't even know what to say. I knew something was going on with you two."

"You don't have to say anything ..."

"Does your dad know about this?"

"No," Mia shook her head. "He doesn't need to."

"I guess," Lilly said doubtfully. "What do you even see in him? He's a murderer, Mia."

"He's given me support, encouragement, and unconditional friendship. All of that has helped me become more confident and through him, it's become truly clear to me that God has called me in a different way than we all expected."

"You still think God called you to Gabriel?"

"Yeah, I really do."

Lilly sighed, clearly defeated. "He can't give you a family," she said, hitting the concern that lay closest to Mia's heart. "You always wanted a family."

"I still want one," Mia said slowly. There was no point in mentioning that they were trying to get him out. Not yet. Lilly's concerns might very well still turn out to be the reality of her future and it was one she was deeply afraid of. She had nothing but her faith to lean on. "I'm just going to trust that God has led me this far and He'll lead me the rest of the way."

Chapter Twelve

Alex didn't comment on his increased masturbation habits, which Gabriel was extremely grateful for. They each tried to give the other what little privacy they could, but there wasn't much to be had and it mostly all came down to them pretending not to be aware of the other's activities. There were some things that they just didn't acknowledge and that included one another's bathroom habits and how often they each felt the urge to take their sexual needs into their own hands. It was as much a reality of prison life as the terrible food and the inescapable smells.

For the three years that they had been trapped in this hell together, Alex had usually been the one with the more intense needs, but that had all changed once Mia realized how interested he was in her.

She hadn't sent nudes, and he knew her well enough to know she wouldn't be willing to have something like that confiscated. The photos that she had sent him with the last letter, however, were ... suggestive. Her dress was cut a little lower, a hint of the top curve of her breast peeking out from beneath the pretty pink lace. She was still smiling, but her lips were slightly parted, and her eyes were soft and welcoming.

He knew that look, the one that invited a man in, and he wanted to pin her beneath him and feel her heat wrapped around him as throaty little moans poured from her lips. His hand was a poor substitute for her body, and he grit his teeth against the futility of the fantasy that drove him as he pumped himself into his fist with the image of her in his mind. She wanted him, she'd told him so, and if he could ever have gotten the hell out of here, he could have touched her and done all the things to her that he thought of doing when he was alone with nothing but his own rough stroking. He could have tasted her, felt her curves under his hands and her legs around his waist, whispered in her ear to tell her how beautiful she was, and everything she made him feel.

He tightened his grip, his mind running over with possibilities and his heart beating a fast rhythm that perfectly matched the punishing pace he set as his hand slid up his length and back down again. He tried to be quiet, but when he was this close it was hard to keep his breathing even and avoid making the sounds that were trapped behind his lips. Sounds he had to keep quiet now, but that he wanted to give to her. She would have known, then, how special she was, how much he wanted her, how much he loved her.

Maybe she would have even said it back.

That was the thought that drove him over the edge, that had his muscles tightening and ecstasy shooting across his mind like the streaks of light behind his eyes.

He laid on his bunk after he had cleaned the mess he'd made and wondered if she ever thought about him like this. It was hard for him to ask her, when their calls were monitored, and all of their letters were read. He didn't want to embarrass her, knew that women that were raised as conservatively as she was were often hesitant to talk openly about sex. She might not even know that she could bring pleasure to her own body.

If she didn't, he wished he could be the one to teach her.

He'd filed his paperwork with the court in mid-November, pointing out that his lawyers had not done a proper job of addressing his claims of abuse and the mountain of knowledge available in the scientific community about the ways that those things affect the brain and people's behavior. It all amounted to a claim that he had not been properly represented, that his council had been ineffective.

If the court agreed, he would either be released entirely or get a new trial. Either way it would be a second chance. All they had to do now was wait.

~

"Merry Christmas!"

"Kennedy!" Mia hugged her and pulled her over to an empty seat. "I'm so glad you're here! You haven't come in a while, and I was getting worried."

"I'm sorry I didn't answer your texts." She picked at the snowflake shaped sprinkle on the edge of her cupcake "Things haven't been so great at home."

"Your parents again?"

"Always," she said, tipping her head back and closing her eyes with a deep sigh like she was offering her troubles up to an indifferent God. "I wish I could move out but every time I think I've got things ready they find a way to ruin it somehow."

"Is there anything I can do?"

"Not really, I've missed all of you and I'm just glad to get out of the house and finally have a little distraction."

Mia looked at the meeting room with its festive garland

and the little tree trimmed in lights and decorations the kids had made in Sunday school. "Well, our Christmas party is something, but other than that we don't have much distraction to offer."

"Oh? I talked to Lilly before you got here, and she said you might have something to talk about?" She leaned forward, cupcake in her hand forgotten as she waited for the latest gossip.

Mia barely resisted the urge to roll her eyes. Lilly had never been good at keeping a secret. "It's nothing, she's upset right now because I'm not seeing James anymore."

"That's all?" Kennedy's face fell, disappointment wiping the excitement away.

"No," Mia sighed. "I guess she probably wanted me to tell you about Gabriel, too."

"The prison guy?"

"Yeah." Mia glanced around to make sure no one was listening nearby. "It's really nothing but ..." She paused, nibbling her lip as she tried to figure out how to explain what had happened between them.

"But?" Kennedy pressed.

"But I might have feelings for him," Mia mumbled. "Feelings that he might also have about me."

"So, he's your boyfriend?"

"I don't know." Mia glanced around again. "Things are complicated and it's hard with him being in prison."

Kennedy frowned and hesitated before asking, "Are you two not ..."

"Not what?"

"Sexting? Phone sex? Sexy letters?" She was clearly appalled when Mia didn't seem familiar with any of those things. "You know?"

"I really *don't* know? Do people really do that?"

"Definitely," Kennedy said, a perplexed mix of shock and pity on her face. "I can't believe you're *not* doing that. He's hot, right?"

"He's attractive," Mia said, but she was blushing profusely. It hadn't been long since she and Gabriel had talked about any kind of feelings between them, but what if he did expect her to do those things? "The guards read all of our letters and record all of our phone calls," she muttered weakly.

"If they want to listen to or read your sexy shit, let 'em," Kennedy continued with a shrug, clearly unbothered by the thought.

The last bit carried in the small room, and Mrs. Newberry glared at them. "Language, please, ladies."

Kennedy gave her tight smile as Mia leaned in and whispered, "Have you ... you know?"

"I can't date, remember? That's the closest I'm gonna get to a real girlfriend until I can move out of my parent's house."

It made sense, but it had never occurred to Mia that even Kennedy had more sexual experience than she did because her parents were so controlling. What had she been missing out on all this time?

The conversation lingered in the back of her mind as she waited for Gabriel to call that weekend, unable to stop turning over everything Kennedy had told her ...

"Gabriel?" she asked, interrupting him as he asked about her day.

"Yeah?"

"Have you had sex before? I know you were young but ..."

"I've had sex before," he interrupted, and she knew that somehow this was one of those mysterious things connected to what had happened to him that he would be reluctant to talk about.

"Do you ..." she hesitated before pressing on cautiously, "Do you think it's wrong for people who aren't married to have sex?" She'd said she wasn't going to demand answers about his past, but she didn't want to drop the subject entirely.

There was a long pause, and she could almost feel the thoughts swirling inside his mind as he tried to figure out how to answer that question. "I don't think so," he said finally. "Especially if they care about each other."

"I care about you," she told him huskily.

"I care about you, too," he said, but there was a note of hesitation there, a hint of confusion. He obviously couldn't see where she was going with this conversation, and she was too shy to announce suddenly that she thought she might want to try having a long-distance sexual relationship.

"If you weren't in prison, you'd be kind of like a boyfriend, right?" she asked instead.

"I think so," he told her. "I don't think we've used that word before, but I would be if I could."

"And, if you were out here with me, would you want to have sex with me?"

"Of course." His voice relaxed a little, like he had decided that she was asking for him to reaffirm his feelings for her. "I'd give anything to even be able to kiss you."

"Gabriel?"

"Yeah?"

"Do you know what phone sex is?"

There was a loud crash on the other end of the line, and she realized with a startled giggle that he had dropped the phone.

"Mia? Are you still there?" He sounded panicked and she couldn't quite stifle another laugh.

"I'm still here," she assured him. "What happened?"

"Nothing. I just ... I know what that is."

"Oh, okay," she said. There was no way to find out except to ask. "I know you probably don't have that kind of privacy and there's always a chance someone could be listening since the calls are monitored but ..."

"Wait, are you asking if there's some way that we could share some kind of sexual relationship?"

"Yes, exactly." She could feel the heat of her blush from her chest to her hairline, but she wasn't backing down now. "You said you wanted me, and I want you, too."

"I do but ... What if I never get out of here? I don't want to hurt you or get your hopes up that we can be more than what we are now."

"I know." She'd thought about that, too, and how much more it would hurt them both if that happened. Eventually they would have to end things, wouldn't they? She'd have to move on, have a life and a family but ... "I know it's selfish of me and we might regret it someday, but I want what I can have now."

"It's not selfish, I just ... Damn it." She imagined him looking around before his voice dropped low, clearly trying not to be overheard as he whispered. "Have you ever touched yourself, sweetheart?"

She whimpered, pressing her thighs together as that honeyed voice flowed over her. "No, I haven't," she admitted. "I was ashamed because it's supposed to be a sin, but I don't think I'd be ashamed of it with you. I'm trying out a rebellious streak, you know?"

"I've noticed, and it makes me so proud of you when you stand up for what you want."

She swallowed and heat bloomed in her stomach. Why did that always happen when he talked to her like this? When he was proud of her and happy because of something she'd done?

"I want you," she said quietly. "I want to do this with you, if you'll tell me how."

"Can you try touching yourself tonight? For me? Think of me when you do, and then write me a letter to tell me if you liked it. Would you like to do that?"

"Yes, I think I'd like to try that. Would it make you happy if I did?"

"Everything you do makes me happy, but this? That would be incredible, baby."

Mia felt like her bones had gone liquid. "I like it when you call me that. Can you do it more often?"

"Baby, I'll call you any name you like."

It was harder than she thought it would be. Without his voice in her ear to encourage her, her mind drifted to the other voices she had heard in her life. Sex outside of the marriage bed, where even touching oneself was frowned upon. It was a sin, an offense against God and her future husband. But if she had a future husband, she realized, it wouldn't be Gabriel and not offending some man she hadn't even met yet was suddenly less important than having whatever she could with him right now.

She'd never noticed how quiet her room was at night, or how clearly sounds traveled when you were trying to be sneaky. Her heart was beating so loud that she was afraid her father would hear it and come to investigate, to find out what was wrong with her. When he didn't appear, she tried to focus on her conversation with Gabriel, on his hastily whispered instructions on what she should do with her hands.

The idea of doing that with her fingers was intimidating, but he'd promised her that if she thought of something that excited her, her body would be ready and it would be pleasurable. She tried to remember the exact sound of his voice when he told her what to do, how it had gotten deep and husky with desire for her, and when she found the places he'd described for her, the slick wetness he'd told her about was there.

It was strange, learning about her own body and experiencing sensations she'd never felt before, but she moved her hand experimentally, rubbing where it felt good and exploring the walls of that hidden place with her fingers like Gabriel had encouraged her to do.

There was a pang of sadness that he wasn't here to see how much she liked it. He would've wanted to touch her here, maybe even join their bodies together in the way she'd read about in health class. It had seemed cold and frightening then, but now she thought it would have been so nice to let him know what it felt like to have someone else touch her the way she was touching herself.

She'd have to do her best to describe it for him. His reaction to that would be worth the embarrassment she'd felt when he had been explaining what she should do.

"You'll need to find your clit," he'd whispered.

"Gabriel," she'd hissed back. "You can't say that word."

"I'm going to get you used to hearing more words than that," he promised. "I want to hear you say it when you tell me all about touching yourself."

"I can't say that!"

"You *can* but I can wait till you're ready."

Now she thought she'd be willing to say it a hundred times in gratitude just for him helping her find it. She'd never imagined it was possible to feel such pleasure, and she was soon biting down on her lips to keep the moans quiet. Gabriel had told her that it might be difficult to orgasm the first time, since she was unfamiliar with her body.

Instead, she wondered if she should be ashamed of how

quickly it happened and how much she wanted it. It washed over her like a rising tide, cresting on a peak that made her shake and tremble. It was the closest she had ever felt to heaven, an odd thing to happen in this little slice of sin. When it was over, she was alone, but she felt more connected to God and to Gabriel than she ever had before.

Chapter Thirteen

Winter

Mia had expected to feel relieved when the semester ended and Christmas break finally arrived, but she had things on her mind that were more unpleasant than finals. She'd put off having this talk with her dad for as long as she could but just the thought of it made nausea swim in her stomach.

"You can do this, baby," Gabriel told her the second time that week. "You don't have to tell him about me, and I understand why you wouldn't, but you have to tell him about college. He's paying for your tuition so he's going to find out eventually and I know you don't want to lie to him."

She blinked back her tears and took a shaking breath. Now was not the time for her to fall apart. "Thank you."

"I'm here for anything you need."

"Anything?"

"You know I am."

"Tell me again how much you liked my letter."

"If I do, will you write me another one?"

She grinned, ready to let him take her mind off her problems with something more fun and flirtatious. "I already did, and I mailed it yesterday. I think you'll like it even better than the first one."

"If I do, I think it might kill me. I loved every single filthy word of the first one. You said clit five times and I was so proud of you. Say cunt next time? For me? Please?"

"Gabriel."

"Fine. Pussy?"

She rolled her eyes, but her heart was racing with excitement and she enjoyed how much her words seemed to affect him. "If I say it, will you be able to die in peace?"

"Yes," he groaned. "Please."

"I wish you weren't in prison so you could touch my pussy."

"Now I'm dead. You've killed me with your dirty talk."

She giggled and pushed down on the urge to tell him she loved him for what felt like the dozenth time. The words were heavy on her tongue, desperate to get out, but she knew it wasn't fair to him to say it. She wasn't sure yet if they were true and even if they were, she'd already asked for too much from him when they both knew how it would inevitably end.

She sat with hands twisted in her lap that night, feet tucked up under a blanket as she watched the flames dance in their small living room fireplace. The winters usually didn't get very cold here, but there had been frost on the ground outside that had crunched under feet when she'd brought in her bags from her last shopping trip before the holidays.

Christmas break seemed shorter than ever this year and she was running out of time.

"Dad?"

He looked up at her from over the top of the book he was reading, nothing more than vague curiosity in his eyes. He had no idea how much she had kept from him, and she suddenly hated herself for not having the courage to speak up sooner.

"I need to tell you something."

"Oh?" He set his glass on the table and turned in his chair so that he could face her directly. He had always been good about that, about listening with his full attention. She'd never felt like what she had to say was less important to him than anything else he might be doing.

She looked down at her knee. "I changed my major."

"You did?" His brows drew together in concern. "You didn't talk to me about it?"

"I wanted to have at least one semester of my grades to show you before I told you. It's a very competitive and demanding field, I wanted you to know I could handle it."

"What did you change it to?"

"Political science." She winced when it came out sounding more like a question than an answer. "I want to go to law school."

"Law school is expensive," he said slowly. "And as you said, very competitive. Have you thought about what your life would look like if you do this? How would you manage a home and a family with that kind of schedule?"

"Maybe I'm not worried about having a family," she asked. She wanted it to sound bold, revolutionary, but they both knew her better than that.

"Mia ..."

"I know," she sighed. "I want a family, but I can do both. It might be challenging but it's possible."

"Does this have something to do with a boy?"

"Dad ..."

"I thought you had a thing with James but then he stopped coming around, so—"

"It's not James."

"But there is a boy?"

"Not really," she hedged. She'd never lied to him when his eyes narrowed on her face, and she squirmed uncomfortably. "It's just ...you know the pen pal program? Remember? Mrs. Newberry threw a fit about it?"

"I remember," he said. "She was convinced that putting young and impressionable minds in contact with criminals would lead to nothing but bad things."

'Well, I think it's led to something really amazing instead." She rushed ahead as he opened his mouth to speak, praying she could make him understand that she understood the futility but couldn't change her feelings. "He's so good to me, so sweet."

Her father shook his head and buried his face in his hands. She'd never seen him look so confused and disappointed. "Didn't you tell me that this man was in prison for something terrible? Murder? You said he was never getting out."

"He probably isn't," she admitted. "I know there's probably no future for us but it doesn't matter to me."

"Well, it should, Mia." She flinched as he raised his voice, something he'd never done before. "It should matter to you. First you decide out of nowhere you want to be a lawyer and now this? As long as you're wasting time on him you won't have a family or a real home. He can't give you a life. You'd be throwing it all away, for what?"

"I don't know." She clutched her knees, curled into herself as her hands began to shake. "I just know he makes me happy."

"I wanted a good life for you, not this empty shell that you're trying to create. Your mother—"

"Was an amazing person, but I'm not Mom."

"No, I can see that."

Mia recoiled, his words hitting directly in her chest and stealing her breath.

He sighed and rubbed the tension in his temples with his fingers. "I'm sorry. That was uncalled for. I know how much you loved her and how proud she was of you. I just don't think she would support what you're doing, and I don't see how I possibly can."

"Dad—"

Her words were cut off when the doorbell rang, and they both looked at one another in confusion. It was late and the roads were icy, neither of them had been expecting company.

He rose quickly, hurrying to the door with Mia close behind him as the doorbell rang again, fast and desperate.

"It could be someone who lost control of their car and ended up stuck in the ditch," Mia speculated. "The roads were getting slick when I came home earlier."

But he opened the door to a familiar face, not a stranger.

"Ms. Daniels? Are you okay? Mia, honey, grab her stuff off the porch. What's going on?"

He pulled Kennedy in out of the cold, her nose and cheeks red from the biting wind and her eyes puffy and watery from the tears that were freezing on her lashes. At her feet were two small bags, stuffed to overflowing with clothes.

She didn't answer his questions, eyes searching wildly until she found Mia and then launching herself forward into Mia's arms.

Mia caught her and shot her father a confused look as she tried to guide her friend into the warmth of the living room. "Hey, let's get you warm, okay? Did you walk here?"

Kennedy nodded, hiccupping through her sobs.

"Dad, can you grab her a blanket? She's freezing."

It took them almost half an hour, several blankets, and a cup of hot cocoa to get her warmed up and calmed down enough to answer their questions about what happened.

"They kicked me out," she said dully, staring into the fire and refusing to look at Pastor Anderson.

"Your parents?"

Kennedy nodded, looking at Mia with fresh tears brimming in her eyes. "Someone saw me in Abilene. I finally got brave enough to go on a date and I guess they told my parents."

Mia looked at her dad, at the confusion on his face. He wasn't putting it together just yet. "She was on a date with a girl," Mia whispered.

His brows drew together, and Kennedy's lip trembled, expecting the worst. "So, they kicked you out into the cold, with nothing but two bags of clothes? They made you walk to … Did they even know where you were going? That you would have somewhere to go? Or were they expecting you to sleep outside tonight?"

"I don't know. They took my phone so I couldn't call anyone. Told me they were paying for it and they wouldn't be spending any more money on …" she wiped her face on her sleeve as another round of tears began. "They called me names," she finished.

"And you came here," Pastor Anderson said.

Kennedy nodded. "Mia told me I could if something ever happened. She said that you wouldn't let me sleep on the streets because I'm … because I like girls." She looked up at him, waiting to see if Mia was right or if she was about to be kicked out into the cold for the second time that night.

"Of course, you can come here," he said, patting her hand reassuringly. "We have an extra bedroom upstairs and Mia can help you get settled. I'll go by your parent's place tomorrow and see if they'll give me the rest of your clothes and personal items."

"Really?"

"Yes, really. Let's get you settled, and Mia can find you

something to eat if you're hungry." His voice was calm, but Mia knew that was only for Kennedy's sake. She could feel the anger he was trying not to show.

She smiled at him gratefully as she grabbed Kennedy's bags. Their own disagreement lay fresh and unhealed between them, but she knew that he would never do this, no matter how much he disliked her decisions. He loved her, and they would work it out.

In the meantime, he would have some unpleasant words for Kennedy's parents about their failures as parents and as Christians, both of which required them to love their daughter unconditionally and not throw her out of their home.

She got Kennedy settled and tucked into her new bed and then crept back downstairs to find him still sitting in his chair, staring pensively into the fire.

"Is she alright?" he asked when he looked up and found her standing hesitantly in the doorway.

"Yes, she's sleeping."

"I'm glad you told her to come here. I hate to think what might have happened to her otherwise."

She sat down on the couch again, tugging the blanket over her legs, and waited.

"I still don't know that I agree with the choices that you're making," he spoke slowly, carefully weighing each word, "but I owe it to you to hear you out about why you think these things will make you happy."

"Thank you," she said quietly.

"And even if I hear all those reasons and I still think that you're wrong, I'm always going to love you."

"I know and I love you, too."

～

He came home the following day red in the face and trembling with anger, but he had several more trash bags stuffed full of Kennedy's clothes and a new phone for her on their family plan.

Mia hugged him, tucking her head under his chin and giving him a quick squeeze before she headed to the kitchen to make lunch. Kennedy smiled twice as they ate sandwiches with chips, and they all relaxed just a little. Kennedy was going to be upset and hurt because of what happened, but those horrible people wouldn't be able to destroy her happiness forever.

She'd just finished the dishes, volunteering so that her dad and Kennedy could sit down in the living room and talk privately about what happened when he confronted her parents, when Gabriel called.

She rushed up the stairs to her room, not missing how her dad's eyes now followed her as she went.

"Hello?"

"Hey, baby, how's everything? Did you talk to your dad?"

"Yeah, I did." She sighed and sat down on the edge of her bed. "I ended up telling him about everything, about you and about school. He wasn't happy about any of it."

"Shit, I'm sorry. Are you okay?"

"Yeah, things kind of took an unexpected turn while we were talking." She pressed a hand to her forehead, struggling against a rising headache and her own confusion about how anyone's parents could be so cruel. "My friend is staying with us now because her parents found out she was dating girls."

There was a silence on the other end of the line, a cold and weighted pause that she didn't understand.

"They found out she was ... and now she's living with you and your dad? The pastor?"

"Yeah, she's—"

"And you're okay with that?" His tone was accusatory, his

voice rising in anger. She felt like she was being held responsible for some crime, but she couldn't figure out what he thought she had done. "She's your friend, Mia."

"Yes?" Mia felt her own voice rising, uncertainty making her defensive. "She's one of my best friends that's why—"

"What about your dad?"

"What about him? Her parents kicked her out of their house with no phone and nowhere to go so we gave her a place to stay. She was pretty shaken up when she got here but she's safe and she has her own room."

He sighed and there was a long pause like he was trying to decide what to say. Just when she began to wonder if he was going to answer at all he said, "I'm glad she has you."

"I don't understand—"

"I know you don't," he agreed. "I'm sorry, it's just that not everyone has a safe place to go. Some people I cared about when I was younger weren't so lucky."

"Oh," she mumbled, nibbling on her lip. He'd never told her exactly what had happened to him and she'd been afraid to ask for details. "Do you want to talk about it?"

There was a pause long enough for her to hope then a soft defeated sigh. "Not yet."

"Okay," she whispered. Not yet, but hopefully he would be able to share everything with her someday soon.

Chapter Fourteen

Mia's foot bounced restlessly, and she chewed on her lower lip as she waited, hands tucked deep into the pockets of an oversized gray hoodie that it was already almost too warm outside to wear. The drive hadn't been long, not much beyond what she made each day for school now that it was back in session for the new spring semester, but today it had taken a lifetime.

Hopes and worries had chased themselves across her mind as she drove. After months of talking to him and losing herself in the increasingly blurred lines that defined their relationship, finally taking this step seemed like unexpectedly reaching the precipice on a long climb. She'd been so focused on each step that she hadn't realized how far she'd come until she'd looked out and found the ground far below her. Suddenly, she was afraid of heights, her heart hammering away in her chest as she finally recognized how far she had to fall.

What if he didn't like her? What if, when faced with the reality of her, he decided she didn't live up to his expectations? Fear and anticipation made nervous nausea roll in her stomach, leaving a bitter taste in her mouth that she couldn't wash away even once she'd made it inside.

She'd done everything she could to make sure she'd actually make it this far. Checked and rechecked with him countless times to make sure that he had added her to the necessary list. Read and followed all the rules and procedures —no loud music in the car, roll up your windows and lock your doors, no cell phones or electronics allowed in the facility. Adhered faithfully to the dress code—no clothing with profanity, no skirts or shorts more than three inches above the middle of the knee, no leggings, no open-toed shoes, no bare shoulders, back, or midriff. She'd opted for tennis shoes, sweatpants, and the hoodie, just in case. She might not have been as polished as she would have liked to be, but she wasn't going to give them any excuse to turn her away.

She'd been scanned through a metal detector and sniffed by a drug detecting dog before she'd even been allowed to walk into the prison, and then they'd inspected her ID before letting her walk through door after door that clanged shut behind her with a terrible feeling of finality.

This would be her world for only a few hours, a temporary confinement that already made her skin crawl, she couldn't imagine what it felt like to hear that sound and know you'd truly never be allowed to leave. Gabriel had been so young then, several years younger than she was now. Just thinking about it made her heart break for him all over again.

The guards led her to a large room with small tables scattered throughout, most of them already occupied by small groups that didn't even turn to acknowledge her as she passed —they were deeply focused on the person they had come to see in the small amount of time they had together.

She found a table of her own, scratched and battered with age and hard use, and sat tensely on the edge of her seat with nothing to do but wait. She had nothing with her except twenty-five dollars to buy snacks and drinks from the vending machine and that, because there were no paper bills allowed, was sitting on the table in front of her in a Ziplock bag full of quarters. It was a sad, silent witness to her anxious trembling.

She looked around aimlessly as she waited, trying to calm her rioting nerves. The facility was somehow more intimidating than she'd imagined. Guards with guns and blank faces, walls and fences topped with barbed wire. Gabriel had been right about the pervasive hopelessness and the smell. They would only have two hours, and still she wasn't sure if she wanted time to speed up or slow down.

Some of the others looked like they were still waiting but most seemed to already have their loved one. There were older couples, parents she assumed, and young women like her, those whose husbands or boyfriends were unfortunate enough to be on the inside. The families broke her heart the most. Toddlers and young children, mothers with clear plastic bags that held a few diapers, wipes, and a sippy cup. Sometimes the children strained away from the now unfamiliar faces, and she could see the pain it caused fathers that wanted nothing more than to spend a few precious hours with the children they barely knew. Other times they ran to them with happy and delighted squeals that made her smile until she remembered that a few hours were all they had.

Most of them were in here for nonviolent offenses. They were often poor, unable to afford to fight the system that clung to a failed war on drugs and its overly punitive sentences. She hadn't needed to see their faces to know that a disproportionate number of them would be young Black men, because a few minutes of research was all it took to know that the war on drugs was really a war on the impoverished and the oppressed.

The weight of everything that needed to be changed about this system weighed heavily on her, but she knew that too many people looked away from the reality, unable to imagine change in the face of the mountainous bureaucracy. Loving Gabriel had given her a glimpse into a flawed world, she couldn't turn away now and do nothing.

She lifted her head as the door once again opened and two guards entered with a new inmate, and her heart tripped over itself in surprise. He was taller than either of the men that flanked him and much broader. The pictures he'd sent her had done nothing to prepare her for his size. She was average height for a woman, but beside him she'd feel impossibly small.

Her gaze roamed shamelessly over him as he walked. He wasn't wearing the white jumpsuit now, but a pair of dark coveralls that stretched tightly over his chest. He'd told her they would strip search him before he entered the visitation room and again when he left. That he was willing to do that, to be subjected to such an intimate violation, just to see her made her heart ache.

The harsh fluorescent lighting made his skin look almost unnaturally pale and his eyes nearly black in comparison. His dark hair was ruffled, like he'd pushed his fingers through it in agitation while he waited.

Was he worried, too? Afraid she might not show up, after all?

The relief that washed over his face when he spotted her was painfully obvious, as was the anxious crease in his brow immediately afterward.

She stood up as they got closer, hands twisting restlessly in her pockets as he approached her. Her heart was fluttering madly, each step that he took pushing it to beat faster until he stopped just beyond arms' reach and everything else in the room fell away. She'd dreamed of seeing him a hundred times, but now that he was in front of her, she was lost, unable to even summon the courage to say hello.

"Can't believe you finally got a visitor," the guard to his left said gruffly. "You're allowed to hug her when you first get here and again before you leave. Other than that, you can hold her hand and that's it." Mia's eyes swung to look at him, taking in the guard for the first time. He was a young man, probably only a few years older than her, blond with a scruffy beard and a tired expression. He didn't seem to be joking and her heart redoubled its efforts to beat its way out of her chest.

Gabriel hadn't known anything about what would happen once they were in the visitation area, and he hadn't dared to hope she'd be allowed to touch him.

Gabriel turned to look at the guard to his right—an older, grumpier man with darker hair—waiting for a nod of confirmation before he hesitantly opened his arms and waited. The confidence that he had in calls and letters when he talked about what he'd do to her body if given the chance, fell away —suddenly he was a broken boy again, unsure if she would allow something as simple as a hug.

She stepped forward, nearly tripping over her own feet in her haste to reassure him. She wrapped her arms around his waist, her cheek pressed tight to his chest as he enveloped her in his warmth. He smelled like strong laundry detergent and the fabric of his coveralls was scratchy against her cheek. She didn't ever want to let go, and she held on until he pulled away first, glancing anxiously at the guards before rubbing her arm reassuringly and letting his lips subtly graze her temple as he reached for her hand.

Mia wiped the tears from her cheeks and sat back down in her hard plastic chair. It was cracked and wobbled when she sat on it, but she couldn't have traded sitting here with him for anything.

He stared at her reverently, his thumb tracing small circles on the back of her hand and she dipped her head, suddenly shy and unsure what to say. "I got a form," she said hesitantly, "from the desk when I came in? I paid for a picture of us together. I hope that's okay."

He nodded, chin jerking unsteadily. "Sure, that's ... Whatever makes you happy."

"You make me happy," she said simply, and he smiled, his face relaxing into a bright grin that made her smile in return. "Thank you for adding me to the list and letting me visit. I know you didn't really want to."

"I wanted to see you," he said softly. "I just wish it wasn't like this. You don't belong here."

She glanced around at the tables that had young wives and elderly parents, the bright innocent faces of the children. "None of us do, but here we are."

There was a moment of quiet between them, where she wished fiercely that she could do much more than hold his hand, her eyes dropping to the plush curve of his mouth, soft and pink and overwhelmingly tempting. She said a quick and fervent prayer that someday she would know what it felt like when it settled over her own. Her mind told her it was useless to hope, but her heart knew nothing was beyond the power of God.

They both laughed awkwardly when a young boy at the table next to them squealed loudly and threw his cup which clattered across the floor to land at Mia's feet. She handed it back to his mother, who muttered a hasty apology, before looking at Gabriel with a rueful smile.

"So ..." He glanced at her, honey eyes drifting over her face as he tried to fill the silence. "How is everything at home? School? Kennedy?"

"She had a bad week last week, ran into her parents at the grocery store and they wouldn't even acknowledge that they'd seen her, but other than that she's been better. Happier, I think, than she's been since I've known her."

He smiled, and she stroked her thumb over his hand, a

moment of silent acknowledgment that she knew it mattered to him somehow and she'd be there for him when he was ready to talk about it.

"And your dad? Was he okay with you coming here?"

She winced. "He wasn't thrilled," she said honestly. "There's been a lot going on and we haven't really had time to talk. He's trying but he doesn't understand why I want to be a lawyer or what I could gain from having feelings for you."

"He's afraid you'll get hurt." Gabriel picked at the scars on the table as he spoke, his blunt fingers tracing the lines. "It scares me, too."

"You didn't hurt me. All this?" She circled her finger in the air to indicate the walls and the prison beyond. "This hurts me, but I probably wouldn't have met you without it, so there's no use dwelling on it."

He looked like he might want to argue but, in the end, he just squeezed her hand.

"Glad we settled that." She didn't think it really was settled but they could deal with their doubts on a different day. "Want anything from the vending machine?"

"Whatever you're having." He picked up the bag of coins, hefting its weight before handing it to her with a chuckle. "I'm not picky."

"I imagine not," she said, her nose wrinkling against the prison smell and what she imagined their food must taste like.

"You really are always hungry, aren't you?" he asked when she came back a few minutes later with her arms piled high with bags of snacks and bottles of drinks.

"Yes, I really am," she said, dropping her hoard on the table and tearing open a package of M&Ms to pour several into her hand before passing it to him.

"This is good, right?"

She looked up at him in surprise. "What?"

"This," he wiggled a finger in the space between them "Us.

It's good. You didn't take one look at me and decide I wasn't what you wanted after all."

"I was afraid *you* wouldn't want *me*," she confessed, squeezing his hand to soothe both of their fears. "But I think we're good."

Her heart was full as he laughed with her and ate half her snacks and smiled at her when she gave the rest of her money to the family beside them so they could buy a few of their own after they overheard them mention how hard it was for them to afford the trip every few months.

She was acutely aware of his body and her need for him to touch her as he stood beside her, awkwardly bumping her as he tried to lean down enough to get both of their faces in the photo she'd paid for. When their time was up, she gripped him tightly in a hug that she knew would have to last them both until she could see him again.

"How was your visit?" Kennedy asked. They'd been busy for the past few days and the Bible meeting was the first time Mia had seen much of her since she'd come home from her first meeting with Gabriel. She leaned forward in her chair now, eyes bright with curiosity, and Mia could tell she had just been waiting for the other Bible group members to leave so that she could finally ask.

Mia smiled, unable to hide the bubbling joy that had been tumbling around inside her and reached into her bag to pull out the picture of her and Gabriel.

Kennedy looked at the picture in her hand and let out a low whistle. "He's very tall," she said, turning the photo around so that Lilly could see it.

"He's huge," Mia agreed, chewing happily on a cookie. "I couldn't believe how big he was when they brought him in."

"Weren't you scared?" Lilly asked her, looking at the picture and shaking her head.

"No," Mia said. "I have no reason to be scared of him."

Lilly's expression was guarded, and Mia felt another small twinge of annoyance. "You're determined not to like him no matter what he does, aren't you?" she asked.

"I just want you to be safe and happy," Lilly said, looking at Mia with a pleading expression. "You know that, right?"

Mia nodded, softening at the genuine conflict that she could sense in the crease between Lilly's eyes. "I know but nothing is easy about this, and I need you to be on my side."

Lilly swallowed hard and looked at Kennedy, seeking something to help her figure out what to do. She'd always been fiercely loyal, fiercely certain of right and wrong, and now she was floundering.

Kennedy smiled and handed her a cookie. "You can't tell someone who to love. It's your job as her friend to let her know that you're concerned and you'll be there for her if she gets hurt, but you have to support what makes her happy."

Mia said nothing, looking at Lilly patiently as she weighed the words in her mind. After a moment, Lilly sighed softly. "You're my best friend," she said. "I want you to be happy more than anything and if you need my support then you have it."

Chapter Fifteen

Spring

Church had been Mia's sanctuary when she was little, a place of peace and welcome where she was sure of the goodness of God and his people. It amazed her how quickly one woman could change that into something unpleasant. Most of the congregation had accepted the news of Kennedy's change in living arrangements at Christmas without fuss, but Mrs. Newberry had been digging from the start, asking questions around town for weeks until she'd finally gotten enough of the story to figure out what Kennedy's parents had done and why. They'd tried to keep it quiet—embarrassed by the existence of their daughter rather than their own disgusting behavior—but it hadn't stopped her from finding out or from telling anyone who'd listen.

Whispers traveled fast in a small town and this one was no exception. Their congregation had begun to turn their heads when Kennedy walked by and even the ones that didn't mutter and gossip behind their hands tended to stare. A pointed Sunday sermon from Pastor Anderson on the importance of loving their neighbors hadn't been enough to stop it entirely and Mia had stayed as close as possible to Kennedy's side since then, both her and Lilly giving stern looks to anyone who's eyes lingered too long or with too much curiosity. It was none of anyone else's business what happened with her parents, and they hadn't tolerated anyone approaching her with a bad attitude or a judgmental heart.

She'd done her best to make the whole unfortunate situation tolerable, but none of that mattered to those who preferred to use God's words as a weapon and Mrs. Newberry did her damage as she always did, with a silver tongue and a cloying smile.

She was tired and uneasy when Gabriel called, and she answered with a knot of worry in her stomach. "Please don't tell me something terrible has happened. I've had the worst night with Mrs. Newberry, and I don't think I can handle any more bad news."

"No bad news," he said quickly, his voice bubbling with excitement. "You're never going to fucking believe what's happened, baby!"

"What happened?" Her eyes were closed, sleep shadowing the lights that crisscrossed the inside of her eyelids.

"They approved it!"

She sat bolt upright in bed, her problems and fatigue forgotten. "What?"

"They reversed the conviction! I'm not getting out, I knew that was too much to hope for and the prosecution made it clear immediately that they intended to refile the charges, but I'm getting a new trial!"

"Okay." She blew a hard breath out through her nose, the air in her lungs electric as her thoughts tumbled over and tried to absorb his words. "I can't believe it. Even if they intend to put you back on trial, shouldn't you be released until then? Bail or something?"

"I hoped so," his tone was bitter, the excitement fading quickly. "They're apparently planning to argue that I can't be trusted not to run. My mother still has money and a lot of influence and that makes me a flight risk."

"She hasn't spoken to you in years! Do you think they'll get away with that?"

"Yeah, I think they will. You should hear the way the guys in here talk. Texas is notorious for the shit they do. Long sentences, shitty defenders, impossible fucking odds on appeal. It's almost a miracle that they approved the writ at all so ..."

"We'll take the miracle," she said firmly. "We take it and do our best to make it into a real opportunity."

"I could get out." It was awed, spoken gently like saying it with too much force could damage it somehow. "We could actually be—"

"We could," she agreed. "Gabriel, I lov—"

"Don't," he said, and she faltered, her chest constricted around the words. "Not yet. I need you to know what happened to me, what I've done, before you say that to me."

"Do you think I'm going to change my mind?" she asked. It was light, a gentle tease as she floated on the joy of their new possibilities, but he was serious when he answered.

"Yes." He took a shaky breath, and she could hear him clench his teeth. "I'm terrified you'll change your mind."

"I won't but I'll wait if you need me to and you can tell me anything you need me to hear."

He was quiet, his breathing soft in her ear as she waited for him to begin. "Can I send it to you instead?"

"Of course."

The letter he sent her was five pages long.

There were names that she recognized—his mother, father, and uncle. There were others that she didn't—Seth, Brittany, Michael. They were all important and together it formed a tapestry, complicated and interwoven threads that told a heartbreaking story of abuse and his own anger and regret. He blamed the adults that failed to protect him or harmed him directly, but mostly he blamed himself. For not being able to stop it, for not being able to protect himself or protect others. His parents said he'd been wild, untamed and ungrateful. He'd internalized that to mean he was to blame for what had followed their decision to send him away.

He described how hopeless he'd felt, how filled with fear and panic, the night he had killed his father and she would've given anything to go back to that moment, to hold that broken child in her arms and tell him that it wasn't his fault, that she would have done the same if she'd been in his shoes. The unfairness of it was enough to make her weep and rage and press her hand to her mouth as sickness clawed its way up her throat to coat her mouth and she slept with his words pressed against her chest and a heavy weight on her heart.

He was waiting for an answer and there was only one that she could give him that would be true to her own heart and reassure him that he had no reason to worry about her being there for him through the process of a new trial. She sat at her desk the next morning, ink flowing over the pages as she wrote her reply.

It would take a few days to get to him, and she spent all of them worried about how he was doing and waiting for him to call.

"Hey."

"Hmm?" Mia looked up to find James standing in the doorway, smiling at her hesitantly as she arranged chairs for the Bible group meeting.

She'd been distracted thinking about Gabriel's last letter and hadn't heard him approaching. She flicked her gaze quickly to check on Kennedy, who was laying out the cookies on the snack table and pasted a polite smile on her face.

"Listen, uh, I know things didn't exactly go well the last time we talked, but since you've had some time to cool down …"

She smiled and straightened to her full height, back ramrod straight. "I'm afraid I'm still not interested, but thanks anyway."

He sputtered awkwardly at her quick rejection; his tone perplexed as he stammered. "You're still mad?"

"I'm not mad, I'm just not interested." She shrugged and decided to give him the whole truth. "I'm in a relationship with someone else."

"Who?" He tapped his fingers on his thigh, the corner of his mouth turning up in disbelief. "I haven't seen you hanging around with anyone. Is it someone I know?"

"No, I'm romantically involved with Gabriel." It certainly wasn't any of his business who she dated, but she wanted him to know. He needed to understand that she had made a choice and it wasn't him.

"Gabriel? The guy from prison that you're writing to?"

"Yep, that's the one." She went back to rearranging chairs and turned her back to him.

"So, you won't date me because you're talking to some guy that won't ever get out of prison? He's a murderer!"

Mia turned to face him, her defense ready on her lips, when she noticed that someone else had come to stand behind James, her eyes now glittering with undisguised malice.

"How interesting," Mrs. Newberry muttered. "It seems those felons have brought sin into our midst, after all. Exactly as I predicted."

Mia smiled stiffly, baring her teeth as Mrs. Newberry flounced away triumphantly without another word. She tried to comfort herself with the knowledge that at least Kennedy wouldn't be the subject of that night's gossip, but by the time they got home she was livid. She'd spoken without thinking and there was no way to stop Mrs. Newberry from gossiping about her relationship and pointing a finger of blame at Lilly for suggesting the program to begin with.

She'd have to have to tell her father about the trial now and her commitment to be with Gabriel through the process, something she might have been able to avoid for months if she'd taken the time to choose her words more wisely.

Gabriel held her letter as his past rose up from his memories to wrap around him, the sounds and the smells of it all almost as real as it had been when it happened. He'd had to tell her, couldn't let her love him or hope for a future when she didn't know the things he had done, but now that she'd read the letter there was no going back.

It might have been enough to finally drive her away and if she was going to reject him now, if he had to find out that she was disgusted by him and the things he'd lived through ... Fear of her disgust was a writhing coil inside him. He was glad he'd decided to write it instead of telling her during a call. Her rejection would be devastating either way but if he heard her say it out loud, he knew he'd never stop hearing it, that it would echo in his mind in the dark silences for the rest of his life.

He would deserve that, but he knew he couldn't live with it, that it would drive him mad.

Opening the letter would be the hardest thing he'd ever done, worse even than standing alone in that courtroom so many years ago waiting to find out his fate. Somehow it felt like there was more of his life resting on the contents of this envelope than there had been on the judge's words. His hands shook as he tore the envelope and inside was a single sheet of paper covered on both sides with the same three words written over and over again, as though she knew he wouldn't believe her the first time and hoped by the end he might.

He put his head in his hands, his heart breaking painfully open to let her the rest of the way inside. She knew the worst there was to know about him and this was her response, to reach out to him with more love than he had ever known.

It was agony to wait, but he called her as soon as he was able, and she answered on the first ring, like he wasn't the only one that had been waiting.

"Hello?"

"Mia! I love you, too."

After that all he could think about was her and what he could do to make sure he didn't let her down. He mulled it over for weeks, holding one copy of the photo Mia had paid for of the two of them together and imagining the way that she had looked as she sat perched on that stupid fucking wobbly orange plastic chair in the visitor's room. She was everything to him and he could have a life with her if he could just have this new trial go his way. He was being offered a miracle, and he wasn't going to turn his back on it even if he did think God owed him an apology.

He didn't know if he could get a decent lawyer in time, six months wasn't long when you had no money and the idea of depending on whoever the court assigned to his defense made him sick to his stomach. There were people he could write to, ones that took on cases for people like him and did it for free, but there were always more requests than they could actually take on and he knew his chances were slim.

There was only one option if he wanted to be with Mia so he did the most humiliating thing that he could think of, because he had meant it when he promised her that he would do anything in the world for her. He picked up the phone and called his mother—whose name he had added to the list of people he could call when he first came to this fucking place and who had never once actually tried to contact in all the years since—prepared to beg for her to help him afford the lawyers and the private detective that he needed to have a real chance at a life.

She didn't answer.

~

"What do you mean she still didn't answer? How many times have you tried calling now?"

"It doesn't matter," he said but there was enough sorrow in his eyes that she wanted to scream her frustration. "We need to focus on trying to find someone who's willing to take the case. Anyone has to be better than another public defender who doesn't give a shit."

Her hand tightened on his reflexively, rage bubbling in her stomach. It was a blessing to know he'd at least have a lawyer now that they were dealing with a new trial and not an attempt to undo the effects of a conviction but depending on overworked and underpaid lawyers had gotten him into this mess in the first place. "We'll find someone. I can't believe how awful and underfunded the public defender program is in this state."

"Hey," he shook his head, nodding slightly at the guard that had turned to look at her as her voice rose in agitation. "It's alright, calm down."

She huffed but settled back down in her seat. "It's just bullshit," she said quietly. "It's already been two months. Have you heard back from that non-profit place?"

"Not yet," he told her grimly. "They're still reviewing my request for help. They have more cases than they can handle, and only take on the ones that are most desperate, with the highest chance of success."

"I'm sure they do have more than they can handle," she

snorted, "that's what happens when the state doesn't provide adequate services."

"Did you expect them to?" he asked gently. "Someone profits off of every aspect of this place—the prison labor, the phone calls, the fees—all of it. They have to keep the beds full."

"Bullshit," she muttered again, but she knew he was right. Prison was a for-profit system that broke families for the bottom line and peddled their wares to the public as a service to keep them safe. Convincing them all that what they did was done in the name of justice instead of the almighty dollar was the biggest con ever pulled.

"Are you sure you want to be a lawyer and get mixed up in all this mess?" He looked sad, like maybe he regretted encouraging her.

"Absolutely," she said fiercely. Every day that she learned more about it, she was more determined to help fix it. "What happens to people like you, people like them," she said, waving a hand to indicate the other tables, "if everyone gives up on you?"

"I love you," he said softly. "You give me hope for the world and I thought I had lost that a long time ago."

"I love you, too," she said, her cheeks flooding with heat under the intensity of his gaze. "What happens if they do decide to take the case?" she asked, trying to smooth over the tension and return the conversation to something more productive than her own frustration.

"I'm not sure. I know my chances are better—if not to get an acquittal to at least get a shorter sentence—if I can get all the evidence admitted this time that the jury didn't hear the first time, but all those witnesses ... I have no idea where they are now."

"There has to be a way to track them down," Mia said with a frown.

He shrugged, clearly uncertain. "I guess we might be able to find them if we had a lot of time to spend combing the internet and social media accounts, but who knows how long that might take."

"We have to try," she said. "Mail me a list of names and I'll start looking."

"You need to focus on your classes," he said, brow creasing in concern. "I'm grateful that you want to help, but you have plans that will help a lot more people than just me so you've got to keep your grades up."

"My grades are fine, and I have plenty of time to help. Lilly spends most of her time with Bryce these days and when Kennedy isn't with her girlfriend, she just hangs out in my room eating snacks so she can do that while I look."

"You can try," he agreed, "but it might not be enough."

It wasn't. She couldn't find any of the people he needed, but she wasn't going to give up that easily. Her next plan was more direct, and it took a few weeks for Mia to convince Gabriel. He was adamantly opposed to her being involved but she wore him down, reminding him that he promised her that he would do anything. If he wanted to be with her, then there had to be no chance that they weren't willing to take.

She took a deep breath and dialed the phone number he had given her.

An unfamiliar voice answered on the third ring. "Hello?"

"Yes, hello. I would like to speak with Senator Miller."

"This is Senator Miller. Who is this?"

"My name is Mia Anderson, I'm calling—"

"If you're lobbying for someone, this is highly inappropriate. This number is only for friends and family." Her tone was brisk and stern, clearly this was a woman used to having and wielding power.

"Yes, ma'am, I know that," Mia said quickly, the words spilling over themselves in her haste to get them out before

Gabriel's mother could hang up. "I got this number from your son."

There was a heavy silence until Lilah spoke again. "I have no son."

"Yes, ma'am," Mia said stubbornly, "you do. I know that there's no way for me to understand the pain that you must be in after everything that happened, but there is more to this story than what was on the news. I'm sure you've heard that Gabriel has a chance to get a reduced sentence. He needs your help."

"Why would I help him?" Lilah said coldly. "After what he did to our family?"

"Because he deserves for his mother to finally know the truth about what happened," Mia said firmly, "and you deserve to hear it."

Chapter Sixteen

Gabriel wasn't surprised that Lilah still refused to speak directly to him—she had never been the type of person that was able to bend easily or often—but he *was* surprised that she had agreed to pay for lawyers and private investigators. And not just any lawyers—according to Mia, Lilah had spared no expense on hiring the best.

Amy Hail, the woman who was now tasked with trying to save what was left of his life, was tall and slim—all long limbs and graceful movements beneath a perfectly polished exterior of pressed fabrics and expensive perfume. There was a hint of red in the brown of her hair and an edge of meanness to the green of her eyes. The impossibly high heels and expertly cut suit jackets reminded him painfully of Lilah on her way out the door to some important government meeting.

It also quickly became apparent that, much like his mother, her fragile appearance was not an indication of weakness. Like Lilah, she was a diamond, polished but unbreakable. She was not unkind, but she offered him no false hope, no platitudes or guarantees. She knew the stakes, and she didn't sugarcoat the odds.

Her familiar abrasiveness soothed his nerves.

"You're sure that you can't think of anyone else?" Her pen tapped restlessly on a legal pad that already had the names and dates of everyone and everything he could remember from the day he was sent to Richard's to the day his father died in his arms. The small room used for lawyer's visits was cold and cramped, with nothing but a few chairs and a small table that was nearly invisible beneath heaps of printed records and hastily scribbled notes.

Every meeting he'd ever had with a lawyer had held this same tense atmosphere of quiet desperation. Unwanted memories dug into his mind, and he rolled his shoulders against the intrusion, trying to focus on the task at hand.

"I'm sure," he told her defensively. "I've been over it in my mind a hundred times since your last visit, and that's everyone."

She leaned forward and her tone was impatient. "I know you're trying, and you want out of here, but the chances of us tracking any of these people down is slim and the odds of them being willing to testify ..."

"Can't you just fucking make them? This is my life on the line here."

"Theoretically?" She shrugged, unfazed by his outburst. "But do you want them to be honest?"

"You think they'd lie," he said flatly.

"I think that what you've described to me are multiple scenarios of abuse and illegal activity of the kind that people want to leave behind them," she said as she flipped through the notes she'd taken. "The more names we have, the greater the chances of finding someone willing to give honest testimony."

He pushed a hand through his hair, helplessness choking him. "I can't think of anyone else."

She flipped the page of the pad again, eyes narrowed on

the list. "We'll pass what you've given me along to the P.I. and then we'll just have to wait and see what we come up with. One way or the other, we have to build you the best case we can."

He fell silent as she wrote, the pen scratching across paper the only sound as the minutes ticked by.

"Do you have any questions for me?" she asked finally, glancing at him as she started to pack her things away. Their time was limited and nearly done for the day.

"How will this be different from my first trial?" He'd avoided asking her during their first several meetings because he wasn't sure he could handle another experience like the last one. Not when Mia was involved.

"Most of it will be the same but primarily we'll have witnesses and expert testimony about your state of mind at the time of the murder," she said, ticking the list off on her fingers. "We won't be arguing that you're innocent, not exactly, but—"

"What are we arguing?"

"We're asking the jury to consider the circumstances of the murder and the role your past played in the events. To be very honest, I don't understand how they managed to get a conviction for capital murder the first time when there was so much to indicate a lack of premeditation at a minimum. This time we'll give the full story. Show the jury you're a victim here, just a kid who was overcome by the circumstances and unlikely to offend again."

"Do you believe that?"

"I have a responsibility to defend you no matter what my beliefs are," she said firmly, "but in this case, I believe you deserve to walk out of this prison someday."

"You think that's possible? Honestly?" He wasn't sure why her opinion mattered to him so much, just that it did.

"You've certainly got the best chance of anyone I've ever

seen in your position and a great support system." She smiled at him and shook her head, obviously bemused. "That girlfriend of yours is going to make a *great* lawyer someday."

"About Mia ... Can we keep the media from prying into my personal life?" His voice spiked, fear setting in as he realized that Mia was on record at the prison for visiting him. The idea of aggressive paparazzi swarming her house made him sick.

"The first thing that I'm going to ask for is no cameras in the courtroom. There's always the chance that someone will be willing to leak sensitive information no matter what the court orders, but media interest is likely to be significantly reduced if they aren't getting trial footage every day. Your first trial was a mishandled media circus."

"That's putting it mildly," he mumbled.

"I'll do everything I can to keep her safe," she promised. "We're all going to do our best for you, but nobody is fighting for you harder than Mia and even if the press shows up, she's not going to get scared off by a few reporters."

The countryside had blossomed since the first time she had been to the prison, the trees bursting with the unfurling leaves that marked the relentless passing of time. The weeks that had turned winter into spring had also made Mia comfortable in her visits. The drive and her arrival were uneventful, the barbed wire and the dogs and the clanging of the doors nothing more than background noise.

It terrified her when she stopped to think through the implications of her acclimation.

She knew the route to the prison, the names of the guards, the smell and sounds of the visitation room so well that she had started to dream about them—her mind replaying the familiar process until she finally made it inside and saw Gabriel as an old man with his hair gray and his back bent with age. In the nightmare, a lifetime had passed, and she knew that he would never leave his cage, destined to die behind the walls that kept him prisoner. He still smiled when he saw her, his face wreathed with wrinkles, and she choked back her tears because she didn't want him to see how badly her heart was broken that they had been denied a life together.

She prayed with clenched fists every day that she would never have to see him like that outside the panicked projections of her mind ... and she did not tell Gabriel. Even if it meant keeping some things to herself, she was unwilling to burden him with her fears when she knew he had so many of his own.

After a subtle and intimate brush of her fingers over his wrist, she twined her fingers with his and took in his appearance as they sat down at the nearest table. He was as handsome as ever, his smile as genuine, but his eyes were shadowed with dark circles.

She had suspicions that she wasn't the only one having nightmares.

"How was the drive?" he asked, already rubbing circles on the back of her hand with his thumb. He was always touching her, like he was trying as hard as she was to soak every bit of their visits in through the skin where it would live forever, an indelibly etched memory.

"It's not as stressful as it used to be." He nodded but he said nothing else, and she frowned, sensing an undercurrent of something dark that made her uneasy. "What's wrong?"

"I spoke to Amy," he said quietly. "They're still looking but without those witnesses ... What if they don't find anyone?" His hand tightened on hers until it was almost painful as he spoke a portion of her own fears aloud, and he looked at her like he might fall apart.

"We just have to keep our faith."

"I don't want you to be alone for the rest of your life because I'm stuck in here."

Mia sighed and pressed a hand to her eyes, willing back the tears there before he could see them. She knew he loved her, that he wanted her, but right now he needed her hope more than he needed anything else. It had been her hope that had finally swayed his mother and it would be her hope that kept him going.

Her pleas to Lilah had earned them an opportunity they couldn't afford to waste in fear and self-pity. Amy had told her plainly, when she had arranged to meet her at a little coffee shop just off campus, that this process would be long and exhaustive, that it would push her to the limits of her emotions, with one day bringing the highest of hopes and the next the dark certainty of failure and despair. They would need as much support from others as they could find, but mostly they would need each other, and she prepared to give him all that she had.

"Hey," she crooned, hating the guards and the rules for preventing her from pulling him into her arms, from running her fingers through the soft waves of his hair and kissing his anxiety away. "We can't think like that."

"I didn't care so much the first time because I thought my life was over anyway, but now I have you and I have a fucking life waiting for me." She started to speak but his head whipped up and she was caught in the tumult of his eyes. "Do you want to know the worst part, though? Even now she isn't here, and she doesn't care."

"Who?"

"My mother," he said, surprising her as the words tore into her to lodge somewhere primal, nestling into her heart. He hadn't spoken at all about Lilah since he had found out about the lawyers and she'd been reluctant to bring it up, afraid of upsetting him.

"Gabriel, I'm so sorry," she said, squeezing his hand and wiping away the tears that she could no longer hold back. "I tried to get her to talk to you, but she said she wanted to hear what the P.I.'s had to say first."

"Of course, she did," he said bitterly.

"She talked about you and your father," Mia told him softly. "She's not a soft woman, obviously, but I think she loved you both."

"And *Richard*? Did she talk about *him*?"

"Yes," Mia admitted, still unsure how much she should say on the subject of his uncle. "I got the impression they were close, and she felt very betrayed by the idea that he might have hurt you."

"They *were* close," Gabriel said. "Richard was able to get away with so much because people trusted him."

"It looks like he dropped out of the public eye around the time your father died, but Amy and my dad told me how famous he was."

"Convincing people that he wasn't as perfect as they thought he was will be almost impossible."

"We're going to be taking on a big legacy," she admitted, "but we *can* do this."

∼

"How was the visit?"

Mia sighed, pausing with her foot on the bottom stair. She'd thought she might be able to get by without her father seeing her, but she hadn't been so lucky.

"It was fine," she said, turning to smile at him as she took another step up the stairs. "Just going over some stuff that we had talked to his lawyers about."

Pastor Anderson nodded absently, still rooted to the spot in the doorway to the dining room. He had been waiting for her to come home, she realized. He hadn't done that since she was in high school, when he needed to talk to her about her mother's illness. It was usually an indication that he had something serious to say.

"Can you come in here, please?" he asked, confirming her suspicions, and tapping his fingers nervously on his thigh.

"Sure," she said, turning away from the stairs and taking a few hesitant steps to follow him into the dining room, where he sat at the table, a cup of coffee sitting untouched in front of him.

Kennedy wouldn't be home from class for another two hours, and without the buffer her presence had provided, Mia had a sinking feeling that this conversation was going to be the one that she had been specifically avoiding for the last three months.

"We haven't had much time to really talk since the unfortunate disagreement we had at Christmas," he said, confirming her suspicion.

"No, we haven't," she agreed. She hugged her arms around her middle, anxiety already prickling beneath the skin and making her thoughts buzz uncomfortably.

He swallowed and shifted his hands restlessly on the coffee cup. "I guess, if I'm being honest, I just wondered if things were still the same as they were the last time we spoke?"

"You want to know if I'm still planning to apply to law school and if I still have feelings for Gabriel?" She knew her tone was blunter than he would have preferred, and he looked away.

"Yes, that's what I was wondering," he confirmed.

"I am," she said simply. "I'm enjoying my classes and I love Gabriel." Her father's face was tired as he nodded and she relented enough to add, "I know Mrs. Newberry's been causing problems because of my relationship with him and I'm sorry you've had to deal with that."

He waved a hand to dismiss her concerns. "I'm not blaming you for that. She's being extremely difficult but ... there's still hope."

He was stubborn about those things, but that relentless hope had once kept him from returning a wide eyed and terrified little girl, so she patted his hand, determined to work out the tension between them now that the conversation had begun.

"I know that you wanted me to follow the path that God had laid for me," she told him with an understanding smile, "and that you always thought that it would be the same path as Mom, but it isn't. I know that hurts you, but I can't change it. I can't change what God created me to be."

"Is that what you think? That I want to change you?" He dropped his head into his hands, shoulders slumping.

"Isn't it?" asked, bewildered when he lifted his head from his hands, eyes red rimmed and cheeks wet.

"I want you to be *happy*, Mia. Happy and safe and loved. I know you have feelings for Gabriel and after everything you've told us, I hate what happened to him, but if he never gets out ..." He took a deep breath. "You're going to be heartbroken. Heartbroken and alone."

"I can handle this."

"I *know* you can achieve anything you set your mind to, but I don't want you to put so much of yourself into your career or into waiting for Gabriel that you miss out on other things in life."

"I understand—"

He shook his head, his face broken and anguished. "You don't understand. I don't think you remember what things were like when you first came to us. You were so touch starved, so scared of even being in a room by yourself, that we couldn't leave you alone. I never wanted you to be lonely again. I wanted you to have a family, Mia, and someone to grow old with."

"I know," she told him. "And I'm fighting to have that. I'm fighting for the person I want to be with."

"What if he hurts you?"

"What if I had married James and had a bunch of babies and then he left me and ran off with a stripper?"

He laughed bleakly, recalling the story she was talking about. A pastor in the next county had done exactly that a few years before, leaving his young wife brokenhearted and alone with three children to raise.

"I always wanted to find a man just like you and somehow I did," she continued, patting his hand at his shocked expression. "He's got a difficult past, but I promise you that I know what a good man looks like, what *love* looks like, because you and Mom showed me. He listens to me, he cares about me, he supports me in everything I do. He looks at me like you looked at Mom, and that's how I know it's right."

He pulled her in for a hug and exhaled a shaky breath. "You're sure that you can be happy? That this is the life that you want for yourself?"

"Yes." She sat beside him, her cheek pressed to his shoulder and her hand on his. "I trust him and I'm asking you to trust me."

Chapter Seventeen

Summer

The June heat was inescapable and clung to Mia's skin with the smell of sweat and sunscreen. She tugged on the hem of the rainbow T-shirt she was wearing, unsticking it from her stomach and hoping to stir a breeze. Bryce and Lilly looked nearly as miserable, hot and wilting as soon as they'd stepped out of the car.

"Mia," Kennedy called, running up to hug first her, then Lilly and Bryce. She was beaming, face vibrant and nose sunburnt as the crowd pressed in around them. Her long blonde hair had been cut short and danced against her cheeks in the slight breeze. "I'm so glad you all came."

"Wouldn't miss it," Mia assured her, looking curiously at the girl that was holding tight to Kennedy's hand.

She was shorter than Mia by several inches, but she made up for it in vibrancy—the glint of silver shone from a piercing in her nose and her long hair was dyed electric pink. Her grin was fierce, slightly on edge like she wasn't sure what sort of welcome she might receive.

To her, Mia and the others were Kennedy's church friends and a note of dull pain echoed in Mia's heart as she remembered what Gabriel had taught her. Faith was not always the guarantee of compassion that she had once thought it was.

"Or the chance to meet your girlfriend, *finally*," Mia said, offering her hand and her warmest smile. "I'm Mia, this is Lilly and Bryce."

"Alison has been a little nervous about meeting everyone," Kennedy admitted, leaning in to kiss her girlfriend's cheek. "But I convinced her."

"We are so happy to meet you," Lilly said, "You've made Kennedy happier than I think I've ever seen her."

At that Alison smiled back at them, some of her tension draining away. "Nice to meet you, too. Is this your first time at Pride?" she asked, voice barely carrying over the noise as she looked curiously at all of them, including the whole group in her question.

"Yeah," Lilly acknowledged, "and it's great!" She turned to Kennedy and gestured at the shirt she wore with its glittering rainbow flag. "If someone had asked you last summer if you'd be here like this in just a year—happy and in love—would you have believed it?"

Kennedy shook her head. "I don't think I would have believed that I *ever* would have been able to do this. I couldn't see a future beyond my parents."

"You're better than them," Alison said fiercely. "They didn't deserve you."

"No, they didn't and that's why we had to come and support Kennedy," Bryce said with a grin. "She's been through a lot and it's good to see her smiling again. I'm glad she has you."

Alison's cheeks flushed as Kennedy leaned in for another kiss.

Mia smiled, her heart full at her friend's obvious blossoming, but her gaze slid from one happy couple to the other and the space between her own fingers felt empty.

She was alone and the hole in her life where Gabriel should have been was becoming a constant ache that had settled deep in her chest. They were all moving on—Kennedy was planning to move in with Alison at the end of summer and that had set Lilly and Bryce thinking about their own apartment—and each beat of her heart was a reminder of the part of her that was missing, each breath heavy with the weight of the passage of time, but how could she admit that to anyone, especially him?

He wouldn't blame her for how she felt, but she blamed herself.

Gabriel watched as Amy settled into the seat on the other side of the table, her face set as she spread the papers in her arms out for him to look at. There was at least an attempt made to keep the air conditioning working in this part of the prison so the suit she was wearing was only slightly wilted as she passed him a neat stack of paper.

"What's this?"

The P.I. report," she explained, pressing a perfectly manicured nail to the first page, dotted with familiar names. "He was able to make contact with Michael Lansing, as well as Vincent Russel, David Hu, and Chris Mendoza. They've agreed to testify."

He swallowed. It was a short list out of all the ones he'd given her. "The others?"

She averted her eyes. "It seems association with Seth Wiseman was as dangerous as you claimed. Andre Lewis died the same year you were convicted. Shooting. Ramon Vasquez committed suicide a few years later and no one can find Thomas Wilson. He's simply disappeared."

Gabriel nodded, unsurprised but heartsore. He had little doubt that whatever happened to Thomas had been unpleasant and irreversible. "None of the others from Richard's?"

"Wealthy families and all that," she said quietly. "Most of them won't even respond to the P.I.'s inquiries, or they've slapped him with legal orders to force him to keep his distance."

He nodded, again unsurprised. Wasn't keeping the family reputation intact the reason most of them had been sent to Richard to begin with? Still …

"Brittany?" he asked, unable to shake the hope that maybe, after all these years, she had forgiven him.

Amy shook her head and he looked away at the unexpected sympathy in her eyes. "She was the first to file for him to desist his attempts to contact her. I know she was key to a lot of this, the final straw that drove you out and into Seth's clutches, but we can't get to her."

"What now?" He sucked his bottom lip between his teeth, worrying the soft flesh as he rapped uneasily on the table with his knuckle. Disappointment and hurt feelings wouldn't help him get out of here, it wouldn't help him get to Mia.

"We wait." Amy leaned back in her chair, regarding him calmly over the expanse of the table.

He nodded wordlessly. He was guaranteed the right to a speedy trial, sure, but both sides needed time to prepare. He wasn't going to have tomorrow, or next week, or next month. There was nothing else he could do, nothing he had been able to do for years.

Just wait.

~

Fall

Mrs. Newberry smirked over the rim of her cup of cider as she approached, and Mia set her teeth. It had been a while since their last encounter, Mrs. Newberry had been mostly quiet the past few months, since she'd realized that nothing had come of her previous gossip. They'd started to believe that she'd given up and Mia had been too busy with classes to pay much attention to her anyway, but the sudden glint in her eye meant she must have found some new bit of information to torment them with.

"Mia, dear," she said silkily, standing just a bit too close so she could lean in conspiratorially, "you look positively exhausted. Those classes of yours sure do seem to be taking a toll on you."

Mia opened her mouth, rage coiling at the tip of tongue, but the other woman flashed a quick smile and plunged on without waiting for an answer. "Have you heard the good news? Mr. Prescott is engaged. It seems he found *quite* a sweet and God-fearing young woman in Emily, and I was just sure that you would want to know since the two of you were such good friends!"

"I hadn't heard," Mia said coldly. "I'm sure he'll be very happy."

"It is a shame that you won't have the same opportunities, isn't it? How are things going with you and that prisoner?"

Mia glared at her, good sense and courtesy falling away in her irritation. "Gabriel is fine. Better than fine, actually, he's waiting now for a new trial. He might get to come home someday."

Mrs. Newberry faltered for a moment, and Mia felt a vicious wave of satisfaction settle over her—one that was quickly followed by a deep and unshakeable dread. Nothing was more dangerous in Mrs. Newberry's hands than information, and Mia was sure that bitterness had just goaded her into once again admitting something that she was sure to pay for later.

"Well, then, perhaps someday we'll get to celebrate your engagement after all," she said with a condescending smirk. With that she sauntered away, leaving Mia standing with her lips pressed together in a thin line of regret.

She'd fallen for the bait. Mrs. Newberry wasn't actually happy about James's engagement; she'd been looking for any reason to make Mia feel inadequate.

"Is she bothering you again?" Lilly appeared at her elbow with a frown and a cupcake.

Mia knew she was worried, and she leaned into Lilly's shoulder, seeking the solace of her best friend's embrace. It was humiliating that she had let Mrs. Newberry push her into making such a careless mistake. She had known that this was the cost of her choices, but she hadn't known that it would hurt so much. "She just loves to remind me of all the things she thinks I can't have. Every opportunity she gets she throws marriage and family in my face."

"You've always wanted those things. A husband. Kids."

"I know." She tipped her head back, stared sightlessly at the ceiling as she pushed back the ache. "I'm not giving up on that. We can bring him home. Right?"

Lilly had no answer.

"Do you ever think about what you're going to do if you actually get out of here someday?"

The question surprised him, coming from Alex, and he sighed, looking at the wall of pictures that held Mia's smiling face.

"All the time," he said honestly. "I just want to be with Mia."

Alex nodded from his position on the bunk opposite. "More than that, though. What about jobs, places to live? I've only got a few more years in this shithole and I don't know what I'm gonna do when it's over."

"You've got your brother waiting for you on the outside, right?" Gabriel knew he did, that Alex had landed himself here when he found his father beating the kid the way he had once beaten Alex. His cellmate had put an end to that with his fists, then drove his brother to the hospital and waited for the police to show up.

Not that Gabriel blamed him. What else was he supposed to do after countless calls to the cops and Child Protective Services had gone nowhere? The local prosecutor hadn't agreed, and, from what he understood, Alex's little brother had ended up in foster care and Alex had pleaded guilty to aggravated assault so he could get a lenient enough sentence to be out before the kid was grown.

"How am I supposed to take care of him with this on my record?"

The uncertainty in his voice was the most humanity Gabriel had seen from him, and he shook his head. "I don't know, man, but I know you'll figure it out."

"Do you worry about Mia? Taking care of her and being normal after all this?"

Gabriel blew out a hard breath. "Every day."

He wasn't even out, and he had already disrupted her life, what was it going to do to her if he actually got out some day? The question kept him up at night, haunting the edges of his dreams and he knew he wasn't the only one struggling. She was already doing so much—classes, homework, church—and now she was talking about getting a job on top of all that.

Anything to keep herself distracted from the time that was passing them by. There were dark circles under her eyes every time he saw her, and he wanted to kiss them away, to hold her so he could make sure she was sleeping at night.

He couldn't do any of those things and time ticked by.

Chapter Eighteen

Winter

Christmas came again quickly, the festive lights an unwelcome reminder of everything Gabriel was missing. Time passed and he still hadn't received a date for his trial.

Mia nibbled her lip and wished she hadn't agreed to stay late and clean up after the church's nativity play. The children in their costumes had been adorable, but all she wanted was to go home. She'd taken on a job before Christmas break, something to do to keep her mind busy, and by the end of her days she was tired enough to sleep with fewer dreams.

"You okay?"

She smiled at Lilly, perched in Bryce's lap now that most of the cleaning duties were done and just the three of them and Kennedy remained. "Christmas is just a little gloomy this year. It's hard to be alone, especially when everyone else is so happy together."

"Sorry," Lilly said. She shifted from Bryce's knee to the chair beside him, face flustered.

"It's fine," Mia assured her. "You don't have to hide your happiness just because I'm a little lonely." She picked at a stray thread on the hem of her sweater, unable to look at them.

"You still have a chance," Kennedy said, wrapping an arm around her shoulder and leaning her head against Mia's. "He might get out someday and then you two can make up for all this lost time."

"I guess we could," she said. "I want to, it's just …"

"Just?"

She hesitated, picking at her thread again. They'd never discussed this part of her relationship with Gabriel before. "We talk about it so often and there's so much *expectation*. What if he's disappointed?"

"With you?" Kennedy's look was puzzled.

"With me and with everything else," Mia said. It was hard to explain the weight she'd carried and how she had come to fear his release as much as she hoped for it. "What if he gets out and we aren't happy? What if he doesn't like being with me?"

"Why wouldn't he like being with you?" Lilly asked.

"He's had sex before," Mia said quickly, trying to get it out before she lost her nerve. "He's been with a lot of people, and I don't know anything." It poured out of her, and she looked at them, swallowing down the vulnerability that sat on her chest, threatening to smother her.

"He was so young when he went to prison," Bryce said, "I doubt he was with that many people."

"He *was*," Mia insisted.

"You don't have to be the first to be the one that matters," Kennedy reassured her. "He hasn't complained about anything yet, has he?"

Lilly and Bryce looked at her curiously. "Oh?" Lilly asked. "What has he had to complain about?"

"Just some letters," Mia bit her lip hard and looked away. "And phone calls."

"*Sexy* phone calls, though, right?" Kennedy asked. "Like we talked about before?"

"Wait, you've been having phone sex?" Bryce sat forward, scanning Mia's face for evidence, and then letting out a low whistle.

"Not exactly," she hedged. "I mean, he doesn't have a phone to himself so it's not really private. And they're sort of recording the calls, so you never know if someone's listening."

"I can't believe you didn't tell me about this," Lilly said. "You two have been talking for so long now and you never said anything."

Mia shrugged, keeping her eyes fixed on the bare ring finger of her left hand. "It's embarrassing," she admitted. "It's all we have, all we might ever have, but we're not married."

"And you feel guilty," Lilly said, pinning the source of Mia's discomfort in a few words.

"Yes."

"You don't judge us," Bryce reminded her, "and we aren't going to judge you."

"Absolutely." Lilly nodded, her hand in Bryce's. "And when he does get out, you two will do just fine. He isn't going to be disappointed in you."

Mia smiled tightly, but the seed of her doubt remained.

Gabriel got the official date on a Tuesday, his world fixing itself to a moment in the summertime that would determine everything about his future ... and Mia's.

She was calmer when he told her than he expected, and he knew she was absolutely focused on making sure he stayed hopeful.

"It's sooner than we thought," she said. "This summer! It could have taken another year. That's a *whole year* that we don't have to worry about. We've come so far."

"Every day I spend in here is a day we can't get back," he said, the time between him and the trial stretching out like an eternity. So much waiting, so much time lost.

"It's worth it," she told him. "Every day that I spend waiting for you is worth it."

He held tight to those words as he spent days staring at the date and time of the trial finally written down in black and white. He'd never thought he'd have this chance and now he resented it taking so long to arrive. It was selfish, but he'd always been a selfish man. He had hope and Mia and witnesses and still he wanted more. He thought about trying again to call his mother, humbling himself to ask if she'd come.

He didn't.

∽

Spring

Gabriel was used to Mia's visits. He still counted the seconds between them, but she had come as often as possible, and he had stopped getting nervous a long time ago. He knew she would be there; knew she would smile at him and link her fingers with his and they would have a few hours where love mattered more than the obstacles they faced.

It was different when her father came.

He followed her to a table and tried to turn his focus to the man who sat beside her. Pastor Anderson looked exactly the way Gabriel had expected him to—neatly dressed, hair combed just the right way, glasses settled sensibly at the bridge of his nose. He didn't have the same hidden edge of cruelty in his eyes that Richard had always had, and the laugh lines at his eyes seemed genuine, but he still frowned at Mia's eagerness for Gabriel's touch, the easy and casual way that she wrapped her hand around his, her fingers slotting comfortably between his own.

She smiled, ignoring the palpable tension in the air as her father stared him down. It was not the way he would have preferred to meet the parent of the woman he loved, but she was insistent that she wanted them to meet before the trial.

"Gabriel, this is my dad," she said, cutting into the silence and looking from one of them to the other. "Dad, this is Gabriel."

He reached out a hand and Pastor Anderson took it, giving it a brief, perfunctory shake. "Nice to meet you finally," Gabriel said, his gaze shifting from the man to the daughter. He knew this was important to her, and his personal feelings about God and religion aside, he wanted to make her happy.

"Mia's quite fond of you," her father said in return—an explanation for his presence more than a return of the greeting. "She's argued very persuasively on your behalf, but I hope you understand that her happiness, her future, is my top priority."

Gabriel pulled his eyes away from Mia, met the blunt gaze of the man who clearly didn't approve of him. "She's everything," he said flatly. "There's nothing I wouldn't give, nothing I wouldn't do for her."

"And if you have to spend the rest of your life in here?"

"Dad," Mia said quickly, shaking her head.

"Then I'll be here for her until she doesn't want me anymore, but I won't try to stop her if she decides she wants to move on. What's between us ... it's for Mia, it's always been for Mia."

Pastor Anderson didn't speak much after that and Gabriel knew he was being judged, his every action evaluated, but he wasn't worried. He knew every expression that Mia made, every shift in her body language. The subtle flow of unspoken communication in the flick of a glance or the caress of a thumb came as naturally to him as breathing now.

"You really do love her, don't you?" Pastor Anderson asked. Mia's seat at the table was empty as she made her customary trip to the vending machine.

"Yes, I really do."

"You wouldn't have been my first choice for her, but maybe I would've been wrong." Her dad sighed, casting his eyes heavenward. "She's never looked at anyone the way she looks at you and it's obvious her happiness matters to you."

"She's my only priority." Gabriel looked at him, his gaze unflinching. "I mean that."

"Well, I guess you had better call me Ryan."

When Mia returned, laughing at the absurdly high mountain of snacks in her arms, there was no tension between them, and when they left, her dad's handshake was warm and friendly.

"I know you're soured on God and faith" he said, "and truth be told after what you've been through it's hard to blame you, but I'll be praying for you, for what it's worth."

Gabriel swallowed hard and accepted the gesture for the kindness it was intended to be. "Thanks, I guess it can't hurt. I heard about what you did for Mia's friend and you're a better man than my uncle ever was."

Mia's arms around his waist were extra tight when she hugged him goodbye, and he saw the tears she tried to hide as she walked away.

He'd never done anything more important than making sure that the two most important men in her life were united in their understanding of how much she meant to both of them.

~

Mia shouldn't have been there, and she knew it. Amy had made it clear that Brittany didn't want to be contacted, that she had put legal barriers in place to prevent them from asking her for help and Mia had been obedient. She'd closed off the possibility that they could reach Gabriel's ex-girlfriend for nearly a year, but the date of the trial loomed, large and final and desperate in her mind, until she broke. If there was a chance she could reach Brittany, as she had reached Lilah, it would be worth the consequence she could face for breaking the order.

Brittany's family was old money, and Mia was surprised when she pulled up to the address in a town several hours away and found the home she lived in was not a mansion, but a quaint two-story house not that different from Mia's own childhood home. The street was neat and tidy, leaves and flowers barely blossoming in the well-tended yards.

A dog barked inside when she knocked, and then the door opened, and she was standing in the warming spring air and staring with wide eyes at the woman she had come to see. Brittany was a slim brunette with soft features, her looks similar to Mia's, but her eyes were brown, dark guarded pools that belied her youth.

That look reminded Mia of Gabriel, and the heaviness he carried.

"You're Brittany," she blurted, and the other woman smiled slightly in surprise. Mia rushed on before she could speak. "I'm Mia Anderson. You don't know me, but I was hoping I could have a moment of your time. I'm friends with Gabriel."

Brittany frowned and crossed her arms over her chest protectively. "I told that private investigator that I don't want anything to do with this. I have a life now, a husband and a child. I don't need my past getting pulled out and examined."

Mia nodded, holding one hand out beseechingly before

Brittany could close the door. "I understand that what I am asking is a lot, but all Gabriel wants is a chance at a life."

Brittany's eyes narrowed on her face. "A friend, huh?"

Mia blushed, heat rushing painfully over her cheeks. "I love him," she said honestly. "So much."

"Yeah?" Brittany flicked a glance at Mia's face again and then shook her head. "Well, come in then and explain to me how the hell that happened when he's been in prison for the last thirteen years. I know you weren't with him when he went in. You look like a baby, and they'd have had your face all over the news if you had been."

Mia stiffened. "I'm not a baby. I'm twenty-one and I'm in college."

"Well, aren't you a fierce little thing? I can see how he'd like you." Brittany smiled as she settled at the kitchen table, waving a hand for Mia to sit, too. "So?"

Mia took a breath and explained how her relationship with Gabriel had begun, how hopeful she had been when they realized that they might have a chance to actually be together and how hard the past year had been on both of them.

"You really do love him," Brittany said when she'd finished. "I can see it all over you. I'm glad. He deserves to be loved."

Mia nodded, nibbling the skin of her bottom lip nervously. "Did you? Love him?"

"As much as I could at fifteen," Brittany said, but the look in her eyes was haunted, and Mia could see it, the ache that she kept deep inside, the place where there was a wound that still wept. "I was emotional—maybe a bit out of control—as a teenager. I landed at Richard's and that just made it worse."

Mia nodded. "He told me about what you all went through."

Heat flashed in Brittany's eyes, but she shrugged. "He's got as much right as any of us to share it, I guess."

"I can't imagine what it was like," Mia said softly, reaching out to lay her hand over the other woman's. Brittany's fingers tightened on it, seeking comfort as she confronted memories that they both knew she would've preferred to forget. "The truth is that none of that should have happened to you, to either of you, and this is a small chance to help make it right for Gabriel."

"I told him I hated him, the last time I saw him." Brittany looked up, a single tear sliding unnoticed down her cheek as she chewed nervously on her thumbnail. "That I would never forgive him for what had been done to me, even though it wasn't his fault and there was nothing he could have done to stop it."

They both turned as a small boy clattered down the stairs, arms full of toys. He waved curiously and smiled, one tooth missing in the front, before letting himself out into the backyard through the patio door.

"Gabriel wanted children. Did you know that?" She looked at Mia, shoulders slumped with a sadness that years of distance could not erase. "Even then, as young as we were, he wanted a real family. The kind where love was just given, instead of earned, and you knew they'd always be there for you."

Mia squeezed her hand, but she didn't interrupt.

"I love my husband," Brittany continued, nodding slightly to herself. "I love my son, too, and I wouldn't undo the life I had to live to get here." There was a spark in her eyes, the rage that she's concealed so well until now. "But someone needs to know what that bastard did, and I guess I need to make up for blaming the wrong person all those years ago. Gabriel was just a kid, and he was half mad with grief and rage when he took off. What happened to his dad was a tragedy, but it was probably Richard's fault more than anyone's."

"Will you help him?"

Brittany nodded and Mia breathed a sigh of relief even as her heart ached. Gabriel had loved this woman years before Mia had known him and maybe it wouldn't have lasted, but what they had made together shouldn't have been taken from them by force. The unfairness of that, the damage that it had left behind, would never completely heal.

She understood, finally, that even if Gabriel came home any happiness they found together afterward would still be built on the back of someone else's pain.

Chapter Nineteen

Summer

Mia's fingers were white at the knuckle when her father parked the car in the courthouse parking lot. It was full, midweek bringing people dealing with marriage licenses and parking tickets, jury duty and drug court. The truly unlucky ones, the ones like her, were here for the court to decide on consequences most people would find unimaginable. Some of the people who had come to watch those proceedings would leave with their loved ones, others with tears and empty arms.

Her dad put the car in park and then waited in supportive silence as she tried to slow her breathing and bring her racing heart under control. He'd insisted on driving, on picking her up every day at her newly leased apartment so that she wouldn't have to face the car ride away from the courthouse alone. She was grateful, honestly unsure if she'd be able to drive herself home if the jury re-convicted Gabriel and he was sentenced to life again. If they left her without hope.

She flicked open the mirror in the visor, checked the

minimal makeup that she'd tried to apply, and sighed. She'd dressed carefully that morning—hair in a sophisticated twist, black skirt carefully pressed, heels low and sensible—but after several nights without sleep there was no makeup that could cover the dark circles exhaustion had drawn under her eyes.

Fear twisted in her stomach, a low roll of nausea that threatened to overwhelm her, but she smiled at her father reassuringly as she reached the door handle.

"It's probably Lilly or Brittany checking to see if we made it," Mia mumbled as her phone started to vibrate in her bag. There weren't many people Gabriel could count on, and the few who were coming had all agreed to meet once they arrived at the building.

"Did you drive by the front of the courthouse on your way in?" Lilly asked when she answered. Her voice was hushed, likely inside the courthouse already, but tense and worried.

Mia frowned, brow creasing in concern. "No, why?"

"There's reporters everywhere," Lilly told her. "They swarmed us when we came in. I don't know what's going on, but we had to make a run for it to get inside. Luckily, security isn't letting them in the building."

Mia stopped and looked around, the stiff fabric of her suit already wilting in the early summer heat as it glinted viciously off the glass of parked cars and looming office windows. The parking lot was around the corner of the large courthouse building, out of sight of the main doors. She assumed they were waiting there since there was no other way for visitors to get inside.

She would have to run through them, it simply couldn't be avoided.

"Thanks Lilly," she said. "We'll be inside in just a minute." She hung up and dropped the phone back into her bag, wiping her sweaty palms on her skirt as she explained the situation to her dad.

He stood for a second, blinking at her in the heat, and then shrugged out of his suit jacket. "Take this," he told her, holding it out at arm's length. "Toss it over your head when we run by so they can't get a picture of your face."

Mia reached for it, her hands trembling. "What about you?"

He lifted one shoulder dismissively. "There's nothing they can do to an old man like me. Everyone at the church knows we're here so it isn't the same as you having to go to school and deal with unfortunate publicity."

She rushed into his hug, quick and light to keep from wrinkling his crisp white dress shirt and tugged his jacket loosely over her shoulders.

The screaming began the moment they turned the corner, an eagle-eyed reporter catching a quick glimpse of her face before she pulled the jacket over her head and ducked down to focus on her own feet as her father guided her through the crowd.

Bodies pressed in on her from all sides, shoving as they each tried to get closer than the rest, and a barrage of unfamiliar voices assaulted her senses.

"Mia, can you tell us how you became romantically involved with a killer?"

"Do you know that Gabriel Myers murdered his own father? Did he lie to you to get you here today?"

"Pastor Anderson! How do you feel about your daughter being in a relationship with a brutal murderer?"

They pushed through, neither of them speaking until the glass doors of the courthouse closed behind them, muffling the sounds of disappointed reporters as they gradually stopped shouting questions and settled in to wait until their prey had to leave the building. The run back to her car would be even worse, but she had bigger issues on her mind now.

After the brief wait to pass through the building's

security, during which the guard that scanned her bag and asked her to step forward through the metal detector gave her a pitying look, they passed into the large lobby and found Lilly and Bryce waiting for them with anxious expressions.

Lilly hurried over, pulling Mia into a tight hug. "Are you okay? Gabriel's lawyer is already here, she went upstairs to settle some of his witnesses in and asked us to wait here for you. She saw us get mobbed and figured out that we must know you. Said she isn't surprised that the media found out about the trial, but we don't know how they found out about you and Gabriel."

"Are the reporters not going after everyone?"

Bryce shook his head. "They went after Amy, but she's his lawyer. The only ones besides her so far have been us and the two of you. All the witnesses made it in without anyone paying any attention so they must not know what they're here for."

It was a mystery that would have to wait, despite the nagging suspicion that planted itself firmly in the back of her mind. She pulled her phone out of her bag, checked that it was on silent and glanced quickly at the time. "Is Kennedy here yet? We should be heading upstairs."

"Not yet. I already warned her about the reporters, but I can send her a message and have her meet us outside the courtroom." Lilly pulled out her phone and began typing rapidly. "Amy said it would be just upstairs on the left."

They found her in the hallway with Brittany and several other people that Mia had never met before, each of them anxious looking but determined to see through the promise they had made to testify. Brittany's hand on Mia's was cold and clammy but she smiled tremulously at Mia's friends and family.

Kennedy and Alison arrived just as Amy began to coach all

of them through what they were likely to experience and how to behave in the courtroom.

"No gum, no phones, so disruptions," she said firmly. "No matter how much of an ass the state lawyers may be. I know we've gone over this already with those of you who will be testifying, but it applies as much when you're just watching the proceedings. I don't want anyone thrown out or held in contempt. Any questions?"

She looked around at the small group, all that could be gathered to show support for the man she had come to represent, and nodded. She was as well dressed and composed as always, but Mia noticed the nervous tap of her perfectly manicured nails against her thigh as they waited for the doors of the courtroom to be opened so they could make their way inside.

Mia waited until they were allowed to go in, until everyone else was busy settling into their seats and looking curiously around the quiet courtroom before she stepped close to Amy's side and whispered quietly, so no one else could hear her, "Do you think he really has a chance? Any hope at all?" She hadn't asked before today because she had been afraid to hear the answer but now, with the decision so close, she couldn't help herself.

Amy sighed and shook her head slightly, as though unsure for once, her eyes drifting to the empty seat at the front of the courtroom where the judge would sit. "I've done my best during jury selection and Judge Turner is tough. She's the youngest Black woman sitting on a judicial bench in the state of Texas, and she didn't get there by letting people run her over, but she's fair. If we were ever going to have a chance, this is the best we could have hoped for."

Mia breathed, her lungs expelling all the breath she had been holding and some of the painful tension. Amy patted her hand and moved to the front of the room, beyond the small gate that barred the audience from approaching too close to the proceedings and began to set up her papers on the table where she and Gabriel sat.

Mia sat on the bench closest to the front, hoping that Gabriel would be able to sense her presence so close to him even though they weren't allowed to speak to him. Her father sat on her right and Brittany on her left, her hand once again clutching Mia's painfully as she looked around with panic in her eyes. Lilly was on Brittany's other side, talking to her about her son and trying to put her mind at ease.

She had just won a hesitant smile for her efforts when the door at the side of the room opened, and Gabriel was led in. Brittany made a small noise, of shock or surprise Mia assumed, since she hadn't seen him in many years and the boy that she had known back then was very different from the man now in front of her.

Mia took in his appearance quickly as he was led to his seat. He was wearing a white prison jumpsuit this time, hands handcuffed in front of him and connected to his shackled ankles with a long chain that also wrapped completely around his waist. Amy had prepared her for that, and for the painful fact that he would remain in shackles as long as he was inside the courtroom. He looked tired and worried, a crease in his brow that faded away the moment he spotted her.

She smiled at him reassuringly and mouthed a silent, "I love you," even though her heart was pounding, and her fingers had gone numb with fear. It took all of her concentration to keep her breaths slow and shallow until he was seated next to Amy to wait for the judge's arrival.

Mia looked down the hard courtroom bench, at the others that had come to testify, all of them uncomfortable in their stiff courtroom appropriate outfits as they stared around anxiously at the cheap wood paneled walls that lined the room. Some of them had been hurt by Richard, though not all of them, a fact that she sometimes lost sight of since he was the devil that made the most sense to her with her upbringing. Seth had done his own damage to the others, just as deep and perhaps even more horrifying, in ways that went far beyond her imagination. And despite all of that, these people had made it through and had chosen, at least for this moment, to fight for a better world and let this small piece of their truths be heard.

Another door opened, this one along the wall in front of them, and a woman in black robes entered the room as everyone scrambled to their feet. Judge Turner was straight-backed and stern-faced as she walked to her seat, and Mia felt a frisson of fear work its way down her spine. All of her hope rested in this one woman and there was little to give any indication that she had any intention of handing out mercy or understanding as she swept the room with a serious gaze and began the proceedings.

The sharp snap of the gavel cut through the silence and Mia squeezed Brittany's hand as they both jumped at the noise. Mia wasn't usually the kind to be jumpy, but every muscle in her body was pulled tight and tense under the skin as though it would be enough to keep the tears in.

The jury in their box watched everything with interest as the state's lawyer—a tall man that the judge referred to as Mr. Price who had stiff mannerisms and a penchant for clasping his hands behind his back as he spoke—laid out the case and the prosecution's evidence.

"The facts," he said, voice echoing against the walls, "are clear. There is no doubt about the guilt of this man. Gabriel Myers stabbed his father to death in an alley. The cold-blooded nature of the crime, the obvious disregard for right and wrong, leaves the state no choice but to keep him in prison. He is too dangerous to be released."

Mia watched with a broken heart as he shrunk down

under the weight of the words, his giant shoulders twisting in and down toward the table as though trying to hold himself together or disappear entirely.

Her free hand, the one not holding tightly to Brittany's, balled into a fist that she hid in the folds of her skirt. She knew very well what Amy had said, and that Mr. Price was simply doing his job, but he didn't know Gabriel like she did, and he was wrong about the kind of person he was.

A gentle hand came to rest over hers with a soft pat that let her breathe and relax her fist. She could always count on her dad to know when she needed him most and she traded her rage for a litany of prayers to repeat inside her mind.

"This was a personal attack," Price said. "One born of rage and hatred. It was overkill, far beyond what was necessary for self-defense even if there had been a need for any. Mr. Myers was a good man, a loving father, and his life was cut short by his own child—an out-of-control teen, with no regard for life. A callous and selfish young man who was throwing a temper tantrum because his parents said it was time for him to stop running the streets causing trouble and come home."

He turned then to look at Gabriel, who was sitting perfectly still and listening intently to some comment that Amy was making to him in hushed tones. His body was still tense and even from several feet away Mia could see the effort he was using to keep an impassive face, the muscle in his cheek that was twitching from the strain.

Mia understood very little of the rest of his opening argument and even less of Amy's. After waiting for so long to be here, it felt as if she were underwater, all the sights and sounds of the proceedings dimmed by the rush of panic. Her head was light, and her body disconnected, rendering all of her senses dull and fuzzy around the edges. Time slowed to a crawl, and she marked its passing by counting her breaths.

In and then out again.

Repeat.

The judge released them all for lunch before Mr. Price began to call his first witnesses—the arresting officers and the coroner that had performed the autopsy on Hugh Myers' body.

Mia couldn't wait to get out of the courtroom and into some fresh air, her head buzzing with anxiety and her hands shaking as she fled down the quiet hallway. It was only when they reached the bottom floor and turned toward the front doors that she remembered the crowd of reporters waiting for her outside.

"Oh," she said, stopping abruptly so that Lilly and Bryce walked into the back of her, bumping her forward an extra step as she swore quietly under her breath. "I can't go out there," she said, wincing at the thought of dodging the questions and the pushy reporters again to leave and then to come back. She'd already have to face them in the return to the car and didn't think she had it in her to do any more than that.

Amy sighed. "I forgot about that," she admitted. "They won't let us bring food back to you. No outside food is allowed in the courthouse."

"I understand," Mia said, pasting a smile on her face that felt awkward and unnatural. "I think I'll get something out of the vending machine upstairs if I get hungry. Not really sure I feel up to eating right now, anyway."

They stood in the open foyer for several minutes, arguing quietly about who should stay behind with her as the flow of people coming and going flowed around them.

"I'm fine to wait alone," she repeated. "If those of you that the reporters recognize all huddle behind the ones they don't, they might not even see you. You need to eat," she urged.

"I'll go out first," Amy said. "I'm used to dealing with them and I'll make an announcement that we're making progress. Everyone else can slip by while they're distracted."

"See?" Mia said firmly. "It'll be fine."

In the end, everyone went except her father, who couldn't be budged. He sat beside her on the bench upstairs, eating a candy bar from the vending machine and sipping on a ridiculously expensive bottle of water.

Mia picked at the label on her bottle, candy bar forgotten on her thigh. She'd peeled it off in tiny pieces and then folded each of those into meaningless shapes, a pile of shiny paper as a testament to her nerves, before the others came back from lunch.

The afternoon was not any easier for her to sit through and she turned her face away when they put up the photos of the crime scene, but the images danced colorfully behind her eyelids. The body lying in dirt and surrounded by trash, the pool of blood dried and black on the ground, and Hugh's hand curled where it had fallen with the glint of a gold wedding ring still on his finger. It painted a damning picture and Mia swallowed back her tears as the information from the autopsy was read. Seven stab wounds. Damage to the heart, the stomach, the liver, the intestines ...

Somehow the prosecution had found several of Gabriel's old teachers, neighbors, people who had known him before he'd been sent to his uncle's, all willing to testify that his relationship with his parents had been strained. That he'd been a wild teen with few boundaries and little interest in following rules or obeying authority. Amy did her best to minimize the damage on cross examination of the witnesses, but Mia's shoulders were slumped by the time Mr. Price finally sat down.

She'd pushed her way to the car after they were done for the day, the jacket over her head hiding her tears. Amy had warned them that today would be bad, but she had never imagined that it would feel this hopeless, that the despair could reach this deep.

Chapter Twenty

Michael was the first person to be called to the stand on the second day. He was unnaturally pale as he walked to the front and took his seat in the small witness box where he solemnly, sincerely and truly affirmed under the penalty of law for perjury to tell the truth.

Mia was not surprised to see that he had refused to swear in on a Bible, but she prayed that he would feel some comfort, some sense of relief once all of this was done. Richard was dead and this was the closest that Michael would ever get to justice for what he had endured.

Amy approached the stand, and the questioning began. "Good morning, Mr. Lansing," she said pleasantly. "Thank you for agreeing to come here today. Let's begin by having you tell us when you first met Gabriel Myers."

Michael glanced at Gabriel and then back at Amy. "I was sixteen," he said quickly. "So, it would have been more than a decade ago."

"You were sixteen," Amy said with an encouraging nod. "And how old was Gabriel at that time?"

"He was fifteen when I first met him."

Amy nodded. "And how did you two meet?"

Michael hesitated, his face draining of what little color it had started with. "I lived with his uncle, Richard Miller. Gabriel was sent to live there, too."

Amy began to pace slowly across the floor in front of the judge, nodding along with his answers and looking back at him when it was time to ask another question. "This was at Richard Miller's house?" she asked.

"No, ma'am. He ran a …" Michael's brow furrowed as he searched for the right word before giving up. "I don't know what it was exactly, but he called it a school. We—all the kids, I mean—lived at the school."

"This was a boarding school?" Amy asked, then continued to the next question without waiting for an answer. "Richard Miller was a pretty famous evangelical preacher, so I assume it was a religious school?"

"It wasn't a school," Michael said bluntly. "He called it one, but it wasn't. We didn't go there to learn—we went because our parents wanted him to fix us."

"Fix you?" Amy shook her head, giving a small, puzzled shrug that Mia knew was theatrical. "What was wrong with you Mr. Lansing?"

Michael took a deep breath, the kind that shuddered a person's whole body and left them hollow on the inside. "I'm gay," he said simply. "My parents didn't believe in that sort of thing."

"They didn't believe you were gay?"

"They didn't want me to be," he clarified. "They wanted Richard to fix it and make me straight. He preached fire and brimstone at them and anyone else who would listen, damnation in every breath. They were terrified that I was going to hell, and they would've done just about anything to stop it."

"I see," Amy said quietly. "Were all the kids there gay?"

Michael shook his head. "No, some of them were there for that kind of thing but most were just doing drugs or sneaking out or even just failing their classes. Richard took in pretty much any kid whose parents thought they were a problem, as long as they bought into his version of God and had the funds to pay for what he called discipline."

Amy smiled tightly. "And were you there the entire time that Gabriel was?"

Michael nodded, shifting restlessly in his seat. Mia knew that Amy had practiced the questions with him before today and she suspected that he knew the more difficult questions were coming. "I was there for two years, and Gabriel was my roommate for just over a year. He ran away a few months before my parents finally came and picked me up."

"So, you were there with him and saw the conditions that he was living in while he was with Richard?"

"Yes, ma'am. We pretty much all lived the same way while we were there."

Mia flicked a glance at Gabriel, at the tense line of his shoulders as he stared straight ahead at Michael. His face, the eyes that were usually so expressive, were like stone as he listened.

"Can you describe what it was like? Living with Richard?" Amy continued.

Michael's mouth moved to form a single word. He breathed it so quietly that the judge had to ask him to repeat himself.

"Yes," he said again, more firmly this time. "It was hell."

"It was hell in what way, Mr. Lansing? Can you be more specific?"

"It was hell in every way," he said, glancing at Brittany and then away again quickly. "Different for each of us but hell, just the same."

"Mr. Lansing ..." Amy began, but he cut her off before she could finish.

"I was abused for two years," he said bitterly. "Most of the time we didn't have decent blankets in the winter, and we never had air conditioning. There was no hot water and there wasn't a single day that I wasn't hungry."

The words settled over them all, stealing some of the air from the room. Mia breathed, slowly and intentionally, as Brittany gripped hard onto her hand. Her father tapped his fingers on the bench beside his thighs and when she looked up at him his mouth was set in a grim line.

Michael continued speaking.

"If we were lucky, we got one meal a day, and that was only if they decided we had been good. If we hadn't been, they just skipped our meal altogether. Sometimes we were locked in our rooms for days at a time and we had to piss in a bucket in the corner."

Amy paused, giving him a moment to collect himself as the courtroom sat in silence. They all watched as he paused, his lip trembling as he composed his thoughts.

"And was Gabriel also treated this way?" she said once he seemed to have gathered control of his emotions.

"He was," Michael said. "But he didn't get scared like the rest of us. He got angry. Richard preached all the time about our sins and how tainted we were. Really awful stuff, you know? But Gabriel would go without his food or his blankets instead of doing what Richard told him to do, so they got rough with him more than the rest of us."

"What did Richard tell him to do?"

Michael shrugged helplessly. "Not to sneak food to people that were being punished was the first thing. He brought me a piece of bread back from dinner that first week he was there, and Richard split his lip wide open."

"What else?"

Another pause, longer this time. "Gabriel was big, even back then he was tall for a kid, so Richard wanted him to help with the rest of us and he wouldn't do it. We were all mad about how they treated us, we all hated Richard, but Gabriel ... Gabriel was stubborn. The more Richard tried to break him the angrier he got."

"Did Richard ask for his help with anything else?"

"Yeah, he ..." a small sob broke from Michael, his breath catching as everyone looked away to give him a moment. "Richard, he thought he could pray the gay away. When that didn't work, they went with more aggressive methods. Gabriel wouldn't help with that."

"I'm sorry, Mr. Lansing, but can you explain to us in more detail exactly what happened and what Gabriel saw when he was there with you?"

Michael pressed his palms to his eyes, trying to stop the steady drip of tears. Beside Mia, Brittany was stiff and tense, her nails digging painfully into Mia's hand. "Um, Richard was ... He was convinced that having sex with a woman would fix me and he wanted to intimidate me into doing it."

"But Gabriel wouldn't do that?"

"No, he wouldn't, not even when they hurt him instead." Michael looked at Amy helplessly. "He came back to the room one night, looking worse than any of us that I ever saw, but he wouldn't hurt any of us."

"And Richard was the one who hit you?"

"Sometimes it was him, but most of the time he just liked to stand off to the side quoting *scripture*," Michael sneered at the word, like it was contemptible in its very existence, "while his buddies did the dirty work. He had a guy, Charles, and he did most of it. That guy was huge, not even Gabriel stood a chance against him."

"Thank you, Mr. Lansing," Amy said, and he visibly

tensed as she walked back to her seat, his eyes never looking up from the floor.

Gabriel watched Mr. Price stand to question Micheal and Mia noticed the clenched set of his jaw, the haunted regret in his eyes as Michael had to defend himself against the prosecution's accusations that he was lying for attention. Mia knew him well enough to know he was blaming himself for what the witnesses were going through and she smiled encouragingly at him when he glanced her way even though he wasn't supposed to interact with them while they were in the courtroom.

Amy called Brittany next, and she stood on legs that wobbled, holding onto Mia's hand until she could stand on her own and make her way to the front. Her steps were slow and measured, a clear reluctance in her stride that was made even more obvious by the pinched look on her face when she turned to face them all.

They waited for her to be sworn in as Mia wrenched her gaze away from the small, terrified woman to Gabriel's hunched form. He was staring straight ahead, his hand holding the arm of his chair so tightly that she was surprised it hadn't cracked under the strain. He hadn't seen Brittany in thirteen years and Mia swallowed her tears and her sudden insecurity as he stared with something close to longing at another woman's face.

"Good morning, Mrs. Townsend," Amy began, and Brittany turned away from looking at Gabriel to look at her instead.

"Good morning," Brittany repeated, her hands twisting and untwisting in her lap.

"You also lived with Gabriel at Richard's school?"

Brittany's face twisted into a scowl. "I would agree that it wasn't a school, but I did live there with Gabriel and Michael."

"Were you there the whole time that Gabriel was there?"

"Nearly the whole time" Brittany clarified. "I think I got there a few weeks after him."

Amy nodded again, continuing her pacing. "And what can you tell me about the living conditions while you were there?"

"The same as Michael," Brittany said, ignoring the tears that slipped down her cheeks. Mia wasn't certain if they were born from sadness or anger. Her tone had plenty of both. "Richard Miller was a bastard who cared more about the rules in some fucking book than he ever did about any of us."

Amy's demeanor remained carefully neutral in the face of her outburst. She waited patiently for Brittany's body language to relax before she proceeded with her questioning. "Can you tell us about your experiences at Richard's? About what brought you there?"

"My parents brought me there," she said with a bitter laugh, swiping at her cheeks in annoyance. "They caught me sneaking out at night, meeting my boyfriend and getting high, and they didn't like it. Richard told them he could settle me down, so they dropped me off and didn't even look back."

"And did he? Settle you down?"

"He certainly tried."

Amy nodded, tapping her finger against her chin. "Mrs. Townsend, how would you describe your relationship with Gabriel during this time?"

Brittany hesitated, biting her lip. "He was protective of all of us, and I gravitated to him when I arrived. I guess I would say he was my boyfriend, or the closest that any of us could come to that kind of relationship in a place like that."

"And was your relationship with him sexual?" Brittany winced at the question and Amy hurried to add, "I'm sorry, I have to ask."

Brittany looked down at her hands. "Yes, it was. He would sneak out of his room whenever he could to come and find me. I loved him," she said, shrugging slightly and glancing up at him before quickly looking down at her hands.

Mia looked at Gabriel, at the single tear that was sliding down his cheek, and then away. She knew the story already but seeing them relive it together made her an intruder in their private grief.

"Can you tell us why you left Richard's school, Mrs. Townsend?"

"I tried to kill myself so my parents finally believed me when I said I would rather die than stay there."

"Why would you do that, Mrs. Townsend? Did something happen at Richard's to drive you to such an extreme method of escape?"

"I was pregnant," Brittany said quietly, looking down so that they could barely hear her. "Richard forced me to get an abortion. I don't know where he found the doctors, but I never even left the school. They came to me, and I don't think either of them ever even looked at me."

Amy stopped pacing, addressing Brittany directly but with great tenderness. "Was the child Gabriel's?"

"I believe so," Brittany said, nodding her head as she glanced up at Amy. "He had just found out and he was ... He was so excited to be a father, even though we were too young and living in that awful place."

Amy shook her head, resting her hand on the banister beside Brittany as she spoke. "Richard was a very religious man. Did he tell you why he would do something that would have been so against his faith?"

"He didn't think Gabriel was the father," Brittany explained. "He thought Michael might have been the father because he made us ... well, you know? To make Michael like having sex with girls."

"He forced you to be physically intimate with Mr. Lansing in an attempt to cure him of homosexuality and you believe

Richard was afraid that the baby would be proof of that abuse?"

Mia looked at Gabriel in surprise. He hadn't told her that he might not have been the father of Brittany's baby and she realized now how much distance Michael and Brittany had put between themselves, the way that they hadn't spoken that morning even though they had known each other so long ago.

"Yes," Brittany confirmed, "I believe Richard was afraid that DNA could prove the child was Michael's and that it could support our stories if we ever came forward with allegations of abuse. Although, I suppose that even if the child had been Gabriel's, it would have looked bad for the school. If any of the other parents found out that I got pregnant while I was staying with him, it would have damaged his reputation."

"What did Gabriel do when he found out what Richard had done?"

"He was angry, worse than I had ever seen. I was angry, too, and hurt that Gabriel had let it happen. I know it wasn't his fault but back then ... We argued, and I was so mad that he hadn't protected me that I told him that I would never forgive him."

"And then what happened?"

"He confronted Richard and when Richard denied it, Gabriel attacked him. There was a lot of shouting, things breaking ... and then Gabriel was gone. He never came back and the next time any of us even knew where he was, it was when he saw him on the news after, well, you know."

Amy nodded. "After his father's death."

"Yes, after that." Brittany turned to face Judge Turner, her eyes clear and earnest. "I tried to kill myself to get away from that place and if my parents had tried to send me back there ... I would be the one sitting in a prison cell today. I would've done anything to not have to go back."

Chapter Twenty-One

The court heard three more witnesses after they had taken their break for lunch, the ones that had lived with Gabriel after he had run from Richard and found his way to Seth. They all went by as barely more than blur in Mia's mind. She already knew he'd run from one kind of monster to another, but Gabriel had been brief on the details. He'd described his time spent with Richard with anger, but his time with Seth had been cloaked in shame. She hadn't pressed him, knowing the overall picture had been enough, but the story that spilled from the mouths of the witnesses was worse than anything she'd imagined. It was an ugly truth that left them all reeling.

Vincent Russel was the first on the stand and he was tense as Amy approached him with an easy smile, walked him through the pleasantries, and then began. "Do you remember when Gabriel first came to Seth?"

"Yeah." His face was impassive, as he brushed blond hair away from his face. "Seth found him living on the streets, just like the rest of us."

"The rest of you?" Amy coaxed. "Who was that, exactly?"

"Seth had a whole house full of kids. Runaways mostly."

"I see," Amy said, tapping her finger on her chin as she appeared to contemplate his response. "You all lived in this house?"

He shrugged restlessly. "Better than living under a bridge, lady."

"I'm sure it was," Amy soothed. "What was it like to live with Seth?"

"Good at first." He glanced at Gabriel and then quickly away. "We had the run of the house and did whatever we wanted."

"And Gabriel had that freedom, too?"

"None of us answered to anyone except Seth."

"And what happened when Gabriel moved in? How did he react to that?"

Vincent smiled, hard and bitter. "Same as any kid with that kind of freedom. He smoked, drank, fucked, did whatever drugs we could get our hands on."

Mia listened tensely; her eyes glued to Gabriel's broad shoulders as Vincent finished his testimony. His words were echoed nearly exactly by David, who took the stand as soon as he was finished.

David Hu was smaller than Vincent, less sure of himself on the stand, but his face was just as stoic.

"What happened once Gabriel got settled into the house?" Amy asked him, waiting patiently as he shifted in his seat. Vincent had been hesitant here, too, but Amy's practice once again paid off, as both were able to answer.

"He got used to the drugs and the freedom and then Seth yanked the chain. Nothing comes without a price, you know? We ran the streets and did his dirty work. Sometimes it was real violent shit, but that part wasn't so bad ... at least, not for us, I mean."

"Then what was bad for you?"

He laughed, humorless. "It started out with rich women. Seth was smart and he eased you in that way because how can you say no to getting money for having sex with a beautiful woman? Sure, he'd sold you, but it was easy to justify it."

"He sold you? You mean that he sold your services sexually?"

"Yeah, and like I said, it wasn't so bad at first but ... then it got worse. Once you were sort of used to it, then he wasn't so picky about the kind of people he sold you to or what they wanted. Nothing you could do by then, of course, so you just take more of the drugs he's handing out and pretend it isn't happening."

"I see," Amy said sympathetically. "And were these people ever violent toward any of you?"

He tapped his face, the sliver of a thin white scar bisecting his chin. "The first time Seth sold me to some guy that wanted more from me than I wanted to give. I learned real quick not to say no to something they paid for. If they didn't hurt me, Seth sure as hell would."

Chris Mendoza was steely eyed on the stand, body nearly unnaturally still as he watched Amy pace the floor in front of him.

"And how did Gabriel react when Seth started requiring him to do these things?"

"Gabriel was different from the rest of us, angrier and more likely to start a fight, even with Seth. He didn't like it, didn't want to do the other things that Seth was asking. He went along with it for a little while, because he was convinced that Seth must know what he was doing, but eventually he decided that he'd had enough."

"And then what did he do?"

Chris's mouth was a thin line. "He tried to leave."

Mia's eyes flew back to Gabriel, sitting hunched and

shrunken in his chair. He hadn't told her that he'd tried to get away.

"Seth wasn't having that, of course," Chris continued, "and when he tried to leave ..." He shook his head and looked down at his feet.

"What happened?" Amy prompted when he had been silently staring at his shoes for several moments.

"They dragged him down into the basement," Chris explained. "Seth and some of the guys who worked for him. There was no one else in the house except for me and even the drugs I took weren't enough to drown out the screams. I still have nightmares about it sometimes."

"Did Gabriel ever tell you exactly what happened in the basement?"

"No, but he never tried to leave again, and he did what Seth wanted after that." Chris said simply. "He knew he'd gotten lucky in a way. There wasn't much room for second chances and a lot of people went missing. You didn't ask about it unless you wanted to be next, but we all knew what Seth was doing."

Chris stepped down and returned to his seat. The courtroom's anxious energy of the morning was now drained and flat. Behind the table across from Gabriel and Amy, the state's lawyer fidgeted, shuffling and straightening papers that didn't need to be straightened.

The state's stance that Gabriel had been nothing more than a typical spoiled teen, too rich and pampered to accept it when his parents placed reasonable limits on him, had been called into serious question.

"Your expert witness?" Judge Turner asked as Amy hesitated.

"She was scheduled in a different courtroom this morning, Your Honor," Amy said with a wince, "and she seems to be running a little late."

Judge Turner tapped a finger on the wooden stand in front of her as she looked at her watch. "We'll take a thirty-minute recess then before the next witness is called," she announced, tapping the gavel so that the sound of it echoed through the room and giving Amy a pointed warning look. "Everyone please be back here by then."

Mia watched in silence as the guards led Gabriel from the room, her jaw clenched anxiously when he didn't look at her at all.

"Take that bathroom break," Amy encouraged. "We still have a long day ahead of us." She walked out then, leading the way as the rest of them shuffled out awkwardly behind her. They had been cordial to one another, all of them polite if a bit distant, but the morning's testimony had drawn them together with a forced intimacy that made them quiet and reluctant to meet each other's eyes.

The witnesses' wounds and secrets had been laid bare and Mia felt like she'd been an unwanted spectator to something sordid and painful. She was distant and numb as they moved through the crowded hallway, exhausted by the emotions that had buffeted her since Michael had first taken the stand.

They all walked together to the bathroom around the corner and Mia watched Brittany in the mirror as they stood side-by-side at the sink. She, too, looked fragile, her eyes weary and fingers shaking slightly as she dried them on cheap brown paper towels that were too stiff and too thin to absorb the water. She tossed them in the trash, already full almost to overflowing, and wiped her hands on the sides of her expensive black slacks.

Lilly and the others had already left, the door swinging shut behind them and leaving the two women alone as Brittany cleared her throat. "Thank you for sitting with me today. It was difficult to relive those things and to hear about everything that happened to him."

Mia bit her lip, her teeth digging in harder than they would normally have done. "You still care about him," she said, "and I understand that, but I love him, and it hurts a little that he still looks at you the way that he does. I just thought you should know that before you thank me."

Brittany smiled and her perfectly even white teeth flashed briefly in the harsh fluorescent lighting that flickered overhead. "All the more reason for me to say it. You've put aside any personal feelings or discomfort about what happened between us years ago because you love him. He's lucky to have you."

Mia sighed, the guilt she felt for the flash of jealousy she'd felt in the courtroom easing just a bit. "Thanks," she said stiffly, but Brittany laid a gentle hand on her arm.

"We went through a lot together and it's been a little overwhelming seeing him again after all this time. It brings back a lot of feelings we didn't have time to process back then. If he's feeling anything right now, it's probably the same kind of weird nostalgia. I loved Gabriel, but I was a different person then."

"I'm sorry," Mia said, shifting nervously from one foot to the other and chewing on the raw spot she was rapidly wearing into her bottom lip. "I know that you're trying to help us."

"I'm a small broken piece of his past," Brittany said, stepping forward to give Mia a gentle-armed squeeze, her arm wrapped around Mia's waist as they walked out of the bathroom together. "You know him better now than I ever did."

Lilly was the only one waiting in the hallway when they came back out and she stood up from the bench she was sitting on when she saw them. "Is everything okay? It's almost time to start so everyone else went back in."

"It's fine," Mia assured her. "It's just been a hard day."

"It has been hard," Brittany agreed, "but it was a long time coming."

Everyone else—missing witness included—was already seated when they returned to their places. Gabriel was back in his chair beside Amy, his head in his hands as she leaned over close to his ear and spoke to him in a voice that was too quiet for Mia to hear. She cleared her throat quietly when Amy finished speaking and turned to go over her notes, but he didn't turn to look at her as she'd hoped, and she shifted restlessly.

He was slouched in his chair, back hunched and shoulders slumped, and he refused to look at her.

She had only a moment to wonder before the door at the front opened and Judge Turner resumed her seat, bringing court back into session with another tap of her gavel.

"Your next witness, please," she said, indicating to Amy to begin before the echoes had faded from the room.

Amy stood, squeezing Gabriel's arm reassuringly and calling for Dr. Engell to take the stand.

The psychologist appeared to be several years older than Amy, though softer in the eyes and less rigid in her posture. She seemed at ease in the courtroom, with a relaxed demeanor that Mia knew must have come with years of testifying.

"Dr. Engell, can you tell how long ago you evaluated Gabriel for the first time?"

"Thirteen years ago."

"And the results of that evaluation?"

"His mental state was as expected for the abuse that he'd suffered and the trauma he experienced from killing his father. His time with Richard and Seth had given him a severe form of chronic post-traumatic stress disorder, known as PTSD. We tend to associate this with those who have seen combat, but it's common after the brain experiences trauma of any kind and is often seen in those who have been abused or sexually assaulted."

"I understand," Amy said. "And what effects does PTSD have on the brain and a person's behavior?"

"The brain changes in structure and function when experiencing trauma at that level," Doctor Engell explained. "It becomes more sensitive and the neurotransmitters that are associated with stress are produced in greater amounts when the person experiences stress. The person may experience nightmares, sleep disturbances, intrusive memories, or anger and irritability. They may react unpredictably to any stimulus that triggers the mind to remember the events that caused the trauma."

"So, you're saying that people with PTSD are dangerous?"

"No, not at all," the doctor responded. Mia knew that the question was asked to give her more of an opportunity to explain the specifics to the judge. "Most people that experience it are not a danger to themselves or others, but in Gabriel's situation it may have made it far more difficult for him to react rationally."

Amy nodded, apparently content with the doctor's explanation. "Dr. Engell, let's back up for one moment. I want to ask you about something else that you mentioned a few moments ago. You said that the first time you evaluated Gabriel, he had recently experienced the trauma of murdering his father. Could you explain further what you mean by that statement?"

"Killing his father was an extremely traumatic event for him. His actions were triggered by the situation that he found himself in and the already existing psychological problems that had been created by the abuse at the hands of both Richard Miller and Seth Wiseman."

"Can you explain the type of reaction that someone that had lived through those experiences might have under those circumstances?"

"The prospect of going back to Richard's would have been

a triggering event in itself. Gabriel had recently escaped from a very abusive situation and the idea of being returned to that environment would have been overwhelming, even without the psychological effects of his time with Seth."

"I see," Amy said. "And how would you characterize his time with Seth?"

"It is evident, in my opinion, that Gabriel was a victim of human trafficking. Runaway teens are especially vulnerable to predation of this type, and Seth used many of the tactics that traffickers use to control and manipulate their victims."

"Tactics such as?"

"They often begin by offering these teens a safe space, somewhere to go where they have freedom and control—both things that would have been intensely important to Gabriel after his escape from Richard."

"This is intentional on the part of the predator?"

"Very much," Doctor Engell agreed. "Once the teen feels safe, they offer them drugs and other illegal substances, both as a means of keeping them compliant and as a hook. It creates a physical dependency and is the first of many things that they can use as leverage."

Amy faced the doctor, her expression one of practiced curiosity. "Why would they need to have leverage over the teen?"

"Each case of illegal activity or morally compromising behavior adds another layer of isolation and embarrassment that prevents the victim from feeling that they would be able to reintegrate into society," Doctor Engell explained carefully. "First drugs, then, in cases such as Gabriel's, it may include committing other crimes or acts of violence, and in many cases prostitution."

"This gives the trafficker control over the teen?" Amy asked.

"It does," the doctor agreed. "Isolating them with shame

can prevent them from reaching out to others for help. Gabriel firmly believed his parents would never accept him, and Seth told Gabriel that he would reveal those secrets if Gabriel ever left."

"But Gabriel did attempt to leave," Amy reminded her.

"The tactics used are effective but not infallible. Gabriel's lucky that he was considered valuable by Seth or it's very likely that he would have simply been killed for attempting to leave. As it was, he was tortured until his abuser no longer feared he would risk escaping."

"And when Gabriel's father came and tried to bring him home? What would that experience have been like for him?"

"He would have felt extremely threatened. He knew what Richard would do to him if he were returned to his uncle's care and what Seth would do if he tried to leave. He believed his parents would never accept him back if they had learned the truth. There was nothing that he wouldn't have done in that moment to prevent those things from happening."

Amy paused, letting the implications of the psychologist's last statement settle over the room before speaking again. "Doctor, have you evaluated Gabriel recently?"

"Yes, we've spoken several times over the past few months."

"In your professional opinion, Doctor Engell, do you believe that he's dangerous?"

Dr. Engell looked at Gabriel, taking time to consider the answer to the question, reassuring the judge that she wasn't rushing her words or failing to properly consider the potential harm he could cause if she were wrong.

"No, I don't believe that he's a significant risk to society," she said firmly. "The conditions surrounding his original offense were unique, an unfortunate combination of the worst possible circumstances, in which an abused young man with severe PTSD was put into a situation where he felt that he had no recourse other than to resort to violence."

"Thank you, Doctor," Amy said, smiling at her politely as the opposing attorney tapped his pen on the table irritably. "I have no further questions for you."

Mia watched, lips pressed into a thin line as the prosecution interrogated the witness, but Dr. Engell spent a great deal of time in the courtroom and her answers remained calm and consistent. No, there was no evidence of premeditation in his actions. No, she did not believe he needed to remain in prison for the safety of the public.

"We will resume tomorrow morning," Judge Turner decided when Dr. Engell was dismissed from the witness stand. The jury looked as tired as Mia felt as they realized they would have to return to the courtroom again for another day of proceedings and they all filed out slowly when the gavel dismissed them.

Chapter Twenty-Two

"Will your client be addressing the court?" the judge asked Amy the following morning.

"He will be, Your Honor."

His progress was slow and awkward, movements artificially shortened by the chains around his ankles. They clinked together with each step, a cheerless jingle that reminded them all of the years of freedom he'd lost as a consequence of that night between him and his father. He settled in at the stand, putting his bound hands in his lap after swearing unenthusiastically on the Bible they offered him, and he looked younger than he was as he waited for Amy to begin questioning him, like the ordeal of sitting through the trial had reduced him once again to the boy he had been the first time he'd sat in a courtroom. The course of his life had already been decided for him once and fear curved his shoulders in and kept his eyes glued to the floor until Amy softly spoke his name.

"Gabriel, why did your parents first send you away?"

He blinked at her for a moment, considering her question. "Too much money and not enough supervision, so I guess I did what rich brats do. I got drunk and smoked weed and chased after girls."

"Is that all?"

"I had a temper," he admitted. "By the time they figured out what was happening and tried to rein me in, I wasn't too happy about it." He looked back at the floor, exhaling on a deep breath that made him shudder and his lower lip tremble.

"Can you confirm the truth of what we've heard from the witnesses on the stand today?" she said, waiting for him to look up and meet her eyes. "About what happened after your parents sent you to live with your uncle?"

He nodded, clearing his throat. "Yes, I can."

"The things that they said, that's the way it happened to the best of your recollection?"

"Yes, ma'am, it is," he confirmed.

"How would you describe your mental state the night that Hugh Myers confronted you?"

"Unstable," he said clearly. "I wanted to go home but I didn't believe that was possible."

"Why is that?"

"I couldn't go back to Richard's after what he'd done, and I didn't think they'd let me go home because I was even worse than I was when they'd sent me away. I drank more, did harder drugs, got paid for the sex and the violence."

"Why didn't you just lie about that?" Amy pressed harder but her tone remained soft. "So they'd let you come home?"

"Seth was going to tell them everything I'd done," he said miserably. "Everyone I'd hurt, everyone he'd whored me out to, all of it."

"In your mind, if you went with your father that night—"

"I would have absolutely been sent back to Richard."

"You couldn't tell them about what happened with Richard?"

He laughed, but it was a cynical sound. "My word against

Richard Miller? He was a legend, the pinnacle of holiness, and I was a teenager with anger problems and a history of lying."

"You'd been dishonest with them in the past?"

"Ever heard the story of the boy who cried wolf?" he asked, teeth flashing in a self-deprecating smile. "No one cares that you're being eaten if they don't believe it's happening."

"If you couldn't go home, why didn't you just leave? Walk away?"

"I tried," he said, pressing his hands to his face and leaving red blotches on his skin from the pressure. "He'd promised my mother that he'd bring me home and he wasn't listening when I told him I couldn't do that."

"And you decided to kill him?"

"I didn't decide," Gabriel said, looking at her pleadingly, begging her with his eyes to believe him. "I was talking to him, and he grabbed me. He was trying to pull me to the car ... I don't remember what happened. He was lying there and there was blood everywhere. On him, on me, on the ground."

"What did you do after you realized that you'd stabbed him? Why didn't you call for help?"

"I ..." He shifted restlessly, tears sliding unnoticed down his face. "I don't know," he admitted weakly. "There was so much blood, and his eyes were open and staring at me. I screamed and screamed but no one came, not for a long time, not till the police showed up and arrested me."

"How did you feel when you realized that your father was dead?"

His lips parted but no sound came out as he stared at her, swallowing reflexively over and over again as he tried to gain control of his voice.

"Gabriel?"

"I was numb," he whispered. "I couldn't understand it and some days I still don't. It doesn't feel real, even though I can picture it in my head. It feels like a dream that I can't escape from."

"Do you regret what you did?"

"I would give anything to go back and change what happened," he said, looking at the ground again. "I didn't just kill my father ...what I did devastated my mother. I destroyed my family, and they didn't deserve it. They weren't perfect, but they didn't deserve that," he repeated.

"If you were given a second chance to be free in society, what would you do with it?"

He looked up, past Amy and the empty table to where Mia was seated on the bench between Brittany and her father. His eyes were still wet, but they were hot with purpose.

"I would spend the rest of my life proving that I'm sorry," he said fiercely. "I would atone, make amends to everyone I hurt and use every breath I took to make up for the ones I stole from my father."

"Thank you, Gabriel." Amy returned to her seat after giving him a reassuring nod but they both looked nervous as the prosecution's questioning began.

Mia tried to focus on the questions, but her hands were shaking and the sound of Mr. Price's voice retreated until it was lost in the buzzing inside her head. Gabriel had done so well answering Amy's questions, but if he fell apart under Mr. Price's much more aggressive scrutiny, it could hurt his chances of ever being released.

It wasn't until the cross examination was over and Gabriel left the stand looking shaken but relieved, that Mia was able to get her emotions under control. Gabriel glanced at her as he returned to his seat, and she was able to force a tight smile that she hoped disguised how close she was to tears.

Nothing remained for them after that but the closing arguments. Mr. Price and then Amy took the floor to give their speeches, a last push that they hoped would sway the twelve people that held Gabriel's future in their hands, and then the prosecution getting the opportunity to offer a final rebuttal after Amy had finished.

"He deserves to be in prison for the rest of his life," Price said, turning back to address the jury directly, "and the state of Texas asks that you continue to protect the public by sending him there. Give him the conviction that he has earned with his despicable actions."

Judge Turner waited for him to return to his seat before speaking. "The jury has heard a great deal of information over the past few days, and they have a lot to consider as they determine a verdict. You'll all be called back when they've reached a decision." She tapped the gavel, and the jury left the room without looking back, giving no indication of which way their thoughts were leaning.

The guards removed Gabriel from the room as quickly as before, but this time he looked over his shoulder as he went, his eyes meeting Mia's as he shuffled out the door and out of sight. His lips were turned up in a hopeful smile, but his eyes reflected the same fear and sadness that she felt inside.

"Well," Amy said, turning to face them all as she gathered up her papers and slipped them into her briefcase, "there's nothing left to do but wait."

"How long?" Mia asked quickly. "How long will it be until they decide?"

"It could be days," Amy said, holding up a hand to silence them all before they could protest, "but I doubt that it will be. We'll get some lunch and then come back to wait. The verdict can be very emotional, best not to do it on an empty stomach."

"Right," Mia muttered, getting to her feet and following Amy out of the courtroom. After several days of being here, they had settled into a routine. The others left to grab lunch as Mia and her father picked at the meager offerings they'd purchased from the vending machine and waited for the others to come back.

Half an hour passed, and then an hour as everyone else filed back in slowly. They didn't speak as they settled into the other benches in the hallway and slid into their own quiet waiting. They stared at the floor, picked lint off their sleeves, flicked aimlessly through the apps on their phones. Each cough or sniffle carried down the long quiet hallways, echoing off the wood paneling and down into the high-ceilinged foyer below.

They weren't the only ones waiting, but Mia felt them with her like all of them existed in the same small bubble that drifted along outside of time and space. It consisted of nothing but them, the cheap carpet with its oddly creeping shadows, and waiting.

"They might not make a decision today," Amy reminded them, not for the first time but, Mia realized as she glanced at the time on her phone and saw it was after four, probably for the last time.

She was steeling herself for that, for having to come back here again tomorrow for more waiting after pacing the floor for all night, when Amy's phone dinged in her hand. She peered down at it, brow furrowed, then looked directly at Mia.

"It's time," she said gently. "They've made a decision."

Mia nodded, words failing her as her legs turned to liquid and harsh buzzing filled her ears, drowning out everyone's words as they led her blindly into the courtroom. She couldn't think, couldn't feel anything except a rising urge to vomit that she wasn't sure she'd be able to breathe her way through. Would the judge hold her in contempt if she threw up all over the carpet?

She swallowed, bile and terror coloring the flavor of her tongue, her mouth as dry as her fingers and toes were numb. Her father had to hold her arm to steady her when Judge

Turner re-entered the courtroom—she couldn't hold her body upright on her own.

There was no air in the room when she asked Gabriel to stand to receive his verdict.

Mia didn't even remember them leading him back in. When had he gotten here? How long had she been oblivious to the world around her as she counted her breaths—one, two, three, four—to keep from screaming?

"This was a very serious crime," the judge began, her gaze traveling from Gabriel to the lawyers at each table. "The magnitude of which was reflected in the charges the defendant faced. Has the jury reached a verdict?"

A white-haired woman in the jury box got to her feet. "We have, Your Honor."

"And how do you find the defendant?"

"On the charge of capital murder, we find the defendant not guilty."

Mia swayed on her feet. Capital murder in Texas was the same as first degree. She knew it wasn't over, Amy had explained that the jury could find him guilty of any of the lesser included charges, but not guilty in the highest charge meant that he could not be given the same hopeless sentence as he had before. He would not serve a life sentence with no chance of parole.

The juror kept talking. "On the charge of murder, we find the defendant guilty as charged."

Guilty. Not capital murder, but murder. A less punishable offense, equal to what most states considered murder in the second degree. They believed he had killed his father, but they did not believe it was a premeditated act.

Amy nodded in her seat, leaning over to speak to Gabriel as the rest of the courtroom shifted restlessly. They'd expected this. Amy knew how much they had hoped for an acquittal, but she hadn't lied to them about the odds.

"Thank you," Judge Turner said as the juror resumed her seat and Mr. Price huffed and reshuffled his papers. "Bailiff, please remand the defendant into custody until sentencing."

Sentencing.

Amy had told them it took the judge an average of ninety days to make a decision in criminal proceedings, but she doubted that the judge would take that long in this case. A few weeks, she predicted, and then they would know. Then they would have answers about their future.

Gabriel didn't look back as he was led away, but she could see the slight droop in his shoulders. It was far from the worst it could have been, but now that the tension of the moment had passed, they were faced with more waiting.

Sentencing was surprisingly similar to the trial itself. There was no jury sitting in the box, but Amy and Mr. Price once again faced the judge, each of them explaining their position and the requests they were making of the court. Mr. Price asked that the judge impose the maximum sentence—life in prison, eligible for parole after he had served forty of those years. Amy made their case for leniency.

Both sides had the chance to present witnesses to support their arguments and Dr. Engell testified again, speaking to the judge directly about the impact of Gabriel's mental state and how she believed he was unlikely to re-offend. The prosecution spoke at length about the rights of the victims to feel safe, to know that their loved ones had received justice, but he was missing one crucial thing that Amy had explained would've been invaluable to the state's position.

Normally this would be the time when the victim's family could address the court and give their impact statements, tell the judge how deeply the loss of their loved one had affected their lives and ask for the imposition of a harsh sentence. But Hugh Myers' parents were dead and his wife, despite the doubts and the anger that she felt toward their son, was not there.

Finally, it was over, and the courtroom quieted as Judge Turner began to speak. "A murder this violent, committed by someone as close to the victim as his own son, is a terrible tragedy, and the public must be protected."

Mia sucked in air through her nose, her body floating, untethered, as she tried to understand the words that would give her hope or turn everything to ash. She was sobbing quietly, her knuckles pressed to her mouth to stifle the sounds until she tasted her own blood on her tongue. Mr. Price was looking quite smug at his table and Amy was rubbing Gabriel's arm as he stared straight ahead, unmoving. If he was crying, too, Mia couldn't tell from her spot on the bench behind him.

"However," the judge continued, "circumstances in this case are extenuating and it is my professional opinion that a blatant miscarriage of justice occurred at this young man's original trial. The sitting judge's refusal to allow the jury to hear crucial evidence about a history of abuse and the defendant's state of mind at the time of the murder was more than enough to warrant a new decision."

Price was looking a lot less smug, his self-satisfied smirk starting to drop at the corners.

"He stands before me now, seeking justice again for the crime he committed. His new conviction shows clearly the inappropriateness of him serving a life sentence without parole, but now I must decide for myself when I believe there is a chance for him to safely reenter society and how much he should be punished for his actions of that fateful night."

She sighed and pressed her hand to the bridge of her nose

and Mia stopped breathing entirely, unable to force her lungs to work or heart to slow its frantic beat.

"My answer to the first question is that I do not believe that he would be a danger to others outside of those particular circumstances and that keeping him in prison is not necessary to ensure the public safety," she said, looking at Gabriel as he stood absolutely still except for the rapid rise and fall of his chest.

His lips were tinged blue at the corners, the air passing through his panicked lungs too quickly to provide him the oxygen he needed. His emotions were written clearly on his face, not the blank slate stare of so many years ago, but the terrified look of a man with everything to lose.

"Which brings me to the question of punishment and what is fair in exchange for the life he stole," the judge continued. "Something must be given, surely, but no member of the victim's family has come forward to urge that this man remains imprisoned, and his crime was committed while he was a minor in considerable distress."

Mia's mind raced, her thoughts forging ahead to count how old she would be if he got a forty-year sentence ... thirty ... twenty-five ...what if he only got fifteen when he'd already served thirteen of those years ...

"It is my decision that the defendant in this case will receive a new sentence of twelve years, to be satisfied with the time he has already served in prison."

Amy was gripping Gabriel's arm so tightly that her knuckles were white as the judge wished them all a good day and tapped her gavel to dismiss them. She began whispering to him, quick and excited, as he looked down at her in stunned silence.

"What does that mean?" Mia demanded, leaning forward over the short barrier that separated them to grab Amy by the sleeve. "What does that mean?" she repeated, afraid to believe what her mind was telling her.

"It means he's coming home," Amy said, hugging Gabriel fiercely as the guards moved forward to take him away.

"Then why are they taking him?" Mia asked, trying urgently to slide by the others as she followed Gabriel toward the exit door. She came up short when Lilly stepped in front of her, Amy's instructions to keep her from following more intimidating than Mia's anger at being corralled.

"He has to go back." Amy explained. "It's normal for them to return him to the prison to collect his belongings while they process his release. The judge's office will file the paperwork, and he should walk out a free man within the next twenty-four hours."

Part Two

Chapter Twenty-Three

G abriel sat on his bunk and watched the sun creep in through the window as the sink dripped. He'd listened to that drip for more years than he could remember. It was there at night when he went to sleep, and it was there in the morning when he woke up.

When it had first started it had been an irritation, one that had only deepened when he'd realized the prison had no intention of fixing it. Alex had complained about it bitterly when he'd arrived, about how the constant repetitive noise made it impossible to sleep or think or breathe without feeling like insanity was one splash away and stored just inside the eardrums.

Gabriel wasn't sure at all how he would be able to sleep without it now. Like everything else about this place, it had slowly gone from something he hated, to something he tolerated, to something that was simply there. They all hated it, groaned about it, wished they could be somewhere else, but those like him who had known that this was all there'd ever be, were resigned to the inevitability of it.

He'd hoped to get out someday, but he hadn't expected it

to be today. Maybe in a year or five, when he would've more time to prepare for his life after prison.

He still wasn't sure he believed there was actually going to be an after. Would the guards come to his cell to release him in a few hours like they'd promised, or would they come to tell him that it had been a mistake? Or a dream?

He thought he remembered it clearly. Walking into the courtroom with his hands and ankles chained and the shame of having Mia and her family, her friends see him that way. Seeing Brittany and Michael and the others as they'd all sat in that fucking witness box and paraded his sins and his failures out into the light for everyone to see.

Brittany and the child they'd lost. Richard. Seth. Hugh and the blood he'd never managed to wash off his conscience.

He hated that Mia had been there to hear it, but he'd known he couldn't keep her away. When he'd asked Amy to try and talk her out of it, she'd laughed in his face. Nothing kept Mia from doing what she wanted to do, what she thought was right and, in the end, he'd been glad she'd been there when the judge had asked him to stand and read him the sentence that would change his life.

The first time, when he was too young to understand the cost of it as they'd taken his life away, he'd been numb with nothing left to lose. This time, there was Mia. The judge had given him a chance to live, but Mia had given him a reason.

He tried to silence the part of him that feared she might not come today, and he would walk out the doors to an empty parking lot and a bus that would carry him away from here and to nothing. Maybe she, too, had expected years longer to prepare and she just wouldn't be ready.

The worry kept his mind occupied as they came to get him and his small box of personal items from his cell and escorted him to the small area where they did out-processing. He was given a change of clothes—a plain white T-shirt and inexpensive jeans—and an envelope with two crisp hundred dollar bills and a few fives and ones that the small woman behind the desk explained was the remainder of what had been in his commissary account.

"There will be someone here to pick you up? So, you won't need a bus ticket or a ride to the station, right?" She was curt, not looking at him as she processed his paperwork.

He swallowed hard, hands shaking as he considered what would happen if she didn't come. "She's supposed to be ... I mean, she said she would ..." He trailed off, swallowing again when the woman pierced him with an impatient look. "Yes," he said, more firmly. "Yes, someone is coming."

She nodded, signing the last form in the stack with a flourish. "You'll be escorted out the front and you'll need to leave the premises immediately."

He nodded, handing over his prison garb and picking up the box containing all of the evidence of the last thirteen years of his life—some art and letters from Mia. He was supposed to get his personal items back, the things that he'd had on him when he was arrested, but they shrugged at him, and he knew the only thing that he'd had in his pockets that night was a knife, and it would stay locked up as evidence in some vault owned by the state of Texas.

He followed the guard out and down the endless passageway, each set of doors that he passed through clanging shut behind him with the same feeling of finality that he'd had when he'd first come in.

It should have been liberating, but it made his knees quake.

The guard barely waited for him to be fully through the last set of doors before pulling it closed with a click and he walked out of the prison and into the bright light of mid-afternoon. There were no chains on his wrists and the jeans they'd given him felt odd and tight around his waist after so many years of wearing nothing but loose jumpsuits. He scanned the parking lot and pushed a hand through his hair as he tried to figure out what to do next. The erratic racing beat of his heart echoed in his ears, drowning out the sounds of birds in the trees and the far-off bark of a dog. He pushed back against a rising panic, a feeling of disconnectedness that started in his ears and spread until it reached his fingers and his toes. He didn't know what to do. Or where to go. He couldn't go back inside and he couldn't breathe …

And then she was there, standing on the other side of the small driveway between the sidewalk and the first row of parked cars, wearing a pretty blue sundress and a smile. He flexed his fingers at his sides as the feeling returned to them and watched as she shifted uneasily from foot to foot, bottom lip caught between the white of her teeth.

There'd always been something between them—guards, handcuffs, walls—and despite all of the times he'd told her that he couldn't wait to find out what she tasted like or see her pretty little body spread out under his, it suddenly seemed like nothing more than an impossible fantasy. How could he do that, when he couldn't even cross the distance between them now?

She took half a tentative step forward and he did the only thing he could think to do, the thing he had done the first time she'd come to visit him, and she'd been looking at him with eagerness and uncertainty. He opened his arms and waited.

There was a quick flick of a glance, right then left as she looked for cars passing in the parking lot, then she bolted, her feet crossing the space in three loose-limbed, bounding steps before she flung herself into his chest with such force that he took a step back to steady them as his arms came around her to catch and hold.

She stayed there for several heartbeats, her face pressed against his chest as they took in each other's familiar warmth and comforting smells, but it was no longer enough and when she tipped back her head and looked up at him with wide wet eyes full of joy and pink lips parted in welcome, there was nothing he could do but press his mouth to hers.

When he'd imagined this moment, he'd expected it to be soft and tender, but she met his kiss with an enthusiasm that surprised him. There was inexperience in the way she fit against him, her hands coming up to grip his face and hold him steady as she pressed her mouth to his just a little too hard, lips barely parted, but he pulled her close and wiggled his head to settle against her mouth more comfortably.

There would be time for her to learn the finer points of kissing and for him to discover the taste of her but for now all that mattered was that he could hold her for as long as he wanted and feel the soft shape of her in his arms and the soft pliability of her lips, and smell of the sweet floral fragrance of her perfume in air that didn't carry the faint traces of bleach and sweat.

He pulled away, rubbing his cheek on her hair as she laughed wetly and wiped the tears from her cheeks. The trembling smile she gave him was the most beautiful thing he'd ever seen, and he wanted to spend the rest of his life kissing her, but there were better places than here to do that.

"Come on," she said, grabbing his hand and leading him across the parking lot. "Let's go home."

Home.

Did she consider her home to be his? Would he be staying with her now that he didn't have to stay here?

The suddenness of it all left him with many questions that they hadn't had time to discuss and he waited until he'd settled into the passenger seat of her little blue sedan to ask her.

"Is that where we're going? Your apartment?"

She looked at him quizzically, reaching for his hand as she turned out of the parking lot and onto the open highway. It was rural and there wasn't much to see, but he found himself watching the window at the sights of passing fields and cows as much as he did her perfectly freckled nose as she answered him.

"Unless there's somewhere else you'd rather go?" she asked, her brows drawing together with sudden uncertainty.

"No," he said quickly. "We hadn't talked about it, and I didn't want to assume. I wasn't sure how your dad would feel about me going there."

She frowned, mouth twisting on a grimace and cheeks pinking. "He's not going to be thrilled with every decision I make but if you want to be with me then I want you there."

He caught the hesitation, the quick uncertain glance. "Mia," he said quietly, pressing her knuckles to his lips for a kiss that lingered. "There is nowhere I would rather be than with you."

"Good." She smiled, setting back in her seat, and relaxing just a bit. "We'll have to hide you just a bit for a while since you aren't on my lease but if I pick up some overtime shifts before the lease expires, I'll have enough saved up for us to move when it runs out."

"Is your apartment not big enough?"

She pulled up to a stop sign, making a show of looking both ways as she subtly avoided his question.

"Mia?"

"It's big enough," she said. "But we need a place where we can put you on the lease. You're not really supposed to have people there that aren't because most places don't want anyone living there who hasn't passed a background check. For the safety of the other residents, you know?"

"Background check," he repeated slowly. "So, they won't put me on the lease at your apartment, even if I have a job by then, because ..."

"Because you have a felony on your record," she said when his question went unfinished. "It doesn't matter which kind."

"I see."

"Don't worry about it," she said, her smile overbright. "There are places that let people with felonies move in and we'll find one."

"You're going to move into an apartment complex where all the people who just got out of prison live because they can't live anywhere else?"

"Yes," she said. "And, yes, it's probably slightly more dangerous than my current complex because most of the people that run them look the other way on pretty much anything if you can afford the ridiculous amount that they charge for rent but eventually we'll buy a house and then it'll be fine."

"It's okay," he agreed. "We can buy a house."

"Exactly," she said, giving him a vigorous and determined nod. "It may take some time on what I make, probably not until after I finish school and get a better job, actually, but it's not impossible."

"Why would we be doing it only on the money you make?" he asked, forgetting momentarily what he had been about to tell her.

She swallowed and squeezed his hand. "Probably not entirely but ... Well, it's just that it can be hard to get a job with a felony on your record, that's all. I don't want you to feel pressured or think I'm going to be mad if it takes a while for you to find something. You should take some time to adjust, anyway. Watch some movies. Eat some ice cream, cookies, and McDonald's."

He sat up straighter in his seat, distracted by the endless possibilities. "Can we?"

"Can we what?"

"Eat McDonald's? Or whatever? Just something that's not prison food?"

"Sure, there's a bunch of places that we can stop between here and my ... our ... apartment."

Twenty minutes later he was peeling the wrapper off a cheeseburger and sipping Coke through a cheap plastic straw. She'd gone through the drive through, deciding not to go in because she didn't want the first place he went as a free man to be the inside of a greasy fast-food restaurant. Instead, she'd set the bag in his lap and handed him his cup and the straws as she'd driven down the street to a small green park where she'd kissed him again, more softly, in the shade of a big tree at the edge of the parking lot before they'd settled in at a concrete picnic table. The air smelled of French fry grease, summer heat and freshly cut grass, simple luxuries that he'd thought he'd never experience again. It took all of his restraint to not lie down on the ground at their feet and stay there all day as the sun crept over his body.

"I can't believe you're actually here," she said. She was nibbling on her food but she hadn't taken her eyes off his face. "It doesn't seem possible."

"I'm here because you gave me hope and a reason to fight for my life when I got the chance. I'm going to take care of you," he promised. "I'm going to give you every single thing you've ever wanted and love you for the rest of your life."

"I know."

"I mean it," he insisted. "I'm going to buy you a house and pay for your school and anything else you need. I don't ever want you to have to worry about anything."

Her brows creased and she stared down at a line of ants parading across the tabletop, collecting what they could from a spilled drop of red liquid from someone else's lunch. "Don't put that kind of pressure on yourself. Our future isn't going to be easy and we'll probably spend more time eating ramen than McDonald's, but we'll figure it out together."

He reached for her hand, wrapping his fingers around hers and caressing the knuckles with his thumb. "My mother figured it out for us."

She looked up, teeth nipping down on the bottom lip that he still wanted to run his tongue over. She deserved more than what he had to give, she deserved everything, but knowing that she would have been willing to live with so much less made him all the more eager to give it to her. "Lilah?" she asked. "What do you mean?"

"I talked to Amy this morning and apparently my grandfather left me a trust fund that Mom never bothered to tell me about. Now that I'm an adult and out of prison, it's mine."

"She was going to let you rot without a lawyer when you had money that was rightfully yours?" There was a bitter spark in her eyes and her mouth was pressed in a thin and hostile line.

"Amy was just as shocked when Lilah asked her to pass along the information to me, but I'm honestly not surprised. Mother doesn't see the world in shades of gray. It's either right or it's wrong. I've almost always been wrong as far as she was concerned."

"That's not how a mother should behave," Mia said hotly. "She should be on your side, helping you, protecting you. If she had been, things might have been different."

"They might," he agreed. "But they weren't and now I'm out and I've got you and my money to take care of you." He threw back his head and laughed. "We've got a trust fund, baby!"

Chapter Twenty-Four

It was late afternoon when she parked the car. She said the apartment complex was the best she could afford on her meager paycheck this close to campus and the paint on the buildings was peeling at the edges of the small balconies. "It's not much but there's a pool and a little workout room that almost never has anyone else in it."

No one looked up as they passed the pool where blue water glimmered, and it was strange how out of place he felt in a world that continued to move along without him when the prison doors had clanged shut.

She watched the line of his gaze. "It's too hot to do much outside right now, but we could definitely go swimming if you want."

The idea that he had the freedom to do that was almost enough to steal the breath from his chest. "I'll need to get a bathing suit," he said as he followed her into the breezeway of one of the buildings and made a mental note of the large number on the side, so he didn't get lost if he had to go outside for anything. When was the last time he had to worry about remembering or finding his way around someplace that wasn't familiar?

She laughed, her voice echoing in the small space as they climbed the staircase. "You're going to need everything. Pants and shirts, socks, underwear. I already let my boss know I'd be out for the rest of the week while you got settled so we can go shopping."

She fit the key into the lock and pushed the door open with her shoulder. She'd said that the apartment was theirs, but she's been living here alone for months, and he was hesitant as he followed her inside.

The door opened to a tiny living room on the left and a minuscule eat-in kitchen on the right. There was a single hallway that he assumed led to the bedroom and bathroom and a sliding glass door that revealed a balcony that he doubted was large enough for the two of them to both stand on at the same time.

She hung her keys on a hook by the door, reaching around behind him to flick the locks as she toed off her shoes. "This is it," she said, spreading her arms wide as she began to walk, chattering about the apartment and expecting him to follow. The living room was tidy, the small space taken up by a small dark blue couch with a low coffee table and a flat screen TV on the opposite wall—but that wasn't what caught his attention as he looked around the room.

"The couch is a little small for you, probably," she said, evaluating it skeptically as he stood next to it, "but we can get a bigger one when we move—"

"Mia," he interrupted, pointing at the wall behind the couch. "You kept all of these?"

His art lined the wall, arranged neatly in rows of thin black frames, all grouped together with others that had similar themes and colors so that it blended from black and white on the top right to a furious explosion of color on the bottom left.

She nodded, tipping her head to look at her arrangement. "There's more in the bedroom and the hallway," she confirmed, taking his hand and leading him through the rest of the apartment, showing him the art she'd hung and the places where she kept pictures of them together in frames on the dresser beside her bed. The worry about invading space that belonged to her faded in the face of just how much of him was already here.

"Do you like it?" she asked, standing in her bedroom and drumming her fingers on her thigh. She was nervous, he realized, afraid that he wouldn't like her home or the things that were important to her.

"I love it," he said, smiling as she relaxed with a nearly imperceptible sigh.

His eyes roamed the rest of the space and landed on the bed that sat beneath the room's lone window. She'd brought him here with the expectation that he would stay, and he thought—hoped—that she meant for him to share that bed with her. If not right away, then at some point. Her letters and the phone calls they'd shared over the months that had passed had been heated, as explicit as they could be under the circumstances, but he knew about Mia's upbringing and her faith. They'd never talked about it, another thing he'd assumed wrongly that they'd have more time to work out between them, but he knew that she's always intended to wait until she was married, and he suspected that would still be true now, even if she did bring him here.

"I was just wondering" he mumbled, raking his hand through his hair. "Where I'm sleeping?"

"Where do you want to sleep?"

"Wherever you are," he said honestly, deciding that it was better to be damned for the truth than a lie.

The tension drained from her shoulders. "Yeah?"

"I want you," he said, leaning down until he could sweep his lips over hers, the barest brush of skin with the heaviest hint of promise, "but I want you to be sure and we're not married yet."

"Yet?" She tipped her face up to look at him, brows lifted in surprise.

"Yet," he agreed. "I know how you feel about that, and I love you too much for you to think we made a mistake."

"I love you, too," she said, reaching up on tiptoe to press her lips against his cheek as her fingers rubbed lightly at one curl of his hair. "And that's why I don't want to wait. I'm not ashamed of wanting you."

He breathed, an intentionally controlled soft and slow inhale and exhale as her meaning entered his mind and went straight to his body. Still, it hadn't been that long ago that she'd been unable to even speak the names of her own body parts out loud. "I'm glad you're not ashamed of it," he said cautiously. "But I won't ask you to do anything that you're not ready for."

"I'm ready," she insisted. "I didn't have time to go to the clinic for birth control yet, but I bought condoms."

"You did?" He tried to imagine how much determination it must have taken for her to overcome her shyness and buy condoms from the store.

"Yeah," she said, and he heard the edge of fierce determination in the statement. "I want this."

She leaned into him eagerly when he tightened his arms around her and pulled her back up on tiptoe to slot his mouth over hers again and moaned, a small soft sound that was somehow fragile, a mixture of unabashed desire and nervous anticipation. It didn't take her long to learn to soften her lips against him and match the erotic movement of his tongue and she shifted closer, pressing against him on instinct, until they both froze when the hard evidence of his arousal unmistakably rubbed into her stomach.

"I'm sorry," he said quickly, pulling away as she looked down at him and then back up with pink cheeks.

"No," she said, her hands holding fistfuls of the t-shirt the prison had given him so he couldn't move any further away. "It's just ... is that because of me?"

"Yes," he breathed, watching intently as her eyes widened and then glanced back down at the straining bulge in his jeans.

"It's bigger than I expected," she said timidly, startling a laugh out of him.

"I won't hurt you," he promised, trying to focus on her concerns and not his own stroked ego. "If you're sure you want this, I'll make it good for you."

A shimmering tear slipped from the corner of her eye to pave a wet path down her cheek as she refused to meet his gaze. "You've done this before, with Brittany and all the others. What if I'm not good at it and you don't like it with me?"

"Hey, please look at me," he beseeched, bending down and trying to peek back up at her face until she finally sniffled and cast a quick glance in his direction. "Nothing that happened with anyone else will ever mean as much to me as doing it with you." He pulled her close to rub his nose against her temple, his voice low and soft as he whispered in her ear. "We don't have to wait but we can go slow, and I can prove it to you."

It hit him again, the glorious feeling of having time to spend. The bed behind them wasn't going anywhere and neither were they. He could take as much time as he needed to show her that his words were true, that he meant it when he said he'd never loved anyone, never wanted anyone, the way he wanted her.

"Can you start showing me now?" Her eyes were still wet with tears and vulnerable. She might be pushing herself to do too much, too quickly, but he couldn't deny her anything and he resolved to use everything he had ever learned about how to please a partner to make sure that she didn't regret it. He bent down, hooking a hand around the back of each thigh and lifting her until she settled against him, her dress pushed up around her hips and her legs wrapped around his waist.

He walked to the bed with her wrapped around him like a vine, nipping and kissing his way across her jaw as he went. By the time he sat down with her on his lap, her body was already quivering, and her lips were parted, her breaths coming in soft pants of confused arousal.

She scooted closer as he kissed her neck and followed the curve of her body down until bare skin disappeared beneath soft cotton. He tugged down the bodice of her dress to reveal the lace of her bra and cupped a breast, squeezing it and rubbing his thumb over the hardened bud of her nipple. Her back arched, pushing her body into his hand as she shifted her hips restlessly, nearly overwhelmed with the newness of what was happening to her.

"Gabriel?" Her voice cracked, fear and desire at odds in her tone.

"It's okay," he soothed. "Just hold on to me."

She tightened her fingers on his shoulders where she gripped him as he changed his hold on her, one finger tracing the curve at the top of her thigh. He didn't dip beneath the fabric of her underwear, but she was already hot, and the cloth was damp against his knuckle.

Her hips bucked against him instinctively, seeking and searching for more as she tucked her face into the crook of his neck.

"Do you want me to stop?" he asked, running his fingers over the ridges and dips of her spine as she nodded against his shoulder. "We can stop but you don't have anything to be embarrassed about. I fucking love it that you're all wet for me."

"You do?" She didn't lift her head from his shoulder, but her voice was hopeful and her whole body shook at his words. Her hips were slowly shifting, trying to get some friction or relief from the arousal he knew she felt, but unable to do so because she was spread so wide around his torso.

Struck with sudden inspiration, he nudged her until his thigh was nestled between her legs, pressing against her center. "This will help," he told her, letting his hands resume their exploration as he guided hers from his shoulders to his hips.

"So pretty," he said, lifting the bra out of the way and revealing the expanse of her breasts beneath the white lace, his fingers plucking her nipples into pebble-hardness and then sucking one and the other into his mouth as she gasped and whined.

She shifted eagerly against his thigh, and he knew the exact moment that she realized the new position allowed her to rub her clit on the hard muscle of his leg because a soft and eager moan tore from her lips.

"Yes," he whispered. "Just like that. Does that feel good?"

She nodded, her breath quickening, and he could feel the tension building in her body. Her face was flushed, and her hair was tumbling down from her bun where his fingers had dug into it.

"Can you come like this?" he asked.

"I think so."

"I want you to." He wanted that more than he wanted anything else, but she pulled him in for another desperate kiss and as soon as he let her go she pulled his shirt over his head and then started working to get his zipper down. He made a mental note to buy something better than the thin white boxers that the prison provided him.

"Christ," he swore, sucking in a deep breath as her fingers brushed against his stomach.

"Did I hurt you?"

"No," he said, gripping her jaw as he pushed his lips roughly against hers. "You're fucking perfect. Keep going ... please."

Her breath slipped from her lips on a shuddering exhale when she tugged him free of his clothes. "Much bigger than I expected," she murmured, tipping her head to look at him as her fingers continued to explore, exploring the new textures and his reactions to her touch. "So hard but the skin is so soft."

"Mia," he said, dropping his head to her shoulder. He wasn't certain if he was begging or praying.

"Show me," she whispered, the edge of need turning it nearly into a whine. "Please."

He urged her to lean back, supported her with his arm as he pushed aside her underwear and explored her folds to gather the wetness of her body. He coated his fingers and began to stroke his hardened length as she watched intently and writhed on his thigh.

After a few minutes of observing, she reached between her legs without prompting, rocking back to make room for her fingers as she copied what he had done and coated her palm with her own shimmering arousal. Her fingers wrapped hesitantly around him, and he let go to put his hand over hers and guide her until her caress became confident. She ground against him harder, her thighs tightening on his and her hips began to move in earnest as she chased her own release.

He grabbed her hip with one and urged her on as she rode his thigh, his other hand coming up to squeeze her breast. His lips found her throat again, tasting the soft flutter of her pulse and the slight tang of sweat on her skin. She was breathing harder, hips jerking erratically, and he knew she was getting closer as he leaned down and captured her nipple between his teeth.

"Come for me," he commanded. "Baby, please." He was

desperate, his own orgasm creeping up as she tightened her grip on him.

The words seemed to be all the encouragement that she needed, and she came with a husky shout, her head tossed back and her body convulsing with the strength of her climax.

The sight of her coming apart in his arms was enough to snap his own restraint and he came before he could warn her. He pulled her in close, his teeth sinking into the soft rounded slope of shoulder as he spilled over them both, coating her hand and his stomach in hot waves. "Sorry," he mumbled quickly, trying to shift her off of him so he could clean the mess off of her, worried that she'd be disgusted or angry.

"It's fine," she said softly, clinging to him as she gathered the fabric of her skirt and used it to wipe them clean, first her hand and then his stomach. She curled against him when she was finished, her lips finding his for a lazy kiss.

"Are you okay?" he asked, rubbing his jaw on her hair and breathing in the floral scent of her shampoo. He'd wanted to go slower, to focus more on her pleasure this first time, but she'd taken him by surprise with her enthusiasm.

"Better than fine," she said with a giggle. "But I think we're going to have to wash your jeans before you can wear them shopping tomorrow. I'm going to have to put them in the laundry downstairs."

"I would help you but ..."

She giggled again. "I don't think my neighbors are quite ready for the sight of you naked in the laundry room. You could make dinner, though, while I toss them in. There's ramen in the pantry so we can clean up and then take care of all that."

He followed her into the bathroom and then watched as she stripped off her clothes, a blush creeping over her cheeks. The shower was barely big enough to fit them both and the meager water pressure delivered a spray that was mostly cold, but he rubbed the soap into her skin and helped her wash away the slickness between her legs.

"I'm sorry," he said, running his hands over the marks his teeth had left in her shoulder.

"Don't be."

He'd been with women that had much more sophistication, but none that had ever looked at him like she did. Like he was something precious and valuable. Stains that he'd thought were permanently embedded in his soul seemed to fade away when she looked at him like that.

He wrapped his arms around her, holding her tight in the shower as the cold water poured over them.

Chapter Twenty-Five

Gabriel sat up quickly, his breath coming hard and fast as his heart raced in his chest. His senses were still lost in his nightmare, fractured pieces of his past slipping through his consciousness and the smell of expensive perfume clinging to his nose. It made him feel like he'd been in some strange woman's hotel bed seconds ago and erased the decade since. He could almost still feel the hands on him, but the memory of Seth's voice was the worst of it.

"Fucking rich women in fancy hotel rooms is a privilege, if you're tired of that, you can start sucking dick in dark alleys with the rest of them."

The hands after that hadn't been gentle and after he'd tried to run ... Even Chris had heard him screaming. He'd learned that at the trial. His shame at what they had done to him was not his own private humiliation, after all.

Desperate to clear his mind, he reached—as he always did when the nightmares came for him—for the grounding familiarity of his surroundings. The hard cot beneath him, the steady drip of the sink, the stink of sweat and ammonia, all usually brought the cold wave of reality to clear away the conjurings of his sleeping mind.

He found none of those things.

Instead, there was the soft dip of a mattress, the steady tick of a bedside clock, and the scent of a different lover than the ones in his nightmares. She was curled on her side beside him, face soft and relaxed as she slept and one hand resting on the pillow beside her face.

The clock beside the bed read 3:27 when he slipped quietly from the bed and left her alone.

Mia found him in the kitchen, standing in the dim green light of her microwave wearing nothing but the thin white underwear the prison had issued him.

"Gabriel?"

He jumped, startled to hear her voice coming out of the darkness of the hallway.

She crept closer, snaking a hand around his wrist when he didn't answer. "It's three in the morning, what are you doing out here?"

"Can't sleep," he muttered. "It's lights on at 3:30 in prison. I've been waking up this early for thirteen years."

"Oh," she said, sleep clogging her mind as she pressed into his side, seeking the warmth he'd taken with him when he'd left his side of the bed empty. "Why didn't you wake me?"

He sighed and rubbed his jaw against her hair. "I didn't want to disturb you. You looked so peaceful."

"What's wrong?" She pulled back to look at him, frowning when he wouldn't meet her eyes. "Are you cold? You're shaking."

He shook his head, hands tightening on her hips to keep

her from moving away when she tried to go and fetch a blanket from the bedroom.

"Just a bad dream," he said. "It happens sometimes."

"What were you dreaming about?" she asked, leaning back into him and offering him her body heat anyway as she wrapped her arms around his torso.

"It's nothing …"

"It's something," she insisted. "I want to help you."

"I know you do," he said, kissing the top of her head. "But there's nothing we can do about it."

She wanted to argue, to tell him that it was normal for him to be feeling unsettled after having to relive everything for the trial and enduring all the changes he'd experienced in such a short time, but he tipped her chin up with the curve of his finger and silenced her with his lips on hers.

This kiss was nothing like the ones before. There was none of the softness and the sweetness that she'd gotten from him yesterday. His mouth was hot on hers, demanding as he parted her lips with his tongue. This was purely about him and whatever memories had haunted his nightmares. He clutched her to him as though her skin on his was the cure for a lifetime of pain, his hands tugging up the hem of the nightgown that barely skimmed her knees until he could reach beneath and cup the backs of her thighs.

She gasped when he lifted her, knocking aside the clutter from last night's dinner where it rested on the kitchen counter. Something clattered into the sink and porcelain shattered as one of her bowls hit the floor and exploded on impact.

"Gabriel," she protested, worried about the shards and his bare feet, but he stepped into the empty waiting space between her thighs and nipped her neck until she shuddered beneath the onslaught of his mouth.

"Buy you a new one," he mumbled against her skin,

unheeding to any damage he might be doing to himself. "I just need you. Need to taste you."

He pressed a knuckle to the core of her, the pressure of his hand a new sensation against the fabric of the underwear. She spread her knees, eagerness and nerves tightening her muscles as she perched at the edge of the kitchen countertop and wondered wildly if this was really happening like this, caught up in some whirlwind frenzy of need with sleep still clinging stubbornly to her mind and inescapable memories still hanging heavily on his. This wasn't like before. This passion was driven by whatever demons dogged his dreams.

He slid his fingers into the band of her underwear, and she shifted as he pulled, lifting her legs one at a time so that he could guide them roughly over her thighs and down her calves to toss them aside. There was no patience here, no gentle path traveled over the slim column of her neck or the soft peak of her breast. He looked at her like he wanted to drown in her, to wash away whatever ghosts still haunted him in the wet pool between her thighs.

Her hips jerked when he pressed a hand to the center of her, his fingers beginning an exploration of her body that made her writhe and drip onto the cheap laminate countertop. She clung to him, one hand tangled in his hair and her face pressed into the curve of his shoulder as she bit down on the soft skin of his neck to muffle her whimpers.

"Lean back," he instructed softly, moving his hands to her legs and smearing her own slick wetness on her skin as he pressed his thumbs gently into her inner thighs, urging her to spread them wider.

Fresh wetness rushed between her thighs at the low rumble of his voice. She'd never been able to ignore that tone, not since the first time she'd heard him speak and he'd left her whimpering on the phone just from speaking her name.

She reached behind her and leaned back into her palms,

reclining enough that he could jerk her hips forward and bring the curve of her ass right up the edge of the counter, her body open and bared to his gaze when he nudged her legs even further apart so that he could look down at her with knowing and hungry eyes.

She shivered when he trailed one finger through the folds of her body, but this time he didn't settle on her clit instead he reached further into the hidden and unexplored depths until he could press persistently against the entrance of her body.

The sudden realization that she felt acutely empty settled over her, and she pushed her hips forward, seeking more as he gently rocked the tip of finger inside her. She clenched down on the intrusion, chasing the unfamiliar sensation of being stroked from within.

"Do you like that?" he asked, his face serious in the odd green light.

"Yes," she admitted, cheeks flaming at being asked to say it out loud but pleased when he grunted in satisfaction and worked his finger deeper inside of her in response.

She squirmed against his hand, seeking more as he curved his finger, pressing against her in new angles that helped her discover the potential of her own body and the places within that sent shockwaves of new feelings shooting through her. His fingers were able to reach places inside her that her own were not and the difference in length and width was enough to make her head spin, especially when he added a second finger beside the first.

She arched her hips shamelessly into his hand as he stroked her, eager to take what he was giving her. Her doubts faded beneath the caress of his fingers, the odd light and the hard edge of the countertop as it dug into her thighs suddenly seemingly the perfect accompaniment to this life changing experience.

"You need more," he said, more statement than question,

and she blinked down at him, ready to remind him of the condoms that she'd stored uncertainly in her bedside drawer, but he pulled her up to give her a quick kiss and then dropped to his knees in front of her.

She peered down at him curiously, trying to draw her knees together now that his height had been diminished just enough to bring him to face level with her bared and glistening core.

"Shh," he soothed, pressing a line of kisses up her thigh. "I just need to taste you, remember?"

"You're not going to ... I mean ... *you know*?"

"Fuck you? Not right now," he said with a soft chuckle, looking up to meet her eyes as he leaned in to skin his lips over her core. His face came away wet, and her cheeks burned with embarrassment, but he never looked away from her, his eyes still hot and locked onto her face.

She bit down on her lip as he parted her folds with his tongue, a long soft swipe that ended with a focused suck on her clit that made her whimper as she tossed back her head and lost herself in the motions of his mouth.

She understood now why such things were meant to be sinful—how could she keep her mind focused on the kingdom of heaven when Gabriel was able to bring heaven to her on earth?

He feasted on her like a starving man suddenly invited to the king's table, exploring each shadowed bit of flesh and gathering up all the wetness he found there before startling her by plunging his tongue inside her.

She huffed a shocked sound through her nose at the unexpectedness of it but was soon swept away by sensation and when he replaced his tongue with his fingers inside her, filling her and stroking the spot that he'd already discovered made her moan, she came apart beneath him.

"You look so beautiful when you come on my fingers."

She stayed splayed across the kitchen counter, chest heaving and breasts bouncing until she could catch her breath. "What about you? Do you want ... I mean, should I?" She glanced down at the bulge between his legs and then away again.

"Do you want to?"

She sat up, pushing the hem of her nightgown down around her thighs. "Don't you think I should want to?"

He shook his head and pressed a kiss to her knee before standing up. "That's not how it works. It's okay if you're not ready for that."

She hooked a finger into the waistband of his underwear, pulling him toward her. "I want to do *something*," she insisted. "We could, I mean, *you* could ..." She spread her knees invitingly, unable to say the words but determined to issue the invitation.

"Not like this," he said, gripping her jaw and pressing a hard kiss to her mouth. "We can do something else."

"What else is there?" she asked, her mouth turning down in a pout.

He smiled and lifted her down, patting her hip once her feet were on the floor again. "Turn around," he instructed, waiting till she shot him a puzzled look and turned to face the counter to lift her nightgown back up around her hips.

Her thighs were still wet and when he pressed them together and she felt the hard press of his arousal at the seam between them she understood what he was trying to do. "Oh," she breathed softly, leaning forward until she could rest her elbows on the counter and pushing her backside toward him.

He was nestled in the space he'd created between her legs, thrusting softly against her, sliding back and forth as she watched him appear and disappear between her thighs. He was pressed against her, chest hot where it met her back, breath ragged and desperate in her ear. He had one arm wrapped around her body, clamped to her stomach like an iron band, as his other hand gripped the countertop beside her elbow, holding them both steady against the motion of his hips.

"Touch yourself," he told her huskily. "Just like you used to do for me in all the letters you wrote. Let me feel you come for me."

Heat rushed through her, and she clenched down on nothing as she fumbled with the fabric of her nightgown, tugging it out of the way until she could press her fingers to the still sensitive area between her legs. Her thighs jumped and tensed around him at the first stroke of her hands, and he swore softly.

"Sorry," she mumbled.

"Don't you dare apologize," he growled. "You're fucking perfect."

"Gabriel," she whined, and he jerked her back against him, bouncing her off his chest and his hips.

He let go of the counter and pushed her hand aside to stroke her with his own fingers. "Say it," he demanded, the movements of his fingers slowing just enough to make her whine in protest. "Tell me this is what you want."

"I want it," she panted.

He sped up, his fingers pressing into her just the way she liked until it ripped a second orgasm from her. Her mouth opened on a wordless cry as she clamped her thighs together, whole body shuddering with the strength of the pleasure that tore through her.

He pushed into her thighs, whispering words that she caught only the edges of. Things like *"so pretty"* and *"amazing"* and then *"oh fuck"* as he pulled her hard against him and coated the insides of her thighs with hot come.

She leaned into the counter with him resting against her

back and his spend cooling on her thighs as she tried to catch her breath. "Well, that was …"

"Perfect?" he asked, pressing a kiss to the back of her neck, just beneath hair that curled, damp with sweat, against her skin.

"Yeah," she said with a giggle, head pressed to the cold smooth surface of the countertop. "Perfect."

"I really fucking love you."

"I really fucking love you, too," she said with a sigh. "But you broke my bowl."

"Shit."

He stood up and let go of her, so she was able to turn around and flick on the overhead kitchen light and survey the damage. "I'll pick this up while you wash off," he said to her, kissing her quickly on the nose before crouching down to grab the first few shards of broken porcelain.

The come was already drying and sticky on her skin when she stepped into the shower, and it was bothersome enough that she was grateful for even the cold stingy spray. Still, she didn't linger, and it was only a few minutes before she was rushing into the bedroom to tug on a clean pair of shorts and a soft t-shirt.

He was digging in the pantry when she came back, and she realized he was probably used to eating breakfast this early, too.

"If we keep this up, we're going to spend a lot of time showering," she said with a laugh, her thighs still shaking as she leaned into his side and pushed the hair back and away from his eyes. Whatever sadness had been there earlier had vanished, leaving nothing but warmth as he leaned into her palm. "Go ahead and hop in and I'll whip up something to eat for breakfast. Pancakes or omelets?"

"Umm," he stammered, suddenly unsure, and she

remembered his frozen silence in the fast-food drive through staring at the menu full of options.

"I'm usually fonder of pancakes," she added helpfully. "Especially for special occasions."

"What's the special occasion?" he asked, pausing on his way to the bathroom to look at her curiously.

"You are," she said, unable to resist the urge to stretch up on her tiptoes and press another kiss to the warm plush curve of his mouth. Soon enough he'd taste like sugar and syrup but for now he only tasted like Gabriel and the tang of her own arousal. Her body clenched on a newly learned greed, but she knew he needed time and they had to go shopping today. He was already going to have to wear the same outfit as yesterday, albeit newly washed.

"But am I pancake worthy?" he asked, lifting one brow at her skeptically.

She bit her lip, pretending to think it over, before looking back at the kitchen countertop, still wet and shiny where he'd cleaned it while she showered.

"Definitely."

The tips of his ears were pink when he left the kitchen.

She set out her ingredients and then turned on the TV on to give her something to listen to as she worked. She grimaced as the morning news came on and then froze as trial footage from thirteen years ago filled the screen showing a young Gabriel, stoic and empty eyed as he faced down the jury. The news anchor was talking fast, and she wasn't able to hear him over the dull buzzing in her ears. The headline beneath the images, however, was inescapable.

Teenage Murderer Freed After Only Thirteen Years in Stunning Court Decision

She didn't want Gabriel to see any of it and she was in the kitchen pouring batter into a pan when he came back, one towel slung low across his hips and using another to dry his dark curls.

"Smells good," he said, pulling her back into his chest and nuzzling his face into her neck.

"No funny business until after breakfast and shopping," she declared, flipping the pancake and turning to kiss cheek. "We should head out pretty soon, before the stores get crowded."

Chapter Twenty-Six

Shopping with Mia was both easier and much harder than Gabriel had imagined that it would be. Following her around the aisles of the nearest Target as she tossed clothes in a red shopping cart held none of the stuffiness that he remembered from his days of being dragged from one fancy boutique to another by his mother, and none of the rush that had come with dashing out the doors with whatever stolen item had caught his attention as he had done during his days with Seth.

He was grateful for the normalcy of it—for the bright florescent lighting and the shopping cart's squeaky wheel and the underwear that she held up for his inspection before shrugging and adding it to the top of the pile—but somewhere between socks and t-shirts he began to notice the looks.

First the odd glance over someone's shoulder and then mothers tugging their toddlers away from him as they entered the aisles or simply turning around and leaving altogether the next item on their lists forgotten entirely in their rush to get away.

"Does it all have to be black?" Mia asked, peeking at him from over the top of a black button down.

"Yes," he said, barely glancing her way before frowning at the old man that scowled at him over a rack of men's jackets. He glanced down at the white shirt he was wearing, checking for the third time to make sure that the prison hadn't stamped the word "felon" on the front without him noticing.

The fabric remained stubbornly blank.

"Why does everyone keep staring at me?" he asked, running a frustrated hand through his hair and turning his back on the old man.

She bit her bottom lip and shrugged. "Impressed by your incredible good looks?"

"Mia," he said, folding his arms across his chest and raising one eyebrow.

"Fine," she said, her mood turning sour as she glared back at the old man, her expression so ferocious that he finally huffed and disappeared into the nearby electronics section. "The news *may* have done a few stories on your release."

He uncrossed his arms and glanced over his shoulder. There were far more people subtly watching him than he'd realized. "A few?"

"A lot," she admitted. "It started out local, but it's been picked up by the national news stations now."

"Didn't they get enough sensationalist bullshit when they locked me up?" he grumbled. "It's been thirteen goddamn years."

"Amy warned me that it might happen after the reporters showed up at the trial. It was a high-profile case back then and you *are* still a senator's son," she reminded him. "Victim's advocacy groups are furious that your case might set a precedent for future rulings."

"Jesus," he said, grabbing the cart and steering it toward the front as she trotted along behind him, trying to keep up with his longer strides. "We're getting out of here before someone decides to spit on you for being with me or something."

"No one is going to hurt me," she said, planting her feet stubbornly and refusing to follow.

"You don't know that. People are cruel and they hate with their whole hearts." He wished he didn't have to explain that to her, that she could keep her innocent belief in their inherent goodness forever, but he knew she wasn't safe with him right now.

She sighed as people turned to watch, as they squinted at him skeptically and waited to see if he'd move to hurt her in the middle of the store at nine a.m. on a weekday morning. More than half of them looked like they expected her to be the first of a new line of victims, the continuation of a pattern that he'd started all those years ago with his father.

"Let's go," she urged, taking back control of the cart and leading him toward the checkout line. "We didn't get everything you'll need but we got enough for now and we'll order the rest online. If you're uncomfortable being out then we'll just stay in for a while, wait till it all blows over."

"What if it doesn't?"

"It will," she said. "Something new will come along and it'll push you out of the news completely."

"I hope so," he said, but he hated the way that everyone's eyes lingered on them as they walked and the cashier's suspicious gaze as Mia loaded everything from the basket onto the little conveyor belt and attempted to make small talk.

They were all watching him, but doing so meant they were also watching *her*, too ... invading her privacy and giving pitying little shakes of their heads as they whispered behind their hands.

And he wondered, for the first time *really* wondered, about what their relationship looked like to the rest of the world. He'd wondered about how it would affect Mia and how it was perceived by people who knew her and cared about her, but he'd never given a shit about anyone else.

The people he'd worried about were people that knew Mia. They knew how stubborn and passionate she was, and they'd seen how happy she was with him. These people, the rest of the world, didn't know Mia and all they saw was a young woman barely on the other side of adulthood that had been sucked into the life of a man nearly a decade older than she was. A murderer. A manipulator. Someone who was taking advantage of her youth and inexperience.

He wouldn't have to hurt her for her to be a victim in their eyes. His presence in her life was enough.

He shifted uncomfortably under the accusatory look of the cashier, his mind flooded with images of Mia's early morning kitchen and the sounds she'd made when he's driven her over the edge into her orgasm, her thighs clamped around his cock before she'd even had a chance to clear the sleep from her eyes. She was a fucking *virgin* for Christ's sake, and he'd been on her like an animal, lost in the memories of his disgusting past life. He'd sank back into the filth in his nightmares and then he'd taken her down with him.

Her cheeks were pink, but her face was defiant as she slipped her bank card into the machine and paid for his socks and new pants, the bathing suit trunks she'd said he was going to need for this afternoon when she took him swimming. He'd have money of his own as soon as he talked to Amy and found out how to access his trust fund, but what if he hadn't been a silver-spoon fed trust fund baby?

No one knew about that, all they saw was her dropping money she'd worked for to feed him, clothe him. Like he was a fucking parasite on her and her life. Living in the apartment she paid for, riding around in the car she was making the payments on. He didn't even have a fucking driver's license, couldn't do a damn thing on his own right now.

He stuffed his hands in his pockets and said nothing else as they walked to the car.

"You're brooding," she said, closing the trunk of the car after they'd tossed all his stuff in.

He rolled a shoulder, not bothering to deny it. "I don't like the way they were looking at you or the things they were thinking."

"You don't know what they were thinking."

"They were wondering if I was going to hurt you," he insisted. "They were thinking that I'm a murderer and a monster who's taking advantage of you because you're young and—"

"And that's bullshit," she said, puffing up in irritation. "What now all of a sudden you think I'm too young for you?"

"I think I haven't let you experience anything else," he said carefully. "You're a virgin and look what I did to you this morning-"

"I *liked* what you did to me this morning," she said angrily, poking him in the chest with her finger. "I tried dating someone else and I didn't like it, but if you'd rather that I got some *experience* with someone else first—"

"Like hell," he snapped. Rational thought and selfless impulses aside, the idea of her being with someone else was enough to have jealousy clawing painfully at his insides. Fuck that. Maybe he didn't deserve her after everything and maybe she would have been better off with someone else, but it was too late for that now.

"That's what I thought," she said quietly. "I don't want someone else, and I don't want you to be with someone else, either. I don't give a shit about what anyone else thinks or about what happened before."

She crowded into him, pushing into his personal space and

resolutely ignoring it as the occasional passerby slowed down to stare at them. She leaned into his chest and pressed up on her toes, curling her arms around his neck and tugging him down until he surrendered.

Her mouth was sweet, and she parted her lips for him without coaxing, heedless of the eyes that watched them or the judgment of those who stared as she teased him with her tongue and tangled her fingers in his hair. She kissed him senseless and then pulled away to place one last peck of her lips to the tip of his nose and smirk up at him in satisfaction.

"I don't know what I could ever have done to deserve you," he said, awed as always by the sheer vibrancy of her, the light that she carried with her into every situation.

"You were just you," she said, "and that was always enough. Let's go home, okay?"

He didn't say anything else until they were settled into the car and the radio was softly playing a song he'd never heard before just loud enough to be heard over the continuous blast of the air conditioner.

"I wanted to take you on a date," he said, squeezing her hand where it rested in his on the center console. "But with the way things went at the store ... And I haven't even tried to call Amy yet to get access to my trust fund. I need money for us, a driver's license. I want to take care of you."

She squeezed back, her smile bright and unconcerned. "You will take care of me, and I'll take care of you. Things will settle down soon and then we'll work on getting you a license. Maybe next week if you feel comfortable? In the meantime, you can work on other things. We'll call Amy's office this afternoon before we go swimming and later tonight we can order take-out."

"Swimming and take-out aren't a date," he argued. "I wanted to do something special for you."

She shook her head. "We've got the rest of our lives for

fancy dinners, Gabriel. We can go if you want but it'll be the same thing that happened at the store. I'm perfectly happy with a movie at home and couch cuddling. That's the kind of thing I imagined doing with you if you ever got out, not eating expensive food with too much silverware."

He thought back over the number of dinners Lilah had made him attend, crammed into a stuffy suit and shoes that pinched his feet as he listened to boring conversations that he'd have done anything not to be a part of. It didn't compare in the slightest to the image of relaxing on Mia's couch with her head in his lap as they watched whatever movie she'd picked out for them on her TV, and he played with the ends of her hair.

"Fine," he said. "We'll stay in and order food."

"I always win," she said brightly. "I'm very stubborn."

"Yes, you are," he agreed. "Lucky for you I like stubborn brunettes with a pretty smile."

She grinned at him, and he lifted her hand to his mouth, pressing a quick kiss to the backs of her knuckles. The soft smell of her perfume lingered in the air and her skin was soft under his fingers. Being able to touch her whenever he wanted to felt like some kind of miracle, the kind of thing that made even someone as jaded and cynical as him wonder if perhaps there might be a God after all. Or at least the beginnings of a run of good fortune that he'd be a fool to turn his back on.

It was a feeling that he carried with him through the rest of the day.

His own incredible good luck.

It hit him as he watched her make them sandwiches for lunch, stacking slices of meat on bread as he stood beside her in the kitchen filling their plates with chips and slices of watermelon. And again, when they went down to the pool before kids got out of school for the day, when the cold blue water was still empty of everyone except the two of them.

Swimming was a pleasure he thought he'd never get to experience again, and they splashed each other like two teens just learning how to flirt before coming up to breathe locked around each other, their mouths hot and hungry.

She tasted of summertime, of sweat and chlorine and sunscreen. Water ran in rivulets down the slim column of her throat, and he chased them with his lips, making her shiver with anticipation before he tossed her back toward the deep end and laughed at her indignant squeal.

When he bought her a house, he was going to make sure it had a pool.

By the time they'd made it back upstairs, he'd forgotten the world outside their little bubble of tranquility. The thoughts that had plagued him in the store earlier seemed like nothing more than a bad dream, a brief lapse of judgment on his part.

All that mattered was her and the love he felt for her, and he was sure that there was nothing outside of them that could tarnish it.

Chapter Twenty-Seven

He grinned and got to his feet, pursuing her down the hallway as she danced playfully just out of his reach. He'd barely cleared the doorway to the bedroom when she stopped running and launched herself into his arms, her mouth already seeking his and her arms locking around his neck.

He was tender as he stripped her down, his mouth barely leaving hers as his fingers worked to unhook her bathing suit and tug the fabric from her skin. "Are you ..."

"Don't you dare," she said. "Don't you dare ask me if I'm sure."

"I don't want you to regret being with me," he said honestly, swallowing hard on the fear that he'd been trying so hard to ignore. "I'm going to do every single thing that I ever told you I would, I'm going to fuck you until you can't breathe, and you forget your own name. But you have to be sure."

"I'm sure," she said, her voice breathy and trembling. "I want you ... *please.*"

She didn't wait for an answer, her fingers gliding over his

chest, her touch still featherlight and uncertain as she pressed her mouth against his throat, her lips finding the erratic beat of his pulse and smiling against his skin. "Mine," she breathed, quiet and awed.

"Yours," he agreed. "Always."

She faltered then, her determination suddenly wavering as she realized she didn't know what to do next.

He felt the burden of responsibility settle over him, as she bit her lip and looked up at him with pleading eyes. He wanted to make it good for her, to be sure that she wouldn't ever regret what they were about to do. There were enough bad memories haunting their bed already and he was determined that she would never be the one with nightmares disturbing her sleep.

"Please," she said again. "Show me what to do."

She was so eager to please and he was lost in her—in her eyes and in the sweetness of her smell and in the slight wobble of vulnerability in her voice. He wanted to drink it all down, get drunk on her and never recover.

He scooped her up, his arms snaking around her, one around her back and the other hooking under her knees to lift her up in his grasp. He carried her to her bed like a bride across the threshold, half naked in wet swimsuit bottoms. Someday he'd carry her into the home they made together. Someday he'd give her his last name and then carry her in his arms in a glittering white dress and lace veil. That day would be perfect, but right now, with her skin bare for him and her fingers tangled in his damp hair she was a vision that he knew he'd never forget. He laid her on the bed, her body settling against the innocent blue and yellow roses of her bedspread.

She was watching him, those sharp hazel eyes dark and wide with desire and she let her knees fall open, an invitation that he desperately wanted to take, but he wanted her to be ready, wanted to pull as much pleasure from her slender body as she could stand and leave her sated and drained.

"Not yet," he murmured, pressing a kiss to her knee and nuzzling his face into her thigh.

"You keep saying that," she protested.

"Almost," he soothed. "I promise. I just need you to be ready for me."

"I am ready," she whined, shifting her hips toward him insistently.

"*Mia*," he said, using the deep and firm tone that he knew she liked and waiting for her to be still before he spoke again. She needed to understand that he wanted to take things slowly and savor each inch of her skin.

"Your body isn't ready," he said when her hips had stopped wiggling, and he dropped a kiss to the mound where heat and wetness were already waiting for him. "But I'll fix that, and I'll make sure you like it."

He skimmed his fingers down and over her thighs before he tugged her bottoms off, and her breath hitched in anticipation. He used his lips and his tongue to wring the first orgasm out of her, worshiping her with his mouth. All thought of convincing her to go slowly left his mind at the taste of her and he barely gave her time to come down before plunging his fingers into her, working her back into a frenzy as he stretched her, preparing her to take the rest of him until she was desperate and he clinging to his own self-control.

"Condoms?"

It was the last coherent thought he was capable of making as he settled himself between her thighs, the slick wet heat of her body so tantalizingly close, but he knew it mattered. She wasn't on birth control yet and he was not going to ruin her, not going to risk it no matter how much he wanted to feel his bare skin slide against her cunt's velvet grip.

Besides, it would probably help him last longer, anyway,

and he didn't want to disappoint her by ending things too soon. He was already teetering on the edge, his dick straining against the skin of her thigh.

A condom would help.

She tapped the drawer in the nightstand, and he leaned over to open it, propping himself up one elbow to peer down inside. The soft rumble of his laughter made her frown up at him and he kissed her forehead, unable to do anything else between the endless chuckles and the wave of love he felt for her.

She'd bought boxes of so many different sizes, colors, and flavors that the whole drawer was stacked full of them. Her skin was flushed pink all the way to the tops of her breasts, her face hot with embarrassment. "I didn't know what kind to get."

"You are perfect," he told her, raining kisses across her face and then lingering over her mouth, nibbling softly on her swollen bottom lip. "You try so hard to always get everything right."

"I wanted you," she countered hotly. "I wasn't going to risk not being able to do this because I bought the wrong one, so I bought one of each."

"That poor cashier," he said, his forehead resting on hers as he kissed her nose.

"Self-checkout," she said primly.

"Right," he said, shaking his head and kissing her again, hard and possessive, before digging back into the drawer to find something usable. He discarded the strawberry flavored and a box that looked as though its contents were meant to glow in the dark before finding the right thing. He tore it open, the gold packaging fluttering down to land on the floor as he rolled the condom on. She watched him carefully, studying his motions, and he suspected that she'd be asking to try it herself the next time.

He sucked in a deep breath when she reached her hand between them to slide her fingertips carefully over his length, experimentally testing the feel of the latex.

"It doesn't hurt? Or bother you?"

"No," he said, his hips bucking against her hand, seeking her touch.

"Okay," she breathed, leaning up to kiss him, her lips lingering on his for a long moment. "Gabriel?"

"Now," he agreed, already knowing what she was going to ask and realizing that there was nothing to stop him anymore from sinking into her.

"Finally," she said, arching eagerly up to meet him as he pushed forward slowly. He'd done his best to prepare her, but he was bigger than anything she'd ever experienced before, and he was afraid of hurting her if he went too quickly.

He kissed her deeply as he rocked into her, each little thrust of his hips earning him a breathy moan from low in her throat and another inch of precious space inside her. She was ready enough that it surprised him how easily she took him in, how encouraging and pleased her little noises were.

He wanted to be soft, but she had no patience, her legs were twined around his waist and holding him close as she begged him for more and harder and deeper and he gave it to her because how could he not? He'd do anything for her with her face so gloriously flushed and her hair all sweaty and perfect little pink lips moaning his name.

There was nothing fake or polished about her, she was unashamed and greedy, and her perfect little tits bounced just right as he fucked into her, and he couldn't believe that this was his life. That after everything he'd done and everything he'd seen, after he'd lived through Richard and Seth and that hellhole of a prison for thirteen years ... that now he was here, and he was with her, and he was buried balls-deep in the hottest and most welcoming pussy he'd ever seen.

He didn't think he'd ever understand how it was possible that this perfect woman loved him, that she wanted him, that she'd given him her heart with the same eager fervor as she was now giving him her body.

He could feel her getting closer as he drove into her, each snap of his hips pushing her nearer. She was clenching around him, her hands scrambling for something to hold onto as she dug her nails into his back.

"You're so fucking pretty," he said, watching her face as the words broke over. "So good. It's so good that you can take all of me like this. Did you know that?"

She tossed her head back and forth on the pillows, a silent denial.

"I love you and I love this pretty little pussy and how good it feels," he insisted, and she clenched around him, her body getting hotter and wetter with each bit of praise. He worked himself inside her, discovering the angles that made her arch and moan. He found all of her sensitive places and the perfect speed, grinding into her so that each thrust pushed him in as deeply as she could take him.

"Come for me," he urged. He wanted it, wanted to feel her as she lost control, but more than that he knew that *she* wanted it. He could feel how close she was, how desperate.

She was tensing as she reached for it, trying to cross that final distance, and when he reached a hand between them to find the sensitive bud of her clit with his fingers, she came apart almost instantly.

The tight and rapid flutter of her body and the sound of her screaming his name as she came around him was enough to push him over the edge with her, his thrusts becoming erratic as he buried his face in the side of her neck and then drove in deep to spill himself inside her.

He held her there, both of them trembling and content as

he pressed a line of kisses across her cheek and down her neck, until he began to soften inside her.

"Sorry," he said, kissing her softly as he pulled out of her. "I have to take care of this."

The confusion cleared from her face when she watched him roll out of bed and take the condom off.

"I'll be back," he promised, heading out into the hallway to dispose of it in the trash can as she waited for him, her chin propped up in her hand. There was a happy smile on her face and she hadn't moved at all when he came back.

He flopped back in bed beside her and gave her a little smack on the ass. "Go pee," he instructed, stopping her in the act of trying to curl back up against him.

"What? Why?"

"You just have to," he explained. "It keeps you from getting UTI's or whatever. Didn't anyone ever tell you that?"

She shook her head, shrugging as she got to her feet. "All we ever got was the abstinence talk, you know?"

"They really didn't teach you shit about anything, did they?"

She shook her head ruefully. "But now I have you, so thank you for being so patient with me."

"Mia." He grabbed her hand as she walked by, not letting go until she stopped to look down at him. "There is nothing that I wouldn't do for you. You're the best thing that ever happened to me and I love you."

"I love you, too," she said, grinning down at him and kissing him quickly before disappearing into the bathroom.

He watched her go, admiring the curve of her naked ass as she went. She hadn't been gone long when he heard the shower turn on and he leaned back against the pillows to wait for her.

He'd nearly dozed off, his body relaxed and his mind lost in a pleasant hum of love and post sex glow, when her phone on the nightstand began to buzz. He glanced at it—DAD—and thought about answering it. He couldn't avoid the man forever, but the timing couldn't possibly have been worse. Would her father be able to tell what he'd just been doing to her? Would he be able to detect the subtle signs of pure masculine satisfaction in his voice? Better not to risk it, he decided, setting the phone back down as he waited for Mia.

She would have to call him back, Gabriel knew. Call him back and reassure him that she was fine, that she hadn't been hurt. She'd have to go back to school, maybe work if she still wanted to. She'd want to go back to church, and he didn't know how to feel about that.

Everything in their little apartment was perfect but the real world was out there, and it wouldn't wait for them forever, wouldn't wait for *Mia* forever and she wouldn't want it to. He'd been in prison where all he had was her, but she'd been out here living a full and happy life. She had friends, family, a faith that was important to her and he wasn't sure suddenly how he would fit into that life, where there would be room for him beside all the other people that she loved.

She came back with a towel draped around her body and her wet hair brushed back away from her face. She looked happy and there was still a soft smile lingering at the corners of her mouth but he felt a hard knot of dread settle into the pit of his stomach.

Chapter Twenty-Eight

The day that Mia had gone back to school had been the day Gabriel found out that an apartment could be just as much of a prison as his old cell.

He'd languished on the couch that day and every day since, his too tall frame forcing him to leave his legs dangling over the arm rest as he flipped through the channels. He'd never been much for TV, that had been Alex's distraction, and he hadn't quite been able to face the box he'd carried out of prison to find his art supplies. It carried too many memories in between the cardboard walls, and he had been afraid that the smell of it alone would somehow take him back there, that he'd wake up and find he was still locked up on the inside and everything that happened since had been nothing but a fanciful dream.

Still, at least the prison had given him a job. A shitty one, but it had helped him pass the time. There was nothing for him to do in Mia's apartment, and even if he'd had a license a quick check of the news every morning had been enough to let them know that his face was still plastered across every channel. They weren't exactly shy about showing Mia, either, from that day at the courthouse, but her part in it had been rendered less important by the stunning verdict and by the time it had hit the national news they'd spent much less time focusing on her.

The few that bothered to mention her painted her as a victim of his manipulations, so they were relatively certain that it was safe for her to go out, that she was less likely to get swept up in an ugly incident if she showed her face in public.

After that morning at Target, he had stayed behind while she went out to get them whatever they needed.

Food.

Dish soap.

Condoms.

Mia's tiny drawer in her bedside table held almost exactly a week's supply at the rate they were using them. A fact that made her blush furiously, but she never turned away when he reached for her, and she'd woken him up more than once with her eyes already wanting and her hand on his dick.

That week had been good for them. Mia had refused to go to work or class, and she hadn't let anyone into the apartment to visit or tried to drag him out to meet her friends or have dinner with her dad. They called, usually several times a day and at odd hours, to check on her, but she remained stubborn about their need for privacy.

It had been a week of bliss, of late-night talks and early morning cuddles and fucking each other senseless on every surface in the apartment.

It had kept him busy—though not so busy that he'd forgotten to call and schedule an appointment with Amy to discuss his trust fund money, and busy meant he hadn't had time to dwell on anything.

Then Mia had gone back to school, leaving him with nothing but his thoughts, the TV, and a cell phone that she'd bought for him so he could call her in class if there was an emergency while she was out. He still hadn't figured out how to use it and his fingers were too big for the buttons.

He was bored and alone.

Lonely.

But not lonely enough to give in to the urge to see or talk to anyone but Mia. She was the only one that had been there for him while he was in, and she was the only one he wanted to see now that he was out.

Amy's assistant had passed along a message when she'd made his appointment for the next week, giving him the contact information for some of the witnesses that had showed up for him at the trial—Michael, Brittany, Vincent. They wanted to keep in touch, now that he was out, but he couldn't find it in him to reach out. He was grateful that they'd come, but bitter about the years that they'd let him suffer in isolation.

This day was no different, and by the time he heard Mia's key slide into the lock, he was restless and frustrated from being trapped in the small apartment.

All of that fell away when he got a good look at her tear-soaked face as she flew into his arms, launching herself at him without bothering to close the front door behind him and nearly knocking him back down onto the couch before he'd fully managed to get his feet under him.

"What happened?"

"They found me," she cried. "On campus. They were waiting for me when I got there, shoving cameras in my face and asking me questions about you. Asking me for interviews. Asking *me* to ask *you* for interviews. It was awful. Campus security had to chase them off the property."

"Shit," he said, tightening his grip on her and trying to nudge the door shut with his foot as she wiped her nose subtly on his T-shirt. "Did they follow you back here?"

"I don't think so," she said with a shake of her head. "I didn't see them when I left campus."

"How did they even find you?" He didn't really expect for her to know the answer, but he couldn't think of anything else to say.

"I don't know for sure," she said, wiping her eyes as she dropped down heavily onto the couch. "But whoever keeps tipping them off seems to know a lot about me. My friends, my school."

"But they don't know where you live," he said, filling in the obvious gap. "So, someone who knows you but not someone close to you."

She nodded and pressed her face into her hands, elbows on her knees as she curled into herself and hiccoughed softly.

"Mia ..." What could he possibly say after everything she'd gone through for him? "I'm sorry. I'm sorry that I've caused you nothing but trouble since the day that first letter came."

She looked up at him, eyes red rimmed and cheeks pink with fury. "That's not all that you've brought me," she said. "You've brought me happiness and love. After all that, one bad day with a bunch of reporters isn't going to make me regret it."

He blinked at her and rubbed a hand over the back of his neck. "Okay, that's fair," he acknowledged. "I just want you to be happy and I would do anything to make sure I wasn't in any way to blame for it when you're not."

She huffed, her pink cheeks puffing as she blew out a frustrated stream of breath. "I know," she agreed. "It's just hard for me to hear you say things like that."

"Sorry," he said, sitting down on the couch beside her and wrapping an arm around her shoulder as she leaned into him. "I want to protect you."

"I don't need protecting," she insisted. "At least not much. I just need you to be on my side with all this, just like always."

"I can do that," he said firmly. "Do you want me to make dinner while you take a nap or something?"

She shook her head. "Can't. We have church tonight. It's Wednesday and I've already missed last week's Bible group and Sunday's sermon. I can't miss it again."

Gabriel stiffened beside her, pulling back to look down at her as she fumbled to put her keys and bag on the coffee table. "Mia," he said, his voice uncertain even to his own ears. "I'm not really comfortable going."

"What?" She turned to look at him, her face puzzled. "I thought you liked my dad?"

"I do but I still—"

She held up a hand, bringing him to a stop. "You don't think my dad is like Richard, do you? Because he isn't. He would never do anything like that."

"I know," he said quickly, trying to placate her long enough to explain himself. "I just don't think I could stand going back into a church."

"You knew this was important to me." Her voice was stiff, lines of conflict scrunched between her brows as she warred with herself. "My friends ... everyone ... they're waiting to meet you."

"I can meet them," he said. "I just can't go to church."

"Okay." She grabbed her keys and her bag off the table after pushing to her feet. Her tone was level, suspiciously so, and she turned her head away and refused to meet his eyes. "I can go by myself. I don't need you to come anyway."

"Mia," he said, reaching her arm and frowning when she shook him off and yanked the door open.

"No," she snapped, hurt and confusion finally spilling over. "You wait till now? Till I'm supposed to be at church in an hour to tell me that you're not going to come and meet the people I care about? After everything else today? *Fuck* this."

He flinched at that, but if she noticed, she didn't

acknowledge it, and it didn't stop her from leaving him alone. The door closed behind her with a final click, and he stood alone in the middle of her small living room thinking he probably shouldn't have taught her to curse.

Mia fumed about it all the way to church, cruising down the small highway that led her back to the familiar turns of her hometown probably just a little faster than was legal or wise. It brought her into town a little earlier than she needed to be and she sat in the church parking lot alone until Lilly pulled into the spot beside her.

"Bad day?" she asked, leaning down beside Mia's window with a worried frown.

"The worst," Mia admitted.

"Come on," Lilly urged, opening the door and pulling her out by her sleeve. "Let's go inside and I'll get you some cookies. My grandma's recipe."

"I love your grandma's cookies," Mia sniffled after they carried in the snacks and supplies. "I could eat a dozen of them."

"I have enough for that," Lilly said, opening a Tupperware bowl and shoving a cookie into Mia's outstretched hand. "But you'll make yourself sick."

"It would be worth it." Lilly's grandma had taught her to make several kinds of Vietnamese desserts, but these honey cookies were Mia's favorite and she shoved half of one into her mouth to keep from crying again.

"What happened?" Lilly asked. And where's Gabriel?"

"He's not coming," Mia said, flopping down in a cracked plastic chair and gesturing aggressively with the remains of her cookie. "He said he didn't think he'd be comfortable in a church! Does he really think that I'd be coming here if it was anything like what he went through?"

Lilly hummed sympathetically and handed Mia another cookie.

"My dad is nothing like Richard," Mia said bitterly. "He isn't even giving you a chance! He knows how much this place means to me." Mia shoved the second cookie in her mouth before she continued, gaining steam as she went. "*And* he didn't tell me he wasn't coming until I was ready to leave, right after I got done crying all over him about getting cornered on campus by reporters."

"Oh, sweetie" Lilly said, setting down the stack of cups she was holding to pull Mia into a tight hug. "Are you okay?"

Fresh tears spilled over as Mia shook her head. "I'd already had the worst day and he just ... He just isn't here," she said. "I probably didn't handle it very well—I *know* I didn't handle it very well—but I was so damn *mad.* It hurt that he'd make me come alone instead of wanting to be part of my life."

"I don't think that's it at all," Lilly said, wiping at Mia's tears with a napkin from the snack table. "He loves you, but he's overwhelmed right now. Church has a lot of bad memories for him, and he might not be ready to face that."

"I know he's overwhelmed but he could have talked to me about it sooner and not after everything that happened today." She looked up at Lilly with a frown. "I just ... I don't understand why we're fighting. It's not like us. We never fight."

"He was in prison," Lilly said with a shrug. "You didn't want to spend the little time you had to talk to him arguing. Now he lives with you and that's different. You can't just hang up the phone and avoid talking about the things that irritate you. You're gonna have to deal with all the problems that you could sweep under the rug before."

"I don't like it," Mia said.

"No one does, but conflict isn't something you can avoid when you have to see each other every day. You're going to disagree about all kinds of things that don't even really make any sense. Did I tell you about the argument I had with Bryce about what kind of toothpaste to keep in our bathroom?"

Mia giggled around a mouthful of cookie. "Who won that one?"

"No one did. We switched to a different kind completely. You have to learn to fight fair and how to compromise." She gave Mia a pointed look. "And how to make up when you've said mean things."

Mia sighed. "I don't think either of us really knows what we're doing here."

"You didn't know how to be a couple while he was in prison at first," Lilly reminded her. "But you figured it out and you did it without any real support from us. Now that he's out it's almost like you two have to start over. You have to learn each other all over again in a different way. It's going to be hard, but this time you'll have all the help I can give you."

"I really love you," Mia said. "Thank you."

"You're welcome," Lilly said. "And I really love you, too."

The good feeling that Mia got from her conversation with Lilly didn't last long. The arrival of the others meant the arrival of curious and judgmental eyes, the worst of which predictably belonged to Mrs. Newberry. Mia's face had been all over the news, so there was no hiding that Gabriel was out and even though she doubted anyone had told the malicious old woman where he was staying, she would have guessed it correctly on her own.

Lilly tried to keep her voice upbeat and the discussions moving as they planned the upcoming Fourth of July picnic, sending supportive and encouraging smiles as often as she could, but it didn't stop Mia's cheeks from burning.

Most of them probably assumed that Gabriel was down

the hall with her father, doing whatever it was that the men did on Wednesdays while the ladies had their Bible club meeting, but they would expect to see him when the meeting was over. When he didn't show up with the other husbands and boyfriends, there would be no way for her to hide that he'd made her come alone.

It shouldn't matter to her what Mrs. Newberry or the others thought. She knew that—she *did*—but even knowing it and understanding why Gabriel felt the way he did about coming with her, didn't dull the hurt or the embarrassment.

She tried to make it to Lilly as quickly as she could after the meeting was over, to say her goodbyes and leave before anyone could stop her or make any comments about Gabriel that she wasn't prepared to deal with, but she found her path blocked almost before she'd had a chance to leave her seat.

"I heard on the television about your young man getting out of jail." Mrs. Newberry's voice was sickeningly sweet, bright to the point of insult. "Congratulations. Of course, the news didn't seem to think it was all that wonderful, what with him being a danger to the community and all."

"He's not dangerous," Mia said bitterly.

Mrs. Newberry nodded, her expression one of forced pity. "I hope not, dear. For your sake as well as the rest of us. Is he here?" She looked around curiously, as though a stranger in a group this size wouldn't have been immediately apparent to everyone.

"No."

"Ah," she said, teeth flashing in a practiced smile. "I'm sure he's probably off talking to your father about wedding plans. Can't live in sin forever, can you?"

Mia snapped her teeth together so hard she was sure that they were on the verge of cracking, forcing her lips to turn up at the corners until her own smile was nearly as blinding and false as Mrs. Newberry's. "He didn't come tonight," she said, surprised at her own polite tone. "As for living in sin ... His dick is big enough to make it worth it."

Mrs. Newberry's jaw dropped, her mouth hanging open comically as she stared silently at Mia.

"And you can tell whoever you want to that I said that," Mia continued in a furious whisper, "because they'll never believe you." She stepped around the still silent Mrs. Newberry and dashed down the hallway and out to her car. She didn't even stop to say goodbye to her father.

It took her three tries to get the door unlocked and her hands were shaking as she put the key in the ignition. She held herself together long enough to leave the parking lot and drive just down the road to the nearest gas station where she parked as far away from the door as she could, put her head down on the steering wheel, and cried.

Chapter Twenty-Nine

Gabriel set his teeth as he watched Mia hurry in the door after class and drop her bag on the couch. He knew she had done nothing to deserve his temper, but it seemed that was all he had to offer her these days outside the bedroom.

The uneasy truce they'd reached the night after she'd come home from attending church the first time without him—when she'd come home still mad and puffy-eyed from crying and thrown herself into his arms to let him soothe her with his mouth and his hands and his body—had held as the weeks began to bleed together, but the strain that their relationship was under, that *he* was under, was becoming more obvious with each passing day.

They'd gotten into another petty argument in Amy's office, surrounded by piles of paperwork that needed to be signed for him to access his trust fund money. Amy had seemed nearly ashamed when she'd had to tell them that Lilah hadn't sent any personal message, just a file with his birth certificate, social security card, and medical records up until he'd been sent to Richard's. It was a blessing, containing all the documents he'd need to start an adult life, but he hadn't even thought of them until he'd seen them and been hit with all the things he didn't know how to do.

He was a grown man, nearly thirty, and he'd never signed his own paperwork or driven his own car.

It had become painfully obvious again at the DMV, waiting in a line for hours while people snuck blatantly hostile glances at him over their shoulders only to discover that he would need a permit to practice driving until he could pass the driving exam. Mia would have to sit with him in the passenger seat, guiding him on the rules of the road and trying not to wince when he cut too close to a parked car. She'd been patient, but he was humiliated and irritable, ashamed that he'd found yet another way to burden her.

The money he knew he'd soon have to give her didn't keep his failures from creeping into his dreams. Mia's face mingled with the women of his past, merging with Brittany's and his mother's, with women whose names he had never known as they swam in and out of his nightmares until he bolted upright in bed and slunk to the kitchen to stare at the time on her microwave as it crept toward dawn. Sometimes she followed him—urging him to come back to bed until he complied or snapped at her with words like daggers that cut them both—but that had become less frequent as his tone became harsh and his eyes bleary from lack of sleep.

She'd gotten more guarded around him, probing his mood before settling in beside him on the couch or telling him about her day. Far too often they ate in silence, his bubbling and impotent fury smothering any words that might have arisen between them. Having the apartment to himself, no matter how lonely, had almost become preferable to the sad confusion in her eyes.

"Will you be okay here by yourself?" she asked, sucking her lip between her teeth as she looked at him.

He knew what she was really asking, the same thing she asked every time she went.

Are you sure you won't come with me?

He answered as he always did, each new string of words always adding up to the same sentiment.

No

"I'll be fine," he said, hating himself as she grimaced at his tone. "Have a nice time."

She nodded, shooting him a weak smile at the barely there attempt at civility that he'd tacked on at the end.

He sat on the couch once she'd gone, his head buried in his hands as the anger faded away and left him with nothing but a hollow hole in the gut carved out of him by the disappointment he'd seen on her face. How had life been easier when he was in prison?

Church had not gotten easier since her last encounter with Mrs. Newberry and Mia crept in late, hoping to avoid being forced to speak to anyone and shrugging a haphazard apology at Lilly as she sank into a seat at the back.

Several heads turned to look at her, their frowns and whispers the only proof she needed that Mrs. Newberry was still spreading word as far and wide as she could about what Mia had said to her. In hindsight, telling the biggest gossip in church that her boyfriend had a big dick might not have been the best decision that she'd ever made but Mia tipped her chin up anyway.

She hadn't had the time to think it through and the whole thing had come at the end of a very bad day. What she'd said couldn't be unsaid, and she refused to let Mrs. Newberry or anyone else make her feel worse than she already did. She was still consistently attending church functions alone, a fact that caused a few more raised brows and suspicious whispers each week.

She always offered, but she knew he wasn't going to come.

Gabriel had been irritable and distant since their fight. He rarely left the apartment even when she was home to help him drive, and he was often out of bed before she woke in the mornings. She wasn't sure how much time he spent actually sleeping at night but the dark circles under his eyes told her that it wasn't enough, and he wasn't willing to discuss whatever nightmares plagued him.

She hadn't expected the transition from prison to be immediate or free of problems, but the longer he was out the more there was an itch under her skin, a thought that ran through her head on an endless loop. It was both frightening and incredibly unhelpful, but she couldn't escape the relentless refrain.

He wasn't adjusting well.

She drummed her fingers on her knee, barely listening to Lilly and the others. She knew it was true, but the way to help him eluded her. Standing with him had been easy when the common enemies had been the prison itself and the state. The bars that had kept them apart were something that Mia could see, the law something that she could understand.

Now the enemy was something else, something far less tangible. It was Gabriel's mind, still carrying his past and all the pain that he'd learned to bury but never learned to live with. It was the skills he didn't have and the life he'd missed and the bitterness that not even her love could fully erase from his heart.

Even after everything, she'd never given up hope, never wavered on her conviction that she was on the path that God had chosen for her—after all, why would God have given her this mountain if it could not be moved?—but she'd believed that the hardest part was behind her. That when he'd walked out of that prison, their lives would get better, and she wouldn't have to be so strong anymore.

Realizing now that getting him out of prison may have actually been the easy part was enough to make her want to scream and rail at the heavens until God answered her and told her why she was the one that had been given the burden of such an impossible love. What had He seen in her, what had He made in her, that she would be the one fashioned to love Gabriel through all these challenges, through all his pain?

It was a question she often wondered about these days and one that inevitably led her back to her own parents. Had they thought that about loving a broken-hearted little girl that had been all skin and bones? One that bit and yelled and hid food in every available crack of her bedroom until the whole thing had smelled of rot? Had they ever thought about giving up when she pushed them away or they'd had to spend yet another afternoon driving her to a doctor or a therapist or another meeting with the caseworker as they tried to adopt a child that they weren't sure would ever be able to love them back?

Mia had forgotten most of that time but some of her earliest memories were of curling up in her mother's lap, surrounded by the smell of home and sweet perfume and listening to another story of how they'd chosen her. How they'd asked for her and fought for her and tried their best every day for her. If they'd ever thought about giving up, she'd never heard them speak of it and she wasn't going to shame them by turning her back on someone who loved her, who needed her. She would not turn her back on the path that God had chosen for her no matter how difficult it was. If there was one thing she knew—that her family had taught her—it was the power of love to change the life of a person and she was counting on that now.

He wasn't adjusting well. That was fine. She'd just have to

keep trying with him until he did. There was no other option for her, no way for her to quit on something that mattered this much.

"You seem distracted today," Lilly said, and Mia jumped, a guilt flush on her cheeks as she realized the meeting had been dismissed and she had been too deep in her thoughts to notice. "Are you okay?"

"I'm fine," Mia said. "Just trying to work some things out in my mind."

"Well, if I was you, I think I'd try and get out of here before Mrs. Newberry corners you again."

"Why? What's happened now?"

Lilly jerked her chin over her shoulder, indicating a little cluster of people near back. "James is in town because his mama isn't feeling well. Rumor has it she's gonna need another surgery soon so he'll be around every few weeks while they're doing all her doctor's appointments and such."

"They?"

"Remember Mrs. Newberry telling us about Emily? His new wife? That's her."

Mia had been too preoccupied to notice the new face in the crowd, but she saw her now. A tall and pretty woman with brown hair that fell around her face in soft waves and a ready smile.

"She looks nice," Mia said with a shrug.

"But Mrs. Newberry isn't, and you know she's going to come running over to point out how lucky James was to end up with her instead of you."

Mia pressed a hand to her temple where a headache was beginning to form. She should be used to this by now but dealing with it never seemed to get easier. "Maybe I can still make it out without her spotting me."

Lilly shook her head. "I think it's too late," she said, shaking her head apologetically. "She was talking to James, snapped him up as soon as he came in looking for Emily, and now they're headed this way."

Mia groaned. It had been a long time since she'd had to deal with James, and it still didn't quite feel like long enough.

"Hey, Lilly, how are you doing?'

Lilly gave James her brightest smile as he joined them and turned her body to shield Mia from his view. "I'm doing fine," she said sweetly. "It's been a long time since you came around and I see you've brought your wife this time. Maybe you can introduce me and tell me about the new church you've got? I hear it's just a few towns over, down the highway."

"It is," he agreed. "I'd be happy to introduce you to Emily."

"It's a shame you two won't be able to meet Mia's ... whatever do you call the man you live with?" Mrs. Newberry faced her with a pasted on puzzled frown.

Mia didn't even pretend to smile, and her voice was flat and unfriendly when she answered. "Gabriel's my boyfriend."

"Oh," James said, looking rapidly between the three women. "I remember seeing something on the news about him getting out of prison, I think. They made things seem ... well ..."

"Right," Mia said quickly, taking a few steps back toward the door. If she left now, she could rob Mrs. Newberry of the opportunity to parade her sins in front of an audience again. "He's waiting for me, so I better go."

"He doesn't come," Mrs. Newberry said to James, leaning in to pass the information along as though they were sharing a secret and letting her voice lilt into something sickly sweet. It was the kind of thing that sounded like concern on the surface but was loaded beneath with pity and condescension.

Mia didn't wait to hear James' response as she turned and hurried from the room, and she didn't give in to the urge to sneak another glance at his wife as she passed. The woman lived the life that might have been hers had things been different, but whatever curiosity she might have felt was buried beneath a mound of shame and frustration.

That feeling stayed with her until she swept into the apartment, door banging roughly on the wall as she tossed it open and swept inside without making eye contact with Gabriel on the couch. She was vibrating with rage, her hands shaking as she replayed the scene at the church over in her mind. She flicked through the stack of mail she'd picked up from the mailbox on her way up, tossing each item across the table with a flick of her wrist. Bills, advertisements, a thick cream envelope addressed in looping feminine script she didn't recognize. She frowned and pulled it from the pile to examine it more closely, momentarily distracted from her anger, but Gabriel pulled it all from her grasp and tossed it on the kitchen table before she could read the name.

"What's wrong?" he asked. "What happened?"

"James *happened*," she said, her voice pitched high and wobbling on each syllable. "Mrs. Newberry *happened*. James was there with his wife and that was all the ammunition Mrs. Newberry needed." She choked down a sob and clung to the anger instead. "It was all she needed to hurt me, to find another opportunity to throw you in my face again."

"What did she say to you?" he asked.

"The same thing she says every time," Mia said. "That if you loved me, you'd be there for me."

"Mia ..."

"I know you love me," she looked up at him through wet lashes, trying to explain with her gaze what she was struggling to put into words, "but it's still hard to do it all alone. I understand why you won't go, but that doesn't change that it hurts when you aren't with me."

"Church is important to you." He stopped, teeth set against the skin of his lip as he, too, tried to find the right words as he weighed his own fears against his urge to support her.

"And so are you," she assured him. "It's just ... It's difficult when the parts of my life that matter the most don't mix and I worry about you. You keep yourself locked in here and I get it, I really do, but you're making our apartment into another prison. You're just sitting and stewing in your thoughts."

"If I've made the apartment a prison for me, then you've let that bitch make church a prison for you."

His assessment hit its target, knocking the breath out of her. Silence stretched between them as she sat on the edge of the couch and dropped her head to her knees.

"You're not the only one who's worried, Mia." He sat beside her and rubbed his hand over her stiff shoulders. "She's not any good for you or that place."

"You could come and chase her away," Mia mumbled. She wanted to argue the point, but she knew he was right. However much her father wanted to give the woman another chance, Mrs. Newberry made the rest of them miserable every chance she got. Maybe it was time they started thinking about the implications of that.

"I'm sorry." He shuddered, his body rocking with the force of it. "I know I'm failing you."

"You aren't." Maybe it would have been easier if he'd shown up and glared at Mrs. Newberry until she ran right out the front door, but was it really his battle to fight? "But even if you were failing me, you wouldn't be the first person or the last. What if I fail you? What if we fail each other and we keep going anyway because we're too stubborn to quit?"

"That does sound like us." He reached for her, tugging her into his arms and resting his chin on her shoulder. "I don't know if I can start with church, but I'll try harder to learn how to live outside the apartment," he said. "You know I love you, don't you?"

"I know," she said. There was still so much that they needed to work out but now that she had calmed down, her body reacted to his proximity as it always did—with want. She could feel the gentle fan of his breath on her neck and the solid muscle of his arm beneath her fingers. The urge to connect, to reaffirm their feelings in the face of their conflict, had her tightening her grip to pull him closer.

"Gabriel ..."

But he had already noticed the change in her breath and the way she leaned into him, and he was lifting her before she could tell him what she needed, carrying her to the bedroom with his mouth on hers. He'd made this walk countless times and he didn't need to see to know where he was going or to find the edge of the bed and lower her onto it.

They'd become practiced and efficient at shedding the layers of their clothing, both of them eager to have the hot slide of skin on skin as quickly as possible, and Mia tugged his shirt over his head in a single smooth motion.

He leaned back against the pillows; his eyes locked on her as she explored the parts of him that she wasn't yet familiar with. She knew what this part of him felt like inside of her, but his hands fisted into her bedsheets as she discovered the taste of it. Her tongue glided over him, learning the texture and the slightly salty tang of his skin. It filled her mouth as well as it filled the rest of her and the sounds he made when she closed her lips around him sent heat curling though her, molten desire turned to fire under her skin.

She lacked the skill to tease him properly and she was probably clumsy, but he didn't complain as she worked her mouth over him, discovering the rhythm and speed that he seemed to enjoy the most. She'd learned enough by now to be able to roll the condom on by herself, a point of pride as she smiled up at him and traced his body with the tips of her fingers.

He helped her line up their bodies so she could sink down onto him, her body opening to take him deeper than she thought he'd ever been. It was thrilling to be filled like this and a roll of her hips told her how much he enjoyed it, too, his eyes fluttering shut and his fingers digging into her skin.

She kept her eyes on his face as she rose and fell above him, each rocking movement met with a thrust of his hips. He'd said she was beautiful but right now, with the thin light of the moon on his skin and his dark hair curling against her pillow as she rode him, she thought he might be the most beautiful thing she'd ever seen. He'd been worth every minute of waiting, every second of worry and when she tipped over the edge into ecstasy with him buried inside, she thought she'd been right after all.

Maybe his dick really was worth the damnation that Mrs. Newberry kept threatening her with.

Chapter Thirty

Fall

"You don't have to come in," Mia said, tapping her fingers in the steering wheel and staring out the windshield at the doors of the church. Gabriel had been working hard on trying to get out of the house more for weeks, but she'd still been caught off guard when he'd announced he wanted to come to church with her for her father's birthday celebration.

"Did you tell them that I'd be there?"

"I said you *might* be there, but I wasn't sure if you'd change your mind, so I didn't make any promises."

He was silent for a moment as he looked out the window at the small building with its faded brick and old windows. He smiled, faint and ghosting across his face so quickly she almost missed it. "This doesn't look anything like the church my mother took me to as a kid, or the place Richard preached when he wasn't at the school with us. This place looks comfortable and those were big and cold and impersonal.

Hundreds of people in expensive clothes hoping to pay their way to forgiveness."

"We don't have any of that here," she said with a shrug. "I've seen videos of Richard preaching and it looked more like a football stadium in there."

"It did," he agreed, and she knew he was acknowledging that on some level things were different here than what he'd feared. "I don't know that I'll ever believe what you do, but I'm coming with you, at least this time."

"If it gets to be too much—" she began, but he leaned across the console and caught her mouth in a quick kiss.

"I'll let you know," he said simply.

"Okay." She tugged him in for another quick kiss before she opened the car door, trying to show as much of gratitude and love as possible in a few fleeting seconds. There would be time for more later, but for now that would have to do.

He was pale as he followed her inside, but the hallway was empty as she led him past the entrance to the chapel with its tidy rows of pews and then the little kitchen where they did their preparations for picnics and parties like this one. She paused by the meeting room and brushed a dark curl off his brow. "Are you sure?"

"I'm sure," he insisted. He was clearly fighting the urge to bolt, and his hand was cold and clammy where it gripped hers. "I can do this for you."

She pulled him in for a quick kiss, her lips brushing his as more of a suggestion than a caress as guilt of kissing her boyfriend in church warred with her desire to comfort him. Somehow knowing what they did when they were alone in their apartment seemed worse when he was with her than it had in the all the time she'd been coming here alone.

"We'll do our best to make sure you're comfortable," she promised.

He nodded and gave her a ghost of a smile as he followed her into the room. Heads turned but he stayed by her, holding her fingers in a death grip as she searched the crowd for her father.

They found him talking to a small group of parishioners and bouncing a toddler on his hip.

"Mia!"

"Hey Dad," she gave him a quick hug. "Just wanted to let you know we're here before we find a place to sit down."

"I'm glad you came." He shook Gabriel's hand and gestured to the rows of tables laden with bowls and trays. "There's still plenty of food so make sure you grab some once you're settled."

"We will," Mia promised. There weren't many seats left but she finally found an empty section and turned to ask Gabriel if he'd like to make a plate only to find him staring curiously back at her father.

"Your dad's good with children," he mused.

"Hmm," she acknowledged. "He loves kids, always wanted grandkids."

"Has he?" Gabriel asked quietly.

Mia met his eyes, heat rushing to her cheeks. "Sure, eventually. Maybe. Someday. Not right away or anything probably ..."

"We never really talked about that, did we?"

"No," she agreed. The closest they'd come was the first day he'd gotten out, when she'd told him she wasn't on birth control. That was something she really should have taken care of by now, but there always seemed to be something else that was more important. "Everything seemed so far away, even after we found out it was possible and then it happened so fast."

He nodded and drummed his fingers on the fancy white tablecloth. "Do you? Want a family?"

"Yeah," she said, watching her dad hand back the

squirming toddler before glancing at Gabriel. "I've always wanted kids."

He didn't flinch away from the revelation like she'd feared he might, and his face was pensive as he considered her words. "Me, too," he said finally. "I wasn't always sure I would—not with the way things were with my parents and after what happened to Brittany—but I think ... I think I might want to try. Someday. I don't know if I have what it takes to be a good dad but ..."

"You're going to be a great father," she said. "How could you not be?"

"I'm still pretty messed up," he said and as much as she loved him, as much as she knew he would love his child, she knew he was right.

"Law school takes a while so maybe by then things will be more settled," she said lightly, lifting her shoulder in a shrug "And if not ... well, I would like to be a mom but not having kids isn't a deal breaker for me."

"Do you have a deal breaker?"

"Hmm," she said, tapping her chin and pretending to think it over, desperate to erase the look of sadness and self-condemnation in his eyes. "Maybe if you start to snore really loudly? Or male pattern baldness?"

He blinked at her for a moment before he cracked a small smile and ran a hand through his hair, tugging on the thick black waves. "Hey, don't even *mention* male pattern baldness."

"You never know ..."

Gabriel opened his mouth, but Mia was spared his retaliation as Kennedy made her way to the table and slid into a seat beside Mia.

"There you are," Mia said. "I wasn't sure you were still going to come. Sorry Alison couldn't make it. Is she feeling sick?"

Kennedy glanced over her shoulder and lowered her voice.

"She's not actually sick. We broke up earlier this week and she moved out of the apartment."

"What?" Mia looked around when she realized how loudly the question had been when it exploded out of her." She lowered her voice and leaned in closer. "Why didn't you say anything? Are you okay?"

Kennedy smiled and nodded. "Yeah, I'm okay. I'm actually the one that ended it."

"Really?" Mia squeezed Kennedy's hand as she tried to remember if there had been any signs that things between the two of them were strained.

"I loved her," Kennedy explained, "but we just ... We got together so fast after everything happened with my parents. One day I was living with them and couldn't even be open about who I was and the next I was in a committed relationship. I never thought about what I wanted out of life or if we had the same goals, wanted the same things. When I did start to think about it, I realized I couldn't answer that question because I didn't know what I wanted."

It reminded Mia of her feelings about James so long ago and how caught up she had been in what she had thought she was supposed to want. It had been painful to examine whether she might want something else instead.

"We're still friends," Kennedy continued. "I don't think she was heartbroken or anything. Maybe we had both been slowly figuring out that we weren't a great match for each other romantically."

"You have plenty of time," Mia said. "Take as much of it as you need to figure out who you are and what you want to do."

"I know it isn't too late but I'm only just now realizing how much what my parents did set me back in life. I had to learn to love myself, figure out who I actually am, so I can be ready to love others."

"We'll love and support you while you figure it all out," Mia promised.

Kennedy picked at her plate as her eyes roamed over the crowd. "I see you finally got Gabriel here, but where's Mrs. Newberry? Or did he already run her off?"

Mia rolled her eyes. "She's on vacation. I'm as glad as anyone that she's gone but *of course* she'd choose to be gone the first time Gabriel decided to come."

"If it was possible, I'd believe she did it on purpose."

Mia would have believed it, too, but truthfully, as much as she wanted Mrs. Newberry to stop making snide comments about Gabriel's lack of attendance, she didn't want him exposed to her cruelty. It was undoubtedly for the best that she wasn't anywhere near him. Especially when she realized he'd gotten up to get another drink and hadn't come back. If Mrs. Newberry had been there, she would have cornered him before Mia knew he was missing.

She found him outside, alone and isolated as he leaned against the wall and looked over the small flower bed with its fading summer blooms. Undeniably handsome in his crisp white shirt, he still gave every impression of a man that was on the verge of bursting at the seams. He'd been restless since he got out, understandably so, but it had gotten worse since the arrival of the letter from Lilah.

She'd forgotten about it entirely the night it had arrived, hadn't had time to read the name before Gabriel had tossed it onto the table and it had been out of sight, out of mind. His lips had been pressed into a thin line of rage when she'd found him sitting at the table the next morning with his coffee in one hand and a letter from his mother in the other. "It's from Lilah," he'd said flatly, waving around the unopened envelope.

"Are you going to open it?"

He'd shaken his head and ripped the thick cream paper, filling their small kitchen with the sound of condemnation.

"Where was she," he asked, "when I needed her most? All my life she gave me money instead of time, instead of support or forgiveness or even love. Fuck my mother."

Mia had only nodded and curled up in his lap, her hand resting over his pounding heart, but his anger—already a problem for them as he tried to adjust to his new life—had only gotten worse, as had his nightmares.

As much as Mia had always wanted Lilah to be the mother that Gabriel deserved, she had begun to wish that the letter had never come. Far from being helpful, it seemed to be making everything worse. Another challenge was the last thing that they needed right now. Gabriel's trust fund had taken the material worries off their shoulders, but it would have been a lie to say that the money had been enough to make anything easy for them.

Gabriel was the partner of her life and the love of her heart, but he was far from healed.

"Hey," she said quietly. "Mind if I join you?"

He shook his head and made room for her at the railing. "I wasn't hiding," he said, "I was just ..." He waved a hand at the party inside. It was a scene of love and laughter and community ...one that he still didn't feel like he was truly part of, she knew. He probably wasn't, truth be told, because he'd lost so much time while the world went on without him.

She sighed and stepped closer, nudging at his arm until he opened his embrace for her to curl into. "Are you ready to go home?"

"I'm sorry ..."

"Don't apologize," she said. "You tried and I can't ask for more."

He stood and held her for another minute, and she didn't think that she imagined the wistfulness of his sigh. He wanted to stay, wanted to be a part of life, but it remained stubbornly just out of his reach.

Chapter Thirty-One

Six weeks after the arrival of her first letter, Lilah knocked on the door of their apartment.

Mia had just enough time to regret her recent life choices in the brief moment between opening the door to find her standing on their welcome mat looking every inch a US senator in a cream-colored suit and hearing Gabriel suck in a furious breath as he appeared at her elbow and found his mother waiting for him. They should have sent a letter back telling Lilah to leave them alone, or she could have called to request it personally. Anything to keep her from showing up unexpectedly and pulling all of Gabriel's issues to the surface with no warning.

Her fingers tightened on the doorknob, and she wondered for one wild second if she could simply close the door in Lilah's face and act like it hadn't happened, simply turn to Gabriel and pretend she hadn't recognized his mother from all the news articles and TV stories. Panicked laughter caught in her throat at the thought of trying to convince him that it had been nothing more than an overly dressed saleswoman.

"Hello Mia," Lilah said, and then, her gaze sliding over Mia's shoulder, "Gabriel."

There was a beat of unbearable silence.

"Senator Miller," Mia said through stiff lips. Her hands were cold and her head was buzzing as she tried to ignore how absolutely rigid and still Gabriel was as he stood behind her. "What a surprise."

"Is it?" Lilah asked. "I sent letters."

"I didn't open them," Gabriel said, his voice this dark and dangerous. "I have nothing to say to you."

"No? Perhaps you might be willing to just listen," Lilah said, and Mia was too stunned to stop her as she brushed both of them aside and stepped into the living room, followed closely by two imposing bodyguards that must have been standing just out of sight outside.

"Please," Mia said dryly, "come in."

If Lilah noticed the sarcasm, she didn't give any indication as she looked around the small living room and the dining room table piled high with Mia's various textbooks and notebooks. She picked an invisible piece of lint from her sleeve as she surveyed the mess, but Mia refused to apologize for the state of the apartment. The new semester was already in full swing, and she had papers to write and exams to study for—if Lilah wanted to visit when things were tidy, she should have waited for an invitation.

"I was afraid you might not be here," Lilah said, turning away from her inspection of her son's home and facing him directly. "I assumed you'd move into something a little more appropriate once you had access to your trust fund."

"It's more appropriate than a prison cell," he said pointedly.

"You intend to stay here indefinitely then?"

"That's none of your business," Gabriel said. Every line of his body was taut with barely controlled rage. The truth was that they were waiting to move until Mia had been accepted into a law school, but he clearly didn't want his mother to know she'd be able to find them here.

"Gabriel, please," his mother said, her tone maternal and condescending and her grip in her purse straps turning her knuckles white. "I don't understand this hostility. Didn't I pay for your lawyers? Made sure you had access to the money your grandfather set aside for you?"

"Did you ever call? Write to me? Do anything to make sure I was okay at all? You've always been this way, thinking money was enough to fix everything and it never was, not once."

Lilah took a deep breath, her smile tight. "I did not," she admitted. "I was angry about ... about what happened with your father."

"And you blamed me," Gabriel said. "I was so young ..."

"You stabbed him," Lilah said, the last word catching on a sob that she struggled to swallow down. "He was my husband and I lost him."

"He was my father," Gabriel reminded her. "I lost him, too."

"You didn't lose him! You were the one that took him away from me!" Lilah wiped furiously at her cheeks as the tears began to flow. "I had to bury him knowing it was because of our own child."

"And you never bothered to ask why," Gabriel said. He was pacing now, his fingers digging groves in the dark waves of his hair. "Didn't you care? Didn't you ever wonder what had happened that could cause someone to do that to their own father?"

"You were always an angry child ..." Lilah began but Gabriel's harsh laugh cut her off.

"So you sent me to Richard," he reminded her. "Did you read the reports, Mother? Did you see what he did to us?"

"Yes," she admitted. "I didn't know about any of that."

"How could you not have known? How could you have been so eager to blame me and so willing to look the other way for him?"

Lilah rubbed her temples and looked at Mia with beseeching eyes. "Richard always presented himself as a good man, a Godly man, someone that you could trust. You know what it's like, don't you? There are certain people in your life that you should be able to trust. Doctors, teachers, preachers ... and Richard, he was so much more than that."

"He was a monster hiding behind a mask of faith."

"He lost his way."

"Lost his way?" Gabriel asked bitterly. "You know what he did to me, what he did to all the other kids that were forced to stay with him."

"Yes," Lilah said, "and instead of telling us what was happening or coming home when you ran away, you lived on the streets. Was that any better?"

"No," he said, his hands curling and uncurling at his sides as Lilah's bodyguards shifted restlessly. "But you already knew that, didn't you? You read those reports, too."

"You should have come home," she said. "If you had come home—"

"What? I wouldn't have been sold to the person with the most money in their pocket? I wouldn't have killed Hugh?"

"If you had let me help you, if you had told me what Richard was doing ..."

"That's bullshit," he snarled. "Fuck that. If I had told you what was happening, ran home to you expecting you to save me, you would have sent me back."

"Gabriel—"

"Don' t lie," he said. "For once in your life, be honest with yourself. You know how much shit I lied about before you sent me away—the drinking and the drugs and the partying. Richard knew it, too. If I'd come to you then and told you what was happening, if it came down to my word against Richard Miller's, who would you have believed?"

Lilah sighed wordlessly and fresh tears sparkled on her lashes, but Gabriel made no move to comfort her. She looked suddenly small and frail, much older than she'd been when she'd arrived as though she'd lost control unexpectedly and it had aged her. "I'm sorry," she said quietly, and Mia thought that the admission had cost her a great deal. She didn't seem like the kind of person to whom an apology would come easily.

"That's not enough," Gabriel said. "Do you think an apology is enough for everything that happened to me?"

Lilah tipped her chin up, her lips trembling. "Have you ever done even that much for killing your father?"

"Get out," Gabriel said flatly. "Get out and don't come back."

For a moment Mia thought Lilah might break, that the sadness in her eyes might be enough for her to let go of her grip on her pride and beg for forgiveness, but whatever emotion had been on her face was soon wrestled into submission. "Very well," she said crisply. "I had hoped ... Well, I suppose it doesn't matter what I'd hoped."

"No," Gabriel agreed. "It doesn't."

Lilah paused in the doorway. "Have a good life, Gabriel. I wish you happiness and whatever peace you can find."

He followed her out, watching as she began to descend the stairs with her bodyguards close behind and then slamming the door and turning on Mia where she still stood at the edge of the dining room.

"I can't believe she had the nerve to come here after everything," he said. His eyes were wild, a lifetime of hurt and anger suddenly pulled from the depths with nowhere to go. "What the fuck did she expect was going to happen? That I'd just pretend all these years hadn't happened?"

"I don't know what she expected," Mia said. "I know you're upset but—"

"She just shows up here, pushes her way into my home, and tells me I'm the one that needs to apologize."

"Gabriel," Mia said, trying to get close enough to pull him into a calming embrace. "She's gone now."

"She's always been gone." He brushed by Mia and pushed both hands through his hair. "I wanted her to leave and now I'm pissed that she left. She can't just do this to me god *damn* it," he growled, his fury exploding as his fist darted out and smashed through the dining room wall.

Mia jumped at the sound and took a few quick steps back, her back bumping against the front door as she stared at him with wide eyes. He'd been on edge since Lilah's first letter had arrived and she'd seen him lost in his nightmares before, but she'd never feared what he might do until this moment.

He swung around to face her, knuckles scraped and bloody, and paled when he saw her face and her hand gripping the door. He held his hands up, palms facing her in a gesture of surrender and shook his head helplessly, as though he was trying to clear it of whatever emotions had taken him over or deny the brief flare of fear she knew he'd been able to read in her eyes. "I'm sorry," he said. "Damn it, Mia, I'm so sorry. I didn't ... I would never scare you, not on purpose."

"I know." Her legs shook beneath her, and she sank to the floor, her back pressed against the door and her forehead pressed to her knees.

"Mia?"

The first sob wrenched itself from her chest, deep and agonized as she curled around herself, tightened herself into a protective ball with her arms wrapped around her torso. There was no way to hide it now, no way to tuck it away and keep the smile pasted on her face. She'd sworn to herself she'd never give up on him, but neither could she watch him continue to go on as he was. They had both done their best, but they didn't have the tools they needed to overcome all their challenges alone.

She heard him hit his knees beside her, his touch hesitant as he pushed her hair out of the way and tried to peer under her arms to her face. "Mia?" He was a supplicant, tears clogging his voice as he waited for her to respond. "I'm so sorry, please, I didn't—"

He opened his arms, his words faltering, and she crawled into his lap. They sat together on the floor, both of them crying as the tension that had accumulated over the weeks since his release finally became more than they could handle. So many things had come between them, and it was more than they could bear.

"I love you," he said when her tears had finally exhausted themselves and she sat quietly hiccupping with her face pressed into his neck.

"I know," she promised. The skin beneath her lips tasted of her own salty tears when she pressed a soft reassuring kiss there, his muscles jumping beneath her touch. "I can't do this anymore."

He froze, unnatural stillness followed by gentle quivering. "Please—"

"No," she hurried, pulling him in for a kiss. "I don't mean like that. I just mean, we need help. We don't know what we're doing, and we need someone to help us figure it out."

He relaxed again, buried his face in her hair. "I can't lose you. I'll do whatever you want, whatever you think we need to do."

Chapter Thirty-Two

Winter

D r. Lucas' office was quiet and relaxing and there was never any pressure to talk about a particular subject. With no set agenda, Gabriel began by talking about the easy topics, about Mia and how much he loved her. How much he worried that he was too damaged to keep her. It seemed natural after that to talk about his fears and why he had them. Weeks passed slowly and he began to feel calmer, more able to engage with people in the world without the panic and guilt that had always swallowed him before.

"Things have gotten better since you started coming here?"

Gabriel shrugged, bouncing his knee to give release to some of his restless energy. The office was comfortable enough —quiet, with soothing blue walls and plush chairs—but it wasn't always enough to settle his nerves. "The nightmares have gotten better, less frequent."

"That's good," Dr. Lucas said. "Is there anything that hasn't gotten better?"

"The anxiety," Gabriel said immediately. "The guilt."

"Anxiety about being out of prison?"

"Some of it," Gabriel agreed. "But also about Mia."

"Are you two still struggling?"

"Not as much now."

"That's encouraging," Dr. Lucas said, his head tipping to the side as he made a short note in Gabriel's file. "What about the guilt?"

Gabriel pushed a hand through his hair and puffed out a harsh breath. "What if I'm not good enough for her? I might be a bad husband, or a bad father and she wants a family. She says she can wait, that she's happy, but I can tell she wants it more than she's willing to even admit to herself. I might ruin her life and I've done enough of that."

"How so?" Dr. Lucas was patient, eyes on the pad and his face impassive. No judgment here, no condemnation for the things Gabriel had done.

"I failed so many people," Gabriel admitted. "People I left behind at Richard's, at Seth's, they suffered because I couldn't figure out how to get them out and then, somehow, I'm the one who gets out of prison? Better people than me are still in there. I couldn't even stop what was happening to me, to the others. They got away with it."

"Who did?"

"Richard, Seth, everyone who helped them or covered up for them."

"And you think you should have prevented them from getting away with it?"

Gabriel stared at Dr. Lucas, at the trim gray beard and unflinching eyes. It made him restless and itchy under the skin, like there was some conclusion that he was meant to reach that remained just out of touch. "Someone should have," he said. "Someone should have done something, and they didn't."

"Yes, but should their failures put the burden on you? You had no power in those situations, and the fault there does not belong to you."

"It doesn't change the need to do something," Gabriel insisted. He wanted to get up and run out of the office. To escape to somewhere far away and never think about any of this ever again. It was the image of Mia crying on the floor of their apartment that kept him in his seat. "I can't live with this helplessness and the anger."

"I understand that you feel helpless and frustrated about what you couldn't change from the past, but you have power now," Dr. Lucas said. "You have power to take care of the people you care about and even the power to help others the way you should have been helped. It's something to think about."

Gabriel nodded stiffly but his mind was already hard at work figuring out what that meant for him. What it might mean for his future and for Mia's.

"Are you still struggling with your faith?" Dr. Lucas continued. He sipped from a can of diet Coke and peered at Gabriel over the rim as he waited for an answer.

"There's no struggle with my faith," Gabriel said. "Mia believes and I don't but it's not a problem for us."

"You don't have any challenges supporting her in her beliefs?"

"Not anymore," Gabriel said. "It used to but now I'm able to go to church with her for events and special occasions."

"Her father being a pastor doesn't bother you?"

"I don't think about it much anymore." Gabriel was a bit stunned at the realization that it was true. "He's nothing like Richard—he doesn't weaponize his authority and he stands up for the vulnerable people in his community, so we get along."

"That all sounds like significant progress for you."

"Yes," Gabriel agreed. "It does."

"Have you talked to any of the others?" Dr. Lucas asked.

"The others?"

"The people that were with you at Richard and Seth's?"

"They've reached out to me," Gabriel admitted, "but I never responded."

"Why is that?"

"What if they blame me for not doing more?" Seeing them at the trial had been almost more than he could stand, and they hadn't been able to talk to him directly. How would he have been able to deal with it if they could have leveled their eyes on him and demanded he account for his failures? "I don't know if I could handle that."

"They helped you at your trial," Dr. Lucas reminded him. "You share a unique bond with them, a shared history, and they may have already had a chance to walk the healing road that you're on now."

"So ... what? You think they might have advice for me?"

"Talking about it might help, with or without advice, but it's possible."

"Hmm."

"You deserve to live a full life and reach for the things that make you happy. Whatever you decide, it's important that you remember that no one else has control of you now. Not your parents, not Richard or Seth, and not the guards at the prison. You're the one in a position of power in your own life now."

Gabriel didn't know what to say to that. All he'd wanted in prison was the ability to make decisions for himself, to live on his own terms. Now he had it, and he had to decide what to do with it. He tapped his fingers on his knee and watched the clock tick toward the end of his hour.

~

"Isn't that right, Mia?"

"Hmm?"

Lilly looked at her curiously and gestured to James' wife, Emily. "I said, it's nice that they were able to come this week."

"Oh," Mia said, sitting up straighter in her chair and trying to drag her attention back to the conversation. "Yes, it's great to have visitors."

Mia had a lot on her mind, and it was hard to concentrate on what they were saying but Emily was soft spoken and had a sweet, patient smile that seemed to put everyone around her at ease immediately. It was obvious that Lilly liked her, and James seemed to treat her well. Mia knew she'd made the right choice in not binding herself to a lifestyle that would never have let her be fulfilled, but she was glad that Emily seemed happy.

"James used to come around quite a bit so it's good to see him back," Lilly agreed.

Mia nodded but she couldn't quite make herself agree with that out loud. "How did Mrs. Prescott's surgery go?" she asked instead.

"It went well," Emily said, her face brightening as her husband came into the room. "She's been very sweet to me since I married James and I'm glad that God watched over her."

"She's a kind woman," Mia agreed.

"Mia," James said as he crossed the room to Emily's side. "I see you've met Emily."

"Yes," Mia agreed. "I don't think I ever congratulated you on the wedding. You make a lovely couple."

"It's nice to see you again," James said. He said it hesitantly and the harsh words they'd exchanged the last time they'd really spoken to one another hung heavy between them.

She might talk to her father about guiding him into a

better way to handle his parishioners, to prevent him from hurting another woman the way he'd hurt her, but she wasn't going to embarrass him in front of his new wife. Maybe he deserved it, but they'd both found what they were looking for and she didn't want to hold that grudge anymore.

"It was nice to see you, too," Mia agreed.

"I know we haven't always gotten along and I'm sorry about that," he hesitated and looked around uncomfortably, "but I just overheard some pretty unpleasant things Mrs. Newberry was saying about you. She didn't seem to think she needed to keep her voice down around me, and maybe I'm not the right person to have said anything, but I think you deserve to know."

"What did she say?" Mia narrowed her eyes, already feeling the blood start to rush. She'd had enough of this. Mrs. Newberry had kept her distance since she'd found out Gabriel had come with her the first time, and an ever greater one once she'd gotten a good look at his size and scowling face the second time he'd come, but obviously he was right. She was never going to stop unless someone stopped her.

"She said that Gabriel should be ashamed of himself for taking advantage of an innocent young girl. That you were going to hell, and it would all be his fault." He looked like he had more to say but Mia was beyond listening. It was time they had this confrontation and there was no better place than right here, right now.

"I'll be right back," she said, only vaguely aware that she'd spoken, her body hot and vibrating with emotion.

"Mia?"

She didn't respond, her head swiveling as she prowled toward the dessert table. Mrs. Newberry had just been there a moment before—she couldn't have gone far. Mia had covered only half the distance between James and the dessert table when she spotted a head of perfectly styled, blonde hair. Her fingers twitched with the urge to reach out and yank it as hard as she was able, but she took a deep breath, prepared to keep her assault a purely verbal one, when a few words of what Mrs. Newberry was saying reached her.

"... actually thinks she's doing a good job helping to run the group! If it wasn't for her suggesting the prison program in the first place, poor Mia wouldn't be in this position. I've said all along that this was going to happen, haven't I?"

The heat in Mia's blood ran cold, the rage that had burned inside her freezing into a cold sense of purpose. Her mind and heart stilled, and her voice was almost pleasant as she asked, "Who put me in this position?"

Mrs. Newberry jumped, a guilty flush on her face as she spun around to find Mia smiling at her, the grin all teeth and no mercy. "I'm sorry?" she asked. "I'm afraid I don't understand ..."

"You're not sorry," Mia said. "Not yet, but you will be."

"Are you threatening—"

"Not at all," Mia said. "We're well beyond the need for threats."

The crowd around them shifted uneasily and Mia knew they were gathering a watchful audience. Lilly was approaching from across the room with Mrs. Mitchell close behind, both of their faces creased with worry, but there was no going back now.

"You can't say these things to me," Mrs. Newberry sniffed. "I'm a parishioner at this church. My family has donated—"

"Absolutely no one here gives a shit," Mia said, interrupting her again just to watch her mouth open and close on her silent outrage. Several onlookers covered their mouths with their hands as though trying to smother a laugh and no one at all seemed inclined to speak up on Mrs. Newberry's behalf.

"Mia, what is going on?" Lilly asked, stepping between the

two women and looking from one to the other like a teacher on a kindergarten playground. "You two know better than to do this here."

Mrs. Newberry's smile faltered when Mia stepped in close and whispered a few words in Lilly's ear. She'd been able to manipulate her way around any real repercussions for so long that the cold look that passed over Lilly's face must have come as quite a surprise.

"So," Lilly said. "Mia told me what happened and she's clearly on the edge of doing something very unpleasant right here in the middle of our Bible group. Fortunately for you, I don't agree with that."

Mrs. Newberry smirked at Mia over Lilly's shoulder. "I knew you'd realize how unreasonable she was being. I thought she was going to attack me, and you have no idea how frightened I was."

Lilly smiled back, and Mia had known her long enough to recognize the look and its implications. "I've got something much better in mind for you," she said, her voice dripping with sugar sweetness. "Go home and don't come back."

"What?" Mrs. Newberry looked from Lilly to Mia desperately. "You can't do that!" Mrs. Newberry said wildly, turning to face the group of onlookers that formed a tight ring around the action.

"I can," Mrs. Mitchell said loudly, and every head turned to stare with open mouths at the small woman as she pushed her thick glasses back up her nose. "You've done nothing for this church that hasn't been to make it worse and, if we're all being fair and honest, we should have kicked you out a long time ago."

"You can't," Mrs. Newberry repeated, her voice rising as though loudness might make them all change their minds. "You can't do this to me."

"I've had conversations with Mia about returning you to

the flock, but you are not a lost lamb. You are a wolf in sheep's clothing. I will protect the people in this church that depend on us to keep them safe."

"Which is what I should have done a long time ago," Mia said, squeezing Lilly's hand in silent apology.

"You've been nothing but a bully to all of us," Lilly added.

"I am not," Mrs. Newberry screeched. "You have no proof!"

"I have no proof that you were the one leaking information about my relationship with Gabriel to the media, either, but we all know it's true."

"I'll go to your father," Mrs. Newberry said, her lips thin and triumphant. "I'll tell him what you did to me today."

"And I'll tell him what you said to me and to Gabriel," Mia retorted. "I'll tell him that you stood in the house of God and spoke cruelly about Lilly because you're a bigot and a bitch."

"You're nothing but that criminal's whore."

"And you," Lilly said, her voice brimming with authority, "are no longer welcome here."

Mrs. Newberry looked around the room for support but was met with only disapproving frowns. Perhaps some of them might have stood with her privately, but they were not brave enough to speak it now in front of so many.

"Go," Mia demanded.

Mrs. Newberry grabbed her purse off one of the nearby chairs and pushed toward the door, knocking aside anyone who was too slow to move out of her way and nearly knocking Bryce over as he entered the room with Pastor Anderson.

"What the ..." Bryce exclaimed. "What happened here?"

"Taking out the trash," Mrs. Mitchell said. "And it was long overdue."

"Was that Mrs. Newberry?" Pastor Anderson asked.

"It was," Mia acknowledged. She sank down into a chair

and smiled up at Lilly thinly when she passed a bottle of water into her shaking hands. "She's not going to be coming back."

"It was time," Lilly said with an unapologetic shrug. "She's made everything as difficult for us as possible for too long. I wanted the chance to prove myself, to give *her* the chance to be a better person, but that's obviously not going to happen."

"She was just biding her time," Mia said. "We gave her enough chances—probably too many. I should never have asked you if you wanted me to kick her out. I shouldn't have put the burden of that decision on you, made you have to be the one to speak up. As soon as I saw her for what she was, I should have told her to leave."

Lilly's eyes were wet with unshed tears as she pulled Mia in for a tight hug. "We all did the best we could," she said. "Next time our best will be better."

"I can't believe I did that," Mia grumbled as she walked into their apartment. She was still riding high on the rush of adrenaline and couldn't stop smiling.

"Did what?"

Gabriel listened with rapt attention as she explained the events of the evening. "Wait, what did you say to her that had her so upset a few weeks ago anyway?'

"I told her you had a big dick," Mia mumbled.

Gabriel laughed as she hid her face in her hands.

"I think she was mad that I wasn't afraid of her anymore." Mia mused.

"She's exactly like Richard," he countered. "She's mean and spiteful to those she can hurt and a smiling face when the world is looking. She uses people and their faith to her own advantage because she's cruel."

"I needed to stand up to her."

"It was time and I'm so proud of you."

She shivered at the praise and kissed him softly as she grasped his shirt by the hem and lifted until he helped her guide it over his head, then pressed another kiss to his chest.

His eyes widened as she sank to her knees, pressing a lingering kiss to the skin just above his waistband, where a trail of dark hair ran from just below his navel to disappear under the fabric of his slacks. He flinched, his skin jumping in surprise when she followed the kiss with a small, painless bite.

"I love you." His voice was strangled and when she found the courage to look up at him, he was watching her with a reverent expression that she'd only ever seen before on the faces of her father's congregation when they were lost in the rapturous love of God.

"I love you, too," she said, suddenly embarrassed at the intensity of his gaze as she struggled to undo the buttons of his slacks.

"Fuck it," he said roughly, pulling her to her feet and then up into his arms as he crushed her mouth under his and carried her to the bedroom.

"Hey," she protested. "I was doing something."

"I saw that, and it was hot," he said as he laid on the bed and began to strip the clothes from her body as quickly and efficiently as possible. "You can do it again later."

She laughed as he nipped softly at her shoulder and threw her bra across the room. "I didn't even do anything."

"You looked incredible," he argued. "Fucking breathtaking on your knees like that."

"Maybe next time I'll actually get my mouth on you."

He groaned and buried his face in her stomach. "You're gonna be beautiful but that's not what I need right now."

"No?" she asked and let her knees fall open, letting him see that she was already wet and ready for him.

"Mia," he breathed. "Have I told you how perfect you are?"

"Once or twice," she teased. "Tell me again."

"Fucking perfect," he said, pushing his pants off over his hips and starting to kiss his way up her legs. "The most beautiful thing I've ever seen."

The awkwardness of their first time was a long-forgotten thing of the past as he moved over her and pushed them both closer to the edge of oblivion with each thrust. When she shattered, her body felt like it carried more than just pleasure beneath the surface of her skin. It was belonging and certainty and home.

Chapter Thirty-Three

Spring

"You're thinking about your father?"

Gabriel nodded. "My father. My mother. I just wonder if they really loved me. I think about all the ways I could make mistakes if I ever become a father, the things I could say or do to mess up a relationship and it seems so endless."

"Parenting is a difficult job," Dr. Lucas agreed. "You still haven't spoken to your mother?"

"Not since she came to the apartment, and we were both pissed off then."

"You said before that you felt like she betrayed you. Do you still feel that way?"

"Yes," Gabriel said, then shook his head. "No? Sometimes I do and then I think, how would I feel if my child ever hurt Mia? I can't imagine it. Can't imagine what I'd do."

"Is that part of why you're worried about starting a family with Mia?" Dr. Lucas asked.

"I'm afraid I won't be a good father because my parents

were distant." Distant was a weak word for what he'd experienced but even now it felt like a further betrayal to tell his therapist that they had been neglectful and emotionally absent. "I don't think either of them had good relationships with their parents, either."

"You're breaking that cycle and learning to have healthy relationships." Dr. Lucas tapped his pen on his knee as he flipped through the pages of notes he'd taken during their session. "I'd say you've mentioned children at least every time we've spoken, so it seems that you and Mia want a family of your own. Perhaps you'd feel better about parenting if you healed the wounds with your own mother."

"You want me to talk to Lilah?"

"I think it's possible that it will help you move on from the past."

Maybe it was, but that was still far from a guarantee, and he wasn't sure how Mia would feel about the whole thing. Especially not after what had happened the last time he'd seen his mother.

"He wants me to talk to Lilah." Gabriel told her the next day as he stood at the counter in their kitchen and waited for his morning coffee to brew. His announcement was met with silence, and he turned back to Mia, unsure if she'd heard him.

She watched him with a crease of worry between her brows. "Is that a good idea?" she asked finally.

"I don't know," he admitted. "He thinks we might be able to work things out, especially if she agrees to go to therapy. I don't know if that's true, but I wasn't sure about reaching out to Brittany and the others and that turned out all right."

"It did," she agreed. "Do you think Lilah would agree to therapy? She doesn't seem like the type who'd be willing to pay someone to tell her when she's wrong."

He chuckled. "When you put it that way ..."

"You're doing so well right now and I worry about how

you'd react if things with Lilah don't go well," Mia said as she tapped a blunt fingernail nervously on the side of her cup, "but if you and Dr. Lucas think this is the right thing to do then I'll support you."

"I told him I'd think about it," Gabriel reassured. "I didn't make any promises and I don't have to decide today."

"You can take as much time as you need," she said.

"I don't know if I can do this," he said into the phone. He'd been working with Dr. Lucas for almost two months to prepare for this and now he couldn't remember a word of what they'd discussed. "I came all this way, and I can't seem to get out of the damn car."

"You can," Mia said. "I know you can."

"What if she won't see me?"

"Then you come home, and I'll be your family."

He was still white-knuckle gripping the steering wheel as he clung to the truth of those words. Months of work with Dr. Lucas had helped all of that feel more real to him, more tangible. He had lost his mother years ago and whether he got her back or closed the door on the possibility forever, nothing would ever take Mia from him.

The large white house just visible through the trees felt familiar to him, but it had never been a home in the same way the house he shared with Mia now was. He stared at the windows, counting the gleaming panes of glass on the second floor until he came to the one he'd grown up in. He had no memories there but loneliness and raised voices and a cold pit of dread settled into his stomach like a lead weight. It was a familiar feeling; the same one he'd always gotten when his mother had looked at him with her characteristic stern disapproval.

He'd always been too loud, too violent, too out of control. The wedge it had driven between them had been deep, the first seemingly irreparable crack in the foundation of his life. Had he been surprised at all when it had come crashing down?

"You're more of my family than anyone else has ever been," he told Mia honestly. "I need to try and fix this but if I can't …"

"I know," she said. "We'll keep going, because that's what we always do."

"I love you."

"I love you, too, and don't forget you can call me or Dr. Lucas if you need to."

"I will," he promised, but he knew he wouldn't. Whatever the consequences were of this decision, it would be between him and his mother, at least for now.

He put the car in gear and crept up the driveway, stopping at the black wrought iron gate to push the button on the intercom. All of the time he'd spent worrying with Mia and he might not even make it through the gate if his mother didn't agree to let him in the house.

He didn't have to wait long, and the woman's voice that answered him was smooth and professional, exactly the kind of employee he would expect to work for an unfailingly professional politician. "Senator Miller's residence, how may I help you?"

"I need to see the senator," Gabriel said. He tried to keep his voice brisk and authoritative, lessons from years ago floating back through his mind, memories of his mother trying to guide him when she still thought he might someday follow in her political footsteps.

There was a pause—checking the daily schedule he assumed—followed by, "She's not expecting anyone today."

"I don't have an appointment," he said. "I'm her son."

This time the pause was longer. "The senator doesn't …"

"Tell her that Gabriel Myers has come to see her," he said, the hard edge of command in his voice apparently enough to send the guard hurrying to obey. He remembered enough about living with Lilah to know how to use his background and connections to get the job done.

Several infinitely long minutes later the gate swung open without another word from the intercom, and he pulled the car up the long driveway. She was already waiting for him on the stairs in front of the massive double front doors by the time he parked.

"Gabriel," she said. "I wasn't expecting you."

"I didn't write," he said with a shrug. "Or call."

"Well." Her pause was a weapon, expertly wielded. "Come inside then."

He followed her in, his gaze wandering over the familiar lines of the furniture and peeking rooms that hadn't changed in more than a decade. It was an odd feeling to be back inside his childhood home after so long, and stranger still to find the walls in the informal living room were still hung with old family photographs. His own face, young and thin with a crooked smile, looked down on him as Lilah ordered lemonade from the kitchen and sat stiffly on the edge of the loveseat cushion.

"Things didn't go so well last time we tried this," she said after a moment. "Perhaps you'd like to speak first this time?"

"I'm sorry," he said without preamble, for what could he possibly say to her except that? "I'm sorry for what I did to Dad."

She inclined her head, a silent acknowledgment, before taking a deep breath to steady herself. "I'm sorry that we sent you to Richard's."

He shrugged. "So, that's the worst of it," he said. "The two of us, both bending our pride a bit to apologize for our mistakes."

"Did you mean it?" Her eyes were nearly the same color as his own and they reflected his own hesitance, his own pride. In the years that he'd lived here, countless people had told him that he looked like his father, but it had always been his mother that had marked him the deepest.

"I've done a lot of things in my life that I regret, but nothing as much as that. I didn't mean to do it and I've spent every day since wishing I could take it back." He let the emotion flit across her face and settle before asking, "Did you? Mean it?"

Lilah turned her face away, searching the green expanse of the lawn outside the window for something he thought only she could see. "I lost both of you the day I sent you away," she said. "I thought I was helping you, but nothing was ever right again after that."

"I don't know if it was right before that," he said.

"At least before that we had hope."

"Maybe we could have hope again."

She looked at him, for once the steel in her spine softening. "I'd like that, and I think your father would, too. You look good, Gabriel."

"I feel good," he said. "I've been going to therapy."

"Really?" There was surprise there, a note of curiosity that he could almost see in her face, though it remained unlined and precisely neutral. Years of practice had made her a nearly unreadable book when she wanted to be, but he had practice of his own in deciphering her.

"My therapist thought you should probably go, too," he said, and he let it hang between them for a moment as he took a long swallow from his drink and watched her eyes narrow fractionally. "Maybe a sort of family thing."

"I can't go all the way—"

"They could do it over video call." He'd anticipated that protest and smiled blandly as he outmaneuvered her.

"Hmm."

"Mia's pregnant," he said into the silence that followed.

Something flashed over her face, quickly suppressed and he wondered if she was having as hard of a time processing the news as he'd had when Mia had told him.

He hadn't been expecting it, though looking back, he probably should have been at least a little more prepared for the possibility. They had been doing the bare minimum to prevent it and Mia hadn't seemed surprised when she'd come to him with big news and vulnerable eyes.

"Are you saying that you're ...?" he'd asked, his hand fisting in the fabric of her loose pajama shirt.

She'd nodded but her voice was wistful and uncertain. "I know we said it wasn't something we wanted right now ..."

"No," he agreed, and his eyes were running desperately over her face, his hand tight on her hip. "Not until ... You wanted to wait until you were done with school."

"I know but—"

"And I'm still messed up," he continued. "Mia, are you ... Do you want to ... Are you going to keep it?" he asked finally.

Mia's mouth opened and then snapped closed, and he watched the wave of realization wash over as she remembered Brittany and the loss he'd experienced. "Of course," she said, pulling him in and holding him tight as a shudder ran through him. "I know I said I wanted to wait but that doesn't mean I'm not happy."

"You're happy." He'd sighed and wrapped her up tightly in his arms.

It had been a revelation. A reprieve. Maybe even a miracle. She was already planning the time she'd need to take off from law school and the best ways to manage the competing workloads of school and parenthood once she returned.

The least he could do was finally make the trip to see his

mother, put into action the plan that he'd been working on in therapy. He needed to do this, so he could be a good father.

Mia was more than happy, she was thrilled, and he knew his mother well enough to know she'd feel the same, even if she was staring at him with narrowed eyes as she contemplated his announcement. She was smart enough to connect the dots about the timing of his visit and he knew she was wrestling with her emotions.

"That's manipulative, Gabriel."

"Offering you access to your grandchild?" Her lips pursed and her fingers tightened on the glass she was holding and he held up his hands in surrender. "Fine, it's manipulative," he agreed. "Is it working?"

She ignored the question, as close to an admission as Gabriel knew he was likely to get and looked at him over the rim of her lemonade glass. "Have you married Mia?"

"Not yet. I wanted to get everything settled first, be a whole person before I asked her."

"And when is the baby due?" she asked.

"Not until this winter."

"Fine," she sniffed. "Though I maintain that it's unfair to use a grandchild against me."

"You've never dealt in fairness, Mother, only in results. Besides, he's a good therapist."

"What's he done for you?"

"I'm here," Gabriel said, looking around at a house he had never planned to come back to. "And it's helped with the anger and the anxiety and the nightmares."

"I'm glad," she said, and he thought she might be. It was always hard to tell with Lilah what was real and what was a careful performance, but there was an uncharacteristic softness in her eyes. She lifted a hand, and for a moment he was almost sure she was going to reach for him, but after a moment of hesitation she let it fall. "I'm glad about all of it, though I hope it doesn't interfere with Mia's education too much."

"She's been accepted to law school—more than one actually—and the timing could have been better, but we'll handle it." He felt a tug of worry, but it was quickly smothered by pride. There was nothing Mia couldn't do once she set her heart on it and he would be there to help her in whatever way he could. He would be an involved father, a supportive husband. "Besides, what do you know about Mia's education?"

She tipped her head, regal and condescending. "I wanted to make sure you were adjusting."

"You couldn't have kept an eye on me before?" It rankled, even now, and he suspected it always would.

"I made mistakes in your youth, ones I did not intend to repeat once you went to prison."

"You never even wrote to me ..." He trailed off, thinking hard as she stared him down over her fine china. Pieces clicked into place, the impossible odds he'd overcome somehow making more sense. "You're the reason my conviction got thrown out."

"Hmm," she said. "I would never do such a thing, Gabriel, honestly."

She would and she clearly had, but to admit it would be more than her pride could allow. She wasn't without her flaws but maybe she loved him more than she had let herself acknowledge, even back then. "I've been thinking," he said, pretending not to notice her moment of vulnerability, "and I want to do something important. Give something back to help people like me."

"And what would that be?" She sat up straighter, her mind seamlessly making the switch to something tangible she could work on.

"Well, I thought I'd ask my mother to throw some of her

considerable influence behind prison and sentencing reform," he said. "At least to begin with. Then I could move on to starting a nonprofit, something to help with the legal complications and helping people get back on their feet once they're released. It's almost impossible for them to find jobs or places to live. It's not surprising how many of them end up back in prison. We've done nothing to help them with the problems that put them there and we've added new, unnecessary challenges on top of them."

She set her glass down, her face taking on a calculating expression that he knew meant she'd slipped into the role of a politician. "Those views aren't exactly popular, Gabriel. Not with donors and not with the public. Our current rules are in place to keep other people safe."

"I know," he said. "But does doing that and not addressing the real causes of crime actually help anyone? Or is it just another way that we can make people miserable without having to feel guilty? We've built an entire system around punishment. We handle people who break the law like they're cartoon criminals instead of real people with real struggles. You don't know how many of the people I was in with had stories like mine. Stealing to survive, killing to survive, doing drugs just to numb the pain of living or to self-medicate for some mental illness because they can't afford to see a real therapist."

"What are you saying?" she asked, sounding as exasperated with him as she had been in his youth. "You want to take on the whole judicial system?"

"More than that," he said, leaning forward and grabbing her hand, cradling it in his as he tried to explain. "I want to challenge the idea of punitive justice as the best way to do things in the first place. The thought that you can lock someone up in a cage and that somehow they pay off their debt to society through suffering ... it makes no sense."

"And what do you think we should do instead?"

"Help people before it comes to that," he said. "Do more to keep people fed, housed, and educated. We can break the cycles that put people in prison and help the ones that are already there get a better chance at a future."

"Gabriel ..."

"I can handle the non-profit," he interrupted. "Mia can help with all the legal stuff once she has her degree and passes the bar and I have just the person in mind to help with the reintegration part of things—but I need your help. You don't just have the platform and the political clout, it's more than that, you have the ability to speak on this as someone who's been directly affected by a horrible tragedy."

"I don't know that I can honestly say that I completely disagree with you being sent to prison," she said. "I can't speak as a victim *and* say the things you want me to say."

"I'm not asking you to advocate for the abolition of consequences entirely or for those who commit violent crimes to go free without an assessment of the risk," he said. "I'm asking that you ask for those consequences to fit the circumstances. I'm asking you to advocate for other solutions for nonviolent offenders, for programs to reduce violence in the first place, and for everyone to have the chance at rehabilitation."

"You've given this a lot of thought," she said. "Is this the only reason you came?"

"I've been working on goals with my therapist," he explained. "Trying to mend our relationship was one of the goals, and the nonprofit was another. I figured since I was already here ..."

She patted his arm. "You got that single-mindedness from me, I suppose, so I can't fault you for it."

"Does that mean you'll help me?"

"I'll do what I can," she agreed.

Chapter Thirty-Four

"You're sure this is the one?" Gabriel glanced around the campus again, the stately buildings and the trees that ruffled in the warm breeze. It was the third campus they'd toured in as many weeks but this time her face didn't have the faint wrinkle of dissatisfaction.

"It's got everything I need," she mused, her hand flat against her stomach as she followed his gaze with her own. "Well, they all did, I suppose but this one feels ..."

"It feels like home," he finished. She'd done a summer internship with Amy, soaking up all the knowledge she could, but she'd applied to several law schools and many of them had been out of state. They were good schools, and her acceptances were impressive, but they were far from her friends and her family, and he knew that wasn't what she needed right now. They would still have to move, but she'd only be a few hours away. Close enough for her to visit them often. Close enough for them to come and visit her when the baby was born.

"Exactly." Tears misted her eyes and she shrugged

helplessly, a confused laugh spilling from her lips. "I'm so emotional about everything lately."

"You're entitled." He grinned and pulled her into his arms. "If this is what you want, then this is where we'll go."

"There's a lovely little house for sale, not far from here." Her smile was wide, unrepentant as she lifted up on tiptoe and pressed a kiss to his lips. "It has the perfect room for a nursery."

"Does it?" He tugged gently on the ends of her hair, rubbing the silken texture between his fingers. "I see you've got it all planned out."

"I wanted to look at all my options, but I think I knew this was the right place."

"And you're happy? About everything?" He had to be sure. There was no room for doubt or uncertainty now, not when he'd given everything he had to making sure she had all the good things she deserved.

"So happy," she confirmed. "And it's not just this—though I'm thrilled about school and the baby—it's everything. You're doing so well now. Your relationship with your mother and the progress you've made with the nonprofit. The interviews you're doing to bring awareness to what happened to you and all the ways the system failed you."

"I know she had to talk me into that last one, but she was right." It was frustrating how often Lilah had already been right about the nonprofit, but she had spent a lifetime learning to manipulate the press and she'd insisted that they use that knowledge to their advantage. "It's drawn a lot of attention to what we're doing and helped us get things off the ground."

"It doesn't hurt that it lets you tell your own story this time, instead of the warped version the press concocted back then."

"About that ..." He puffed out his cheeks and huffed an embarrassed breath. "She thinks I should write a book."

"You should." There was no hesitation in her voice, no worry in the delicate lines of her face. "I always believed God helped us find each other for a reason and I still believe that. We are meant to help people, and this is how you're going to do that."

"It might help—I think the part of the idea is publicizing what I know about Seth Wiseman and hoping that it encourages other victims to come forward since the statute of limitations has passed for me now—but it would mean less privacy for us."

"Maybe a little." She nibbled her lip and considered it. "I know you're worried and I don't blame you. Your parents didn't do such a good job with you—parading you in front of cameras for your mother's campaigns and spending so much time worried about their ambitions that they forgot about you —and maybe you're afraid we'll go down the same road."

"How do you know we won't?"

"I guess I just have faith."

"That's all we've ever had, and it's worked out pretty good for us so far." He tucked a lock of hair behind her ear, his heart racing. "Listen, Mia—"

"I'm proud of you," she said. "Proud of us and everything we've accomplished."

He laughed, heart fuller than he'd ever imagined possible. All the years of loneliness, all the pain, and his failures. Everything he'd done and all the ways he'd let people down and *she* was proud of *him*. "You're the one that pulled us through," he assured her. "Look at what you've done, at everything you've achieved."

She beamed at him, fresh tears on her lashes as she sniffled.

"I thought there would be a better time for this," he

fumbled in his pocket, his fingers closing on a small black box, "but this seems like the right moment."

"Gabriel—"

"Please, let me finish." He flipped open the lid and held it up for her to see the ring inside, the shadows dancing over the cut angles of the sapphire set in platinum. It was classic, timeless, and had been the only ring in the store he could imagine on her finger. "Everything we've become is because of you. You've made me a better man. You're making me a father. You've given me love and a reason to live."

He placed a kiss on each corner of her mouth, soft and gentle as he wiped away the tears on her cheek with his thumb.

"I can't imagine spending a single day of my life without you," he continued. "I wanted to do this when I was a whole man, one you could depend on, and I think ... I think I'm finally that man."

"I've always been able to depend on you," she said fiercely. "You were always the only one, the only man that mattered."

"I love you, Mia." He pulled the ring from its velvet bed, once again painfully conscious that his future hung on a single moment, a single decision. He'd come up lucky since the moment she'd started to push her way into his life, and he just needed that luck to hold a little longer. "Will you marry me?"

She laughed and threw her arms around him, pulling him close to rain kisses over his face. "I love you," she said, repeating it again and again and punctuating each word with another frenzied kiss.

"Sweetheart," he pulled her away, his own laugh rising to meet hers as she struggled against letting go of him. "Is that a yes?"

"Oh!" Her eyes went wide, caught between horror and amusement when she realized she'd forgotten to give him an answer. "Yes! Absolutely and with my whole heart."

He swept her off her feet, ignoring the stares as he spun her around, both of them laughing wildly until he set her back on her feet and slid the ring onto her finger. When he kissed her, he kissed like a man who truly believed they had forever, and he didn't need to rush.

Several Years Later

It wasn't the first time that Mia had walked across the stage at graduation, but it was the most important. It was the culmination of years of work, of determination, of learning and compromise and difficult prioritizing. It was the product of her rebellion and the calling of her God.

She'd passed the bar already, taking advantage of the state's willingness to let her sit for the exam prior to graduation so she had nothing left to worry about by the time they called her name. All she'd had left to do was show up and be acknowledged for her efforts. Well, more than acknowledged. Celebrated, really, if her husband had anything to say about it.

She scanned the crowd as she descended from the stage, searching the sea of faces for the ones most familiar to her. Even in a crowd, Gabriel was easy to spot—his dark hair and large frame always stood out among the rest. She waved as she passed him, blowing a subtle kiss to him and the toddler he was holding as he pointed her out to their daughter. Lyra had her father's fair skin and dark hair, short curls bouncing around her cheeks as she waved and tugged on her twin brother's arm.

Brekker was already long and lean, restless as he wiggled in his grandfather's arms. He had his father's wobbling, crooked grin as he stretched up to clap and wave to her. The three of them, the miracle family that had been given to her through God's grace and second chances, would have been enough. If they were the only ones that had come to see her achieve her dreams, it would have been enough.

But her father was also there, tears in his eyes and a proud smile, and on Gabriel's other side was Lilah, fussing over her granddaughter and looking dignified in a pale blue suit.

All of them had come to celebrate with her, to wait through the long ceremony even though there was going to be a party later. Lilly and Bryce would be there, as well as Kennedy and her new wife—at this point she was certain the guest list had expanded to include almost everyone she'd ever met. If anyone had ever doubted Gabriel's support for her career goals or the pride he had in her accomplishments, they wouldn't doubt it for long. He'd gone as overboard as she would allow before she finally had to put her foot down and insist that he not include a firework display or the release of live doves.

He'd given in on those points but made up for it when she'd woken before dawn, anxious and full of nerves about the day to come.

"I'm proud of you," he'd said, voice still husky with sleep as he whispered against her neck.

She'd nodded against his chest, her breath too far gone for anything else. Her fingers were tangled in his hair, her knees spread wide around his hips, full of him as he rocked up into her. In the still light of morning, he'd shown her nothing but aching tenderness as he'd held her, keeping her close as he reclined back on a stack of pillows that kept him sitting mostly upright, his mouth close to her ear and his hands drifting over her body as she leaned into him, her breasts pressed against his chest.

The need for him was still there, the edges unblunted with time and undaunted by the early hour and her nerves. Her fingers had found purchase in his skin, gripping to hold him as he filled her, and her skin had come awake under his caress.

He'd cupped her thighs, his thumbs lingering in the creases where her legs met the curve of her hip, then reached farther to knead the round flesh of her behind before rediscovering the dimples in the small of her back and tracing the lines of her vertebrae. His mouth had moved from her lips to the curve of her cheek, over the ridge of her brow and the line of her nose before trailing fire and warmth down her neck and over the width of her shoulders.

All of her worries had disappeared, drowned by the pleasure of his touch and the scent of his skin. There was nothing to fear in a world where she was loved like that, where she was worshiped so openly, with such a lack of shame. She'd broken over him with a soft cry, ecstasy and warmth flooding her, words of love tumbling from her lips and the taste of her lover on her tongue.

The memory of it made her cheeks heat and a low heat rekindle in her blood, but it was soon forgotten as Gabriel put his fingers in his mouth and let go with a long whistle as she passed that made heads turn all across the large auditorium and his mother to elbow him in the ribs.

Mia's face, already pink, flamed hot and red but she couldn't withhold a laugh as she settled back into her seat to wait for the procession of graduates to end. Over the years since he'd been released it had gotten more normal to have him around, and sometimes she lost sight of how lucky she was to have him beside her at all. Occasions like this were a good reminder of what she might have missed, that this day might have come and gone without him, without their children.

She would take his embarrassing over-enthusiasm with gratitude.

He'd given her all of himself, made her life and the lives of so many others far better than they would otherwise have been. The program they had started had given hope where there had been so little. Every day new letters crossed their desks, begging for help dealing with a system that they had no idea how to navigate, and newly released inmates shuffled through the door, unsure of themselves and where they fit into the world. Gabriel welcomed them all, doing his best to help as many as he could.

He'd given purpose to Alex, given him a job at the nonprofit and helped him regain custody of his brother. Alex knew what it felt like to be cut adrift when the prison spit you out and he used that knowledge to connect with the newly released, guiding them to resources and a brighter future.

It hadn't ended there.

Kennedy was working with Lilah to make changes to the law, partnering with Brittany and Michael to speak to Congress about the challenges facing LGBTQ+ youth and their need for specification legal protection to keep them safe from guardians that did not respect their identities. A national ban on any kind of conversion therapy was the prime goal, one that seemed more possible with each passing day.

Now that Mia was finally able to practice law herself, she'd be able to contribute even more to the legacy they were building. A legacy of hope. Of love. Of second chances and radical forgiveness and foundational change.

She caught Gabriel's eye as the ceremony drew to a close

and the graduates let out a collective sigh of relief. He grinned down at her as she pulled the cap from her head and tossed it high with the others. It felt like the end and carried the bittersweet flavor of a monumental task finally done, but it also felt like a beginning, like the deep breath taken right before the sun rises.

Acknowledgments

Many people believe that writing is a solitary activity and while it may be true that the act of writing is something you do alone, the act of publishing is more like a team sport. There are many people without whom this book would not exist and I am deeply and personally grateful to all of them.

I have to begin by thanking Jean Lowd and Creative James Media for taking a chance on me. I wasn't entirely sure there was a home for Gabriel and Mia, their story is not an easy or comfortable one in many ways and I knew from the beginning it might be difficult to find others who were excited to tell it as I was. Thankfully, Jean saw the potential and the entire CJM team helped to make it shine. I would like to thank Abby Orlandi, my incredible editor, and Diana TC, who designed my amazing cover, for going above and beyond to help make this book the best it could possibly be. All of your work is so important to me!

Before I could even dream of trying to find this book a home, I had a full team of supportive, encouraging, and amazingly talented people. Thank you so much Maria for devoting so much of your time to talking me through all of my late-night panic attacks and moments of self-doubt. This book is a labor of love and you loved it just as much as I did. There are no worlds to express what that means to me. Also, all of my love and gratitude to Tristen for being such an amazing beta and for being so patient with me. You're amazing and I can't wait to hold your book! I know it's just a matter of time!

You're both wonderful people and I appreciate you more than you'll ever know.

Thank you so much to Hana and the Reylo Creatives Discord server. Hana, you are an amazing friend and you have created a truly wonderful space with amazing people. Thank you for giving me a place to belong and trying so hard to teach me how to properly use a comma. The entire Reylo community has been so supportive and I truly would not be a writer without all of you. Also, Liana and the entire group in the 3,2,1…Write! server, you have given me so much knowledge and support that I would have been totally lost without all of you. So many of you are going to do great things and I can't wait to support all of you.

On a more personal note, it's absolutely necessary for me to thank my mother, who gave me life, love, and all of the encouragement any kid could ever need. Thank you, from the bottom of my heart, for always seeing the best in me, even when I was at my worst. To my father, it is undeniable that I got large chunks of who I am from you, and for that I will always be grateful. I love you both and hope I have managed to make you proud.

No list of acknowledgements would be complete without my Sassy. You were there for me as I discovered who I was and there is no one else in the world I would rather have gone through adolescence with. You are the sister of my heart and I'm blessed to have you as part of my life no matter how far apart we may be.

Last, but certainly not least, I have to thank my incredibly supportive family. My amazing kids, who think they have the world's weirdest mom and still do everything they can to cheer me on. My oldest, who specifically requested to be known as Eldest Hellspawn, it's in print now and you can't take it back. You have always enjoyed challenging me and I can't imagine a life without you. To my youngest, never let go of your chaos.

It keeps me on my toes and is the best thing a person can have if they want to live on their own terms. Mothering both of you has been the greatest privilege of my life.

For my husband, well, you're still (probably) not Batman but I definitely consider you to be a hero. Marriage isn't always easy to handle, especially when your wife decides to put all her free time and energy into writing a book, but you are always there for me. I look forward to a lifetime of falling in love with you over and over again.

There are so many people I wish I could thank more specifically, beloved grandparents, siblings, friends, and more but there are a lot of you, so please know I hold you all in my heart and I'm grateful to each of you for simply being part of my life.

Ashley Hawthorne is a shameless introvert and lifelong lover of stories. A homeschooling mom for more than a decade, she needed a new challenge when her rapidly growing students began to become more independent. After a lot of consideration and a few false starts, she decided to start writing stories of her own. Her favorite tales have always been those of love and loss, hope and heartbreak, and that's what she hopes you will find in the worlds she creates. Most of her time is spent writing or hanging out with her family, but she also enjoys outdoor adventures and baking. She lives in a very tiny house in Texas with her husband, two teenagers, and far too many rescue animals, including a cat named Fish Stick and ball python named Root Beer.